ON AMERICAN SOIL: JIHAD

PRESERVE, PROTECT AND DEFEND Book 1

D. S. Wall

Russet Leaf Press

Russet Leaf Press

ON AMERICAN SOIL: JIHAD

Lor,

Thanks for your help and
encouragement in getting
this book done. I needed
it!

Love,
Dave

Chapter 1: Max

When the foreigner sent Max's cousin to arrange a meeting, Max agreed. He met the man in the bar of Hotel Ciudad Juárez, near the international airport. It was not a long drive from his home. The well-dressed gentleman wore gold jewelry, including a large watch on his wrist. This man should not flaunt his wealth in Mexico, he thought.

"Sir, please sit with me. You are Maximo Lopez, the fellow who guides people across the American border?"

Max felt an obligation to help those desperate people looking for work and a better way of life for their families. America was the land of promise, full of opportunities to work hard and earn good pay. He knew firsthand the poverty they were trying to escape. His parents were poor, scraping a living any way they could. He grew up with almost nothing.

He found his way across the border when he was a young man, and earned a decent living working construction jobs. He stumbled into his calling as a coyote, crossing back into Mexico a few times a year to visit his family. He learned the best routes — easy to travel if prepared for the journey — and where the border has no pedestrian wall. Friends and family asked Max to bring them back with him to the U.S. so they too might earn money. He obliged, and the word spread that Max would get them to America.

He started doing it full time, asking for payment that he felt his charges could afford. Aware there were other, unscrupulous men who take thousands of U.S. dollars to guide unfortunates into the U.S., Max did not do that. But when people he didn't know, who appeared to have money, offered him thousands of dollars, he took it. Lord knows he and Juana needed it, for their children were growing and needed nutritious food and decent clothes for school.

"I am Max. Who wants to know?"

"My name is Abdulaziz Ali. I need to arrange passage to the United States for three men. I am told you are highly successful doing this." He waited for the Mexican to respond, but the man seemed wary. Abdulaziz continued, "I shall pay you 1,000 U.S. dollars now, to reserve your services for a few days in October of this year. When you deliver my colleagues to their destination in Texas, they will give you another 10,000 dollars."

Max sized the man up and wondered who these people were. Eleven thousand dollars — *that is a lot of money for a poor man like me.* October was a decent time for the trek — not too hot in the daytime and not too cold at night.

"We will drive most of the way, but these men will have to walk 5 miles in rough terrain and must carry what they bring with them." Max cautioned.

"Of course," Abdulaziz agreed. "They must travel alone. Only you will accompany them."

"In this business, we take payment before we start the journey," Max tested the man. When he helped friends, he accepted what they could offer when they offered it, but with foreigners, it was different.

"Agreed. The travelers will check-in to this hotel on the 12th of October and contact you when they arrive. You should be ready to guide them the next day."

"Si — yes, I can do that." Max agreed to the deal, and the foreigner passed him $1,000.

As planned, Mohammad and his two companions landed in Juárez on October 12th and sent word to Max they had arrived. They instructed him to bring them to an address in Las Cruces, New Mexico, and he agreed. One of Max's normal trails led him there, anyway. Las Cruces was close enough to the border to make it a simple journey, but far enough away from El Paso to avoid crossing paths with the U.S. Customs and Border Protection.

It was easy money for Max. Mohammad paid him

the $10,000 when he got to the hotel, and he then passed it to his cousin, who would deliver it to his wife. The cousin understood she would reward him.

Juana did not want Max to do it. She believed these foreigners were dangerous and wanted no part of them. But Max was thinking of her and the children, and besides, she didn't know their intentions.

And Juana was left to worry for her husband's safety.

Chapter 2: Lightning

"Jace, come in the house!" Charlotte called to her husband from the deck. The sky was dark, and the weather had turned blustery. *He always does this,* she thought. *I can't trust him to use his own brain. Once he gets wrapped up in something, he doesn't want to quit!*

"Yeah, I'm comin'. I just need to get this one branch." Jace finally got around to cutting out those dead branches in the oak tree in the backyard — at least those he could reach with his pole saw. He considered getting his eight-foot stepladder to get a few feet higher, but decided against it. He did that last summer trying to prune the Bradford pear. That turned out to be a bad idea. He lost his balance and had to jump from five feet up with a saw in his hand. He threw the tool away from him, landed in a crouch, and rolled forward in the grass. Charlotte was there watching and was not amused. As a younger man, Jace might have laughed it off, but at 43 years old it hurt a little, and scared him too. But he wouldn't say that to his wife.

Charlotte's right. I need to pack it in, Jace admitted

to himself. The wind had gotten worse and there wasn't much more to do anyway.

The approaching storm announced itself with a deafening, bone-rattling thunderclap. Lightning struck the oak and splashed over to Jace, taking only milliseconds for the supercharged bolt to course across his body. He stung as if he were being probed with a thousand needles at once. After several seconds, he realized he was lying face up on the ground. The erratic thumping of his heart beating in his ears was the only thing he heard. He sensed daylight, but felt only a tingling sensation, as though he was in a numbing fog.

Charlotte had turned to walk inside when the lightning hit. She felt the brittle crackling of an electric charge in the air. Blinding light and a concussive boom enveloped her, throwing her to the deck. Her initial reaction was, *what did he do?* but just as quickly she realized that this was not of Jace's making.

"Oh my God. Jace," she said as she saw him lying in the grass under the tree. Fearing the worst, she ran to him and was relieved to find him awake and breathing.

Jace knew Charlotte was next to him, touching him, and then heard her. "Jace, Jace, are you okay? Can you hear me? Jace!"

He rolled his head slightly, haltingly, afraid to move. His eyes met Charlotte's. He always seemed to get lost in those beautiful, turquoise eyes like when he saw her for the first time — even now. Gazing into those eyes made everything seem perfectly fine. He didn't notice the horrified look on her face.

"Are you okay?" She said again, and then he grunted a, "yep."

"You were hit by lightning. I don't think you're okay." Charlotte dialed 9-1-1 on her iPhone that she somehow still gripped in her left hand and told Jace not to move until help arrived.

Chapter 3: The EMTS

Virginia Beach is the largest city in Virginia, with a population of around 450,000 people spread over 500 square miles. Fortunately for Jace and Charlotte West, they lived in a well-populated part of the city and just a mile from the fire and rescue station on Nimmo Parkway. The emergency medical technicians arrived minutes after Charlotte called 9-1-1.

Lightning-strikes are rare, but there have been enough of them in summertimes past that Tony, the attendant-in-charge, had seen a couple before and knew what to do.

"Where was he?" Tony asked Charlotte. "Was he in the tree?"

"No, he was under the tree, cutting branches."

"Was he awake when you found him? Was he responsive?"

"Yes — he complained of numbness."

"My arms and legs feel kinda tingly," Jace added.

"That's good to know. Do you have pain, sir?" Tony continued to assess.

"My body hurts."

Tony suppressed a little chuckle, "Yes sir, I imagine so."

"You have a slight burn on your shoulder." He pointed to Jace's left shoulder. The lightning tore away his shirt,

and his skin had a pencil-sized, red lesion. "We'll take care of that in a minute."

Tony knew that 90% of lightning-strike victims survive, but the ones that don't, die from cardiac or respiratory arrest. He made sure the patient was breathing without difficulty and checked his central pulse at the same time.

"Stabilize the spine," Tony instructed his crew. Getting struck by lightning can cause traumatic injury, and he needed to be cautious. "Let's do a 12-lead EKG once we're en route. Respiration is okay, but put him on oxygen."

Tony worried they were exposed to more danger outside, and he wanted to get the patient to the hospital, so they worked quickly.

"Where are you taking him?"

"Virginia Beach General," Tony told Charlotte. "He looks stable, so we're good to go. I'll need some information from you."

As Charlotte gave him Jace's medical background, the other EMTs loaded Jace into the ambulance. Charlotte told him she'd meet him at the hospital. She needed to call the kids and grab some things, then hurry over there.

It seemed to Charlotte that the EMTs swept in and whisked Jace away in just minutes. Suddenly, they were there, and then they were gone. The whole thing was a blur. The rain hadn't even started to fall by the time they had him in the ambulance and on his way to the hospital. Charlotte was still in the driveway when another thunderclap startled her back into the moment, and she ran into the house.

Chapter 4: The Arrangement

Mohammad arranged for one of his American followers to meet him in Texas and escort him and fellow jihadists to Virginia. He tasked his lieutenant, Bilal, to instruct the American to find a safe place to hide near El Paso and to provide transportation to Norfolk such that authorities would not notice them.

Kent Green was a young black man, a college student disenchanted by what he thought was disregard white America had for African Americans. He found Islam recruiting sites on the internet that promised loving and inclusive communities. The more he read them, the more he became dissatisfied with American society. One website guided Kent to a mosque in Norfolk that welcomed him and offered the opportunity to convert to Islam. Most who worshipped at the mosque were families wishing to practice their faith of peace and devotion to God and to integrate into the pluralistic society that is America.

Unknown to its members and leaders, Mohammad recruited three Muslims who occasionally attended services at the mosque, into his jihad. He
guided Kent to these few who had formed a jihadi
cell at his behest.

Most Muslims believe that jihad discussed in the
Quran refers to a Muslim's personal struggle to
practice Islam, particularly when faced with op-
pression. Mohammad's jihad was the more modern,
extremist ideology brought about by the rise of
political Islam. Osama bin Laden popularized the
violent holy war when he fought against the So-
viets with the mujahedin in Afghanistan. And later
when he declared a jihad against the U.S. 'occupying'
Saudi Arabia. Mohammad's was the never-ending
holy war to create and expand the political Islamic
State.

Kent was told to find a house on the outskirts of
El Paso that ensured the privacy of his guests. So, a
few months before they needed it, he found a place
on the internet. It was an older home off Interstate
10, closer to Las Cruces, New Mexico. It was fur-
nished and isolated, but close to civilization. With
help from his friend Bilal, he paid two months' rent
to the leasing agent and asked him to leave the keys
to the house under a doormat at the back door.

While Kent was looking forward to meeting Mohammad, he was wary about driving for two solid
days, and then back again, to escort him to Norfolk.
Why couldn't the dude just fly? Kent thought to him-

self, but he didn't object. As instructed, he rolled into town a day ahead of the scheduled meet-up date to ready the place for the rendezvous. He found the keys and opened the house. He had only to buy groceries and supplies — enough for four men to rest and recharge — and wait for his guests to arrive.

Chapter 5: The Charming

Millicent saw him right away. They were in the same Flow of Fluids class. He was tall-ish — around six feet — handsome with tan skin and a black beard kept closely cropped like a 'five-o'clock shadow.' Millicent thought Bilal must have been physically fit as he wore his casual, but stylish clothes especially well. Unlike most guys at school who throw on some combination of t-shirts, sports gear, and jeans, he dressed and carried himself as though he had money, but not in a flaunting way. She couldn't stop looking at him.

On the first day of class, Bilal scanned the classroom to find a seat. At a table on the far side of the room, he noticed an attractive African American woman staring at him. He looked her in the eyes, but she didn't look away, or look down as the females do back home. American women are different — they wear tight jeans and tight blouses and hold their ground. He wouldn't admit it to his brothers, but he enjoyed the boldness. Bilal imaged he would enjoy living in America — if circumstances were different. He made to the chair next to the pretty girl and politely introduced himself.

"Hello, my name is Bilal Khalil. May I sit at this table?"

"Yes, please do." Millicent felt a little flutter in her stomach. *Woooow,* she thought, *how nice!*

"And you are called?" he prompted.

"Oh — sorry. I'm Millicent, Millicent Jackson."

"What a lovely name," and the charming had begun.

Chapter 6: The Emergency Room

Dr. Susan Killam was the attending physician on duty when the EMTs wheeled Jace West into the emergency room. She loved emergency medicine. It was what she wanted to do since she was 10 years old when she experienced it as a victim of a car accident. The medical equipment, the doctors and nurses making critical decisions, and rushing to save lives was thrilling to her.

Her energy level kicked up a notch, as though she just had a shot of espresso, when she heard a lightning-strike victim was en route. It sounded as though the patient was stable, but at least it would be more exciting than the typical sun-sick tourist they get during the summer. Victims hit by lightning are both injury and medical patients. Blunt trauma, neurologic disruption, cardiopulmonary arrest, and burns — a smorgasbord of injury and illness she must look for — all in one patient.

Dr. Killam and her team met Jace at the ambulance crew entrance. As they rolled him to the treatment room, Tony, the lead EMT, called out his vitals for the hospital staff.

"Forty-three-year-old male, awake and responsive, complaining of numbness in his limbs, muscle soreness, especially in his left shoulder. His BP is elevated at 144 over 85. His heart rate was rapid but is down to around 75 now."

"Arrhythmia?" Dr. Killam asked.

"His heartbeat was irregular but self-corrected."

"Okay — thanks, guys." Tony and crew took that cue and faded back toward their rig, but hung around for a few minutes just in case there were more questions.

"What's your name, sir?" Dr. Killam assessed the patient herself.

"Jace West."

"So, your arms and legs are a little numb?"

"Yes, but it's feeling better now."

"How about your muscle aches?"

"Feels like I got it by a Mack truck."

"That's normal for getting struck by lightning. Your muscles contract forcefully when that current hits you. We'll check it out. We also expect numbness. It's a good sign that it is subsiding already.

"Let's do a comprehensive metabolic panel," the doctor instructed her team. "Meanwhile, we'll examine for bone fractures, and then, Mr. West, I'll do a few simple neurological tests."

Chapter 7: The Tasking

Millicent was uneasy every time she thought about it. Bilal's friend was coming from Saudi Arabia to visit him and his friends, and he was very on edge. He told her that Mohammad is his mentor and he wants to please him with their progress, but he didn't offer details. She tried to ask, but he became irritated when pressed.

Millicent didn't understand his relationship with his friends, Haider and Owais. They were less mature, and he was clearly in control of their little group. They did what he told them to do and were tense about Mohammad's visit only when they were with Bilal. Otherwise, in her mind, they were typical grab-ass, college-boy fools. When he wasn't watching, they'd look her up and down, undressing her with their eyes. They were creepy, and she didn't like them. Unfortunately, they lived with Bilal.

They rented a house together in the Park Place section of Norfolk, near the trendy West Ghent. Millicent loved West Ghent, and had an apartment nearby, so she and Bilal saw a lot of each other since they first met in Fluids class. Bilal was charming, mature, and handsome, and she fell for him. She liked that he was foreign, giving him a refined mystique.

"What will Mohammad say about your hot, African American girlfriend?" Owais teased Bilal. Haider and he flashed mischievous, schoolboy grins at each other, daring to question their leader.

Bilal knew his compatriots had lustful thoughts of Millicent. They didn't respect women as he had grown to respect Milli.

"Mohammad will say nothing because he understands she is part of integrating into this culture," he replied tersely, in a manner they understood not to continue with the foolishness.

He had fallen for the strong, alluring woman, captivated by her emerald eyes, framed by perfectly smooth skin and long flowing hair. She was unlike any other woman he had met — beautiful, and his intellectual equal. He could not help but be intrigued by her bold independence — behavior that he would normally reject from a female. *American men don't deserve to have such women.*

Bilal asked Kent Green to pick up Mohammad.

Millicent had seen him around campus, but she had no idea they knew each other until she met him at Bilal's house. She liked him. He was a sweet and thoughtful guy, but he was outwardly troubled by racial inequalities in American society. Kent would cite white privilege and how he thought black people were still on the plantation. She understood how people felt that way, but never fully bought into the narrative. She grew up on the other side of Kent's tracks and enjoyed the privilege he believed unjust. He declared he was converting to Islam, but she didn't see the connection between that and his ideas of racism. Millicent guessed that must be how Bilal and Kent became friends — at mosque.

When Kent knocked on the front door, Owais answered.

"Green, come in," Owais said as he opened the door.

Kent knew the house well by then. Ahead of him was the stairway that led to the bedrooms upstairs. On his right was the dining room, but Bilal used it as a study, and to the left was the living room. This morning was like most other times he visited. The twins, as he called them — not that they looked much alike — were playing Counter-Strike in the living room on the 50-inch flat-screen. They were scary good, and they always played as the terrorists — something that left him with an uneasy feeling.

Bilal came down the stairs and motioned Kent into the study. He closed the pocket door behind them to block out the noise.

"Kent, I have exciting news for you. Mohammad is arriving in Texas and I want you to pick him up and bring him here," he said proudly.

"Me?" Kent was surprised. He had sensed the visit was very important to Bilal, and it confused him why Bilal chose him to meet Mohammad.

"Yes! This is a great honor for you."

"Why not you, or one of the tw... um, others?"

"I have many matters to handle here, and I do not trust that they can navigate across the states without trouble. They are new to the U.S. and don't understand how things are." Kent agreed with that. He wouldn't depend on them to go a mile down the road to McDonald's.

"What do you need me to do?"

"We'll rent a luxury vehicle for you to have a comfortable drive. You'll collect Mohammad near El Paso and return here."

"El Paso? That's a long way. Why not just fly into Norfolk?"

"He will be in Texas and wishes to travel by car from there. Airplane travel wears on him." Kent didn't know how far away El Paso was, but he knew *that's a long-ass drive.*

"When do I go?"

"It won't be until October, so we have time to prepare. I think during fall break from school is an ideal time."

Chapter 8: The Hospital

"**M**r. West, you're extremely lucky. It appears you have no serious injuries." Dr. Killam reviewed her examination results with Jace. "Your bloodwork came back great; everything is within the normal range. You have no broken bones or other trauma injuries, and your neurological tests are fine. Your numbness is subsiding on its own, but it may take a while — days, maybe a week or two, to resolve completely. You had an irregular heartbeat, but that's resolved.

"Great, I'm ready to go home."

"Well, I'd like to hold you overnight and have a cardiologist and a neurologist examine you tomorrow. Lightning-strike survivors suffer all kinds of maladies, and some develop over time. Frankly, I'm surprised you are in such good shape, and I want to be safe." That news was not what Jace wanted to hear. Charlotte saw his expression and interjected.

"Good idea. We definitely want that reassurance that everything is okay."

"Great. We'll find a room and transfer him out of Emergency. It should only be a few minutes." Dr. Killam smiled and hurried out of the treatment room.

Jace just wanted to get home, shower, and get something to eat. He had been working in the sun and felt dirty, and he hadn't eaten. He looked at Charlotte and let out a long sigh.

"Well, that's excellent news! You'll get out of here tomorrow. It could have been so much worse." She tried to comfort him. "I'll feel better when the specialists take a look."

He made it to his room in time for dinner and had a surprisingly satisfying meal. And he convinced the nurse to allow him to wash up before they connected him to the monitors for the night. She agreed, provided Charlotte kept an eye on him.

After he settled in, Charlotte suddenly felt exhausted. The events and the stress of the day caught up with her, and she needed to go home. The nurse said the doctors would see him early the next day, and Charlotte wanted to be there. Jace didn't remember details when it came to doctors. As long as they said he's good to go, then that's enough for him, but Charlotte needed to know details. She decided to get up and over to the hospital first thing in the morning.

Jace slept little during the night and was glad when morning arrived. He had a doctor, and two nurses examine him at different times, doing the same neurological tests. The monitors beeped continuously, and nursing assistants recorded his vital signs every hour, making it difficult to rest.

Charlotte showed up as the neurologist was finishing her exam.

"There are no signs of neurological damage." Dr. de Havilland turned to Charlotte, acknowledging her, and speaking more to her than to him. "Lightning strikes can fry the nervous system and cause serious damage, but Mr. West seems to have weathered the storm." The doctor smirked at what she just said. No pun was intended, but Charlotte couldn't help laughing. "The numbness in the extremities is normal and will go away, but if it doesn't, in say two weeks from now, you need to have it checked out. Eyesight and hearing are normal, eardrums are intact."

"Please set a follow-up visit with your primary care physician. Tell them what happened, and I said you should go as soon as they can schedule you."

"We'll do that."

"At this point, there is no reason to run a CT scan." Turning to Charlotte again, "Mr. West told me he has a headache. That's expected. Give him a thousand milligrams of Tylenol when he needs it. Give it a few days. If it persists, call me, or his primary care, but it needs to be checked."

As the neurologist finished, the cardiologist walked in and asked how he was doing. Dr. de Havilland informed him of the results of her exam and then excused herself to continue to her next patient. The cardiologist explained the potential damage to the heart caused by lightning, but Jace's EKG was normal. The doctor said there was no need to keep him in the hospital and asked him to schedule a follow-up examination at Jace's convenience.

It took the staff an hour to process Jace's discharge and wheel him to Charlotte's car. The last two days had been crazy, and they were both relieved to be on their way home. As they pulled out of the parking lot, he called the kids. They were both out of town and he wanted to let them know everything was fine.

Chapter 9: The Fourth

Jace popped two extra-strength Tylenol and tried to relax. Three days had passed since he got home from the hospital. His head still hurt, and his shoulder and chest muscles ached too. He took off the week leading up to the Fourth of July weekend, hoping to unwind, and get a few honey-dos checked off his list. Now, he didn't feel like doing much, and just wanted to sit back in a quiet room and maybe play some music. He was in sensory overload and needed to block everything out.

Charlotte left him alone in the study. He was irritable since the accident. *Understandable*, she thought. "Do you need me to get you anything?"

"No, I'm good." He appreciated his wife. She always looked out for him.

"Okay, I'll close the door for you."

"Thanks, Char," he said as she left him alone.

It was Saturday, the Fourth. Jace and Charlotte had been looking forward to the holiday. The kids were home from summer school for three days. Jace was cooking spiedies and corn on the cob on the grill, and she made potato salad. Spiedies — heavily marinated chunks of meat, skewered, grilled, and served on a slice of Italian bread — have been a Fourth of July tradition in his family ever since he could remember. He used to stock up on the special sauce when they visited his family in upstate New York, but he could buy it at local grocery stores in recent years. A relaxing weekend with his family and his favorite Independence Day food was just what he needed.

Jace still had a headache. It had been a week since the lightning strike, and it hadn't gone away. Charlotte made the follow-up appointment with his primary care physician for the next Tuesday, and they were eager to have it checked out. But they intended to make the best of the weekend.

The kids were anxious to see their father after the accident, but the family agreed it was better for them not to miss classes. That's difficult to recover from in summer sessions. Besides, Dad was okay, and they were going to be home for the holiday, anyway. At 19, Olivia was one year older than her brother Alec, and a second-year student at the University of Virginia. Alec stayed closer to Virginia Beach and was a freshman at the College of William and Mary, just an hour away in Williamsburg.

Charlotte warned the kids when they got home. "Dad still has his headaches and is not himself. He's overly sensitive. It's strange."

"What do you mean?" Olivia asked the question before Alec could.

"He smells and hears things that I don't. And he says he senses things…"

"Like what?"

"Sometimes he seems to know what I'm thinking. He'll answer a question before I ask it. It creeps me out. And he'll get sudden waves of emotions."

"What? Dad getting emotional?"

"He says they're not his; he just feels them. It's as if there are ghosts in the house or something. It gives me goosebumps."

"That is very weird." Alec agreed with his sister and mom. "Dad has always been level-headed, steady as she goes."

Jace had a quiet and calm demeanor. Some people might think he was standoffish, but family and friends knew him to be a likable guy with a subtle, dry sense of humor. He found it easier to connect with people by joking with them. It's one reason Charlotte married him — she had a funny bone, too.

"It must be the headaches," Olivia said with a shallow breath, not sure she believed that herself.

The West's wanted to start the holiday celebration, so they enjoyed their spiedies dinner in the early afternoon on the deck, and then went inside to escape the July heat. While Olivia and Alec shared how summer school was going with their mom, Jace used the time to nap. When the sun was lower in the sky, Charlotte and the kids were enjoying cold drinks under the umbrella by the pool.

"Mmmmmmmm, that smells good!" Jace said as he walked outside to join the family.

"What does?" Alec asked.

"That steak. Someone's grilling steak — fillets."

"You can smell someone cooking fillets?" Olivia said with a subtle hint of disbelief, as she scanned the neighbors' backyards, looking for the telltale smoke coming from a grill. There was none. Most folks already had their days' cookout.

"Yeah, you can tell because there's less fat burning than other cuts of meat, like a New York. I wish they'd turn down that music..." Jace added with a sigh.

Alec and Olivia looked at their mom. Charlotte returned their gaze with wide eyes as if to say, *see what I mean?!* The kids weren't sure what to do, so they followed their mom's lead and said nothing. There was no music that they could hear.

"I can do without the heavy metal at the moment," Jace finished his thought.

Olivia got a pit in her stomach. *What the hell?*

"Why do you say that?" Jace reacted.

"Say what?" Charlotte asked, trying to stay calm. *He's doing it again.*

"Olivia said, 'What the hell?'"

"She — didn't say anything, Hon."

"I thought it." She stared at her mom with a look of fright in her eyes, "I thought it, Dad," turning her head to look at her father.

Jace felt the sudden rush of alarm coming from his family. Those unexpressed emotions hit him as though they were his own. They were afraid — and so was he.

Chapter 10: Almost Fun

Tuesday could not come soon enough for Jace and Charlotte. Until then, Jace tried to stay away from everyone. The only time he was at ease, despite the headache, was in the study with the door closed. He'd put on soft music or run a fan to drown out noise coming from outside the seclusion of his study. It disappointed him he could not spend more time with the kids before they drove back to school. But he knew they understood and felt their relief when he was able to relax. When he said goodbye to them Monday morning, their anxiety for him was palpable. He sensed Olivia wanting to cry.

"Everything will be okay," Jace hugged Olivia, and then Alec. After they witnessed the smelling and hearing thing on Saturday, both kids searched the internet for the aftereffects of lightning strikes. They found plenty of cases where people claimed to experience heightened senses after getting struck by lightning — even extrasensory experiences. They also found cases of personality changes, sometimes severe. "Don't worry, I'm not changing. I'll get used to this. I'm the same old Dad."

As reassuring as that was, no one mentioned anything about heightened senses and personality changes. Things were getting freaky.

***

Charlotte didn't normally go with Jace to his doctor appointments, but there was no way in the world she wasn't going with him this time. She was glad she made the appointment for early in the morning. They were in the doctor's exam room by eight o'clock.

After Jace, but mostly Charlotte, explained what happened, including everything since the lightning strike, Dr. Roberts gave him a quick exam and reviewed online the other physicians' notes and hospital records from after the accident.

"Physically, everything looks normal," the doctor concluded. "It's common for victims like you to suffer headaches for many years after the event. There is much we don't know about how and why lightning strikes affect the human body. We know victims get headaches, but don't understand why, and so we don't know how to treat them. I'll prescribe a pain killer..."

"No. I don't want that," Jace replied hastily.

"Well, I'll write a prescription in case you change your mind. You realize you must be very careful with opioids. If you're not, you'll get hooked quickly, and I won't be able to prescribe more for you."

"Isn't there anything else we can do?" Jace's tone had a hint of frustration.

"I want you to see Dr. de Havilland, the neurologist. She mentioned she'd like to follow-up with you. She has more experience with this and will be able to help. Our office will do a referral and get you an appointment as soon as possible."

"What about the other stuff? I smell things, hear words, sense things I didn't prior to the accident." Jace was reluctant to ask.

"I've read that there are people who claim to gain increased senses after getting hit by lightning, but they are unsupported by medical findings. There are some studies, but those are rare. The medical community doesn't invest time and money into studying the phenomena. Dr. de Havilland will have more information on that." The doctor was more apologetic than helpful.

Disappointed, they left the office thinking they need to do some heavy research. *Doctors don't know everything. You have to look out for yourself*, Charlotte thought to herself. *I've seen this too many times.*

"Yeah, I know. I'll do some research," Jace said out loud.

She looked at him and smiled. "This is getting to be almost fun!"

He stared at her, realizing what he had done. She let out a laugh, and suddenly he felt so much better.

Chapter 11: Mohammad

On the battlefield, the United States and its allies have eradicated thousands of Islamic extremists and destroyed the Islamic State's caliphate in Iraq and Syria. Sophisticated intelligence techniques and military action kill terrorists and disrupt their attacks worldwide. Yet in 2020, there were more jihadists fighting in more countries than there were on September 11, 2001. Spiritual leaders indoctrinate pious, young Muslims into political, radical ideology and send them into the holy war.

Wahhabism is an ultraconservative form of Islam that insists on a literal, intolerant interpretation of the Quran. It is the heartbeat of jihadism and teaches that those who do not practice it are heathens and enemies. It is the dominant religious force in Saudi Arabia and is taught in its schools. It is this environment in which Mohammad was born and raised.

At an early age, his schooling taught him there are two kinds of people — Wahhabis, like himself, and everyone else. They scorned and persecuted — even killed — those who did not practice their form of Islam. Madrassas, funded by Saudi charities, spread this doctrine throughout the world. These teachings lay the foundation for Muslims to become jihadists.

As did his hero, Osama bin Laden, Mohammad came from a wealthy Saudi family — one of privilege. He believed his calling was to recruit young Muslims into jihadism, to guide them, to fund them, and to compel them to kill non-believers. Like bin Laden, he loathed the U.S. His aim was to continue the jihad his idol had declared against the U.S., and strike at the American homeland.

To do this, he needed soldiers — jihadists — who could live in America, blend into its diverse society, and then strike at his command. Mohammad found his lieutenant in Bilal Khalil. Bilal's father owned a company that worked for Mohammad's family construction business. The business arrangement made the Khalil family well-to-do, and Bilal was to become a construction engineer by attending university in America.

Most Saudi's have grown comfortable with the trappings of western societies and do not outwardly show disdain for them. Most are not jihadists, but at their core are the underpinnings of Wahhabism. So, it is easy to persuade young Saudis like Bilal, Haider Khan and Owais al Omani to join the cadre of the true believers. Mohammad trusted Bilal, a smart, mature young man being groomed to take his father's place, to be his lieutenant. Haider and Owais came from the Saudi middle class, members of the enormous government bureaucracy, and their parents earned the right to send their sons to American universities.

Mohammad built his jihadist cell with these three men destined to go to the U.S. on student visas. He pointed them to Norfolk, Virginia — the home of the largest naval base on Earth, belonging to the most egregious infidel state.

Chapter 12: The July Call

At the prearranged time, Bilal placed the call to his mentor's cell phone. Mohammad answered after one ring with the customary Saudi greeting, "My friend, salam alaykum," peace be upon you.

"Wa alaykum as-salam," *And upon you be peace*, "my brother," Bilal responded, and their conversation began. They were careful not to use names, and they talked in generalities. They could never be sure whether their conversations were private.

"How are the arrangements for the visit proceeding?"

"All is well. A minor issue has been raised." Mohammad understood that meant to check their secret place on the dark web for more information. Only those two knew how to find and access their encrypted message board where they discussed details of their plans without prying eyes. Using two methods of communication added another layer of security. Mohammad felt it necessary to converse with Bilal, and not rely solely on the internet, even if the length of the phone calls was short.

"Will our young man be ready to do his part?"

"Yes, he is willing and able."

"Is the timing still as we discussed?"

"It remains the same."

"Thank you, my friend. Alhamdulillah," *praise God.*

"Of course, my brother. Until next time, Alhamdulillah," and Bilal ended the call.

Their discussion was brief, but they exchanged important information. They knew American intelligence agencies are capable of listening to telephone communications between the U.S. and the Middle East. Mohammad and Bilal were good at keeping their secrets. Bilal relayed Kent is on track to meet him at the border. He also gave the signal that he has a problem and Mohammad needs to read their message board. If agents from the FBI heard what was said, they would have no idea what the two comrades had communicated.

It was the first contact Bilal made with that phone. As an added measure of security, he would make three more calls with it, and then discard it. He kept several prepaid telephones handy. They are inexpensive and can be purchased with cash from many stores. Even if the authorities discovered his phone number, it would not be useful to them for long.

Chapter 13: Millicent

Millicent Jackson was always one of the smart kids in school. Math and science came easily to her — a trait inherited from her father. Dad was a mechanical engineer by degree, but joined the Navy after graduating from college and became a nuclear engineer. After 20 years of deployment on aircraft carriers, he retired and settled his family in Norfolk. Like many retired naval officers in a military town, he started his second career as a defense contractor. Millicent got her outgoing personality from her mother. Mom graduated with a degree in the humanities and attended law school. A reason Millicent's father retired rather than move the family to the west coast is that his wife had become a thriving, highly respected lawyer in Virginia.

As a high school senior, Millicent wasn't sure what to do with her life, so she picked the logical path of going to college to study engineering. If she liked it, then a plethora of interesting options would be available to her. If she decided not to be an engineer, then the degree would be a useful steppingstone to many other career paths: medical school, law school, or business school — she could do whatever she wanted.

She was excited to land an internship with an energy firm in Virginia Beach, hoping for a rewarding experience. She started full time after the semester ended and could work part time when classes resumed in the fall. It was a thrilling opportunity to venture into the professional world outside of school.

After two weeks off in July, the boss returned to the office. He had been in a terrible accident, and people in the company speculated that he would never be back. When she heard he was okay, a tear formed in the corner of her eye, and she dabbed it away before it could fall, thankful for his recovery. It pained her when people around her were suffering, and she was relieved to know when they weren't.

Her dad told her to always be to work early. "If you're not early, you're late," he said. "Make sure everyone knows you are serious and responsible." So, Millicent showed up 30 minutes before start time every day, and she liked to pop in to say hello to the boss.

When she got to work Monday, people were already in his office. Millicent had decided to give him space to let him get settled when he arrived, but since others were in there, she popped her head in the doorway.

"Good morning, boss! I'm glad you're here," she

said in her cheery and genuine way.

"Thanks, Mil. So am I!"

Chapter 14: The Neurologist

J ace received a call from Dr. Roberts' office shortly after he and Charlotte returned from their appointment with him. They scheduled a referral visit with Dr. de Havilland and to their relief, they found themselves in her exam room the next morning.

She ran the standard neurological exam, testing his reflexes, strength, balance, sensations, memory, and ran simple hearing and vision tests.

"Mr. West, I see no reason for concern," the neurologist validated Dr. Roberts' diagnosis. "There is no sign of anything wrong with you. This is a very intriguing case. So much can happen to a person's nervous system when suffering a lightning strike, but other than your headaches, you show no deleterious effects."

"I read on the internet a direct strike could literally cook the person's brain," Charlotte said. "Fortunately, the lightning hit the tree first."

"Right, it's what they refer to as a splash-over. It

jumped from the tree over to Jace, then followed the more electrically conductive sweat on his skin rather than entering his body. Jace, you were out in the summer heat, working up a sweat. That saved you from experiencing severe effects."

"What about the headaches?" He wanted a resolution.

"Dr. Roberts prescribed a pain killer. That should offer temporary relief, but it's not a suitable solution. I'd like you to stick to Tylenol and try to relax with meditation. I'll give you literature on that — it's effective and offers continuing respite."

"Why can I sense things now, that I couldn't before the lightning strike?" Jace asked, less afraid to bring it up than the previous day.

Dr. de Havilland explained, "I've read reports regarding victims claiming similar things — a heightened sense of smell, taste, hearing, and sight. There is no medical explanation. In most cases, the patients reported those things were temporary. I've heard victims claimed their presence disrupts electrical appliances. People said streetlights go out when they walk under them, or computer screens flicker when they pass by them."

"Scientists have documented the other phenomena you described — that you sense thoughts and feelings of other people. Folks have shown they developed clairvoyance. They could see events in their minds that have yet to occur."

"There is a well-known case of an MD — an orthopedic surgeon in New York — hit by lightning while making a call in a telephone booth. He died and had an out-of-body experience, but a nurse on the scene revived him. Soon after, he heard classical music playing in his head. He eventually quit his career as a surgeon to compose music and became a concert pianist. There's a name for it. When someone exhibits a talent after a serious brain injury that they didn't have before, they are called an 'acquired savant.'"

"Most in the scientific community typically write these cases off as unsubstantiated anecdotes, but there have been attempts to explain them. One theory is the massive electrical current causes a flood of neurotransmitters in the brain, opening parts of it that were previously inaccessible. Some speculate that the part of the brain that regulates how information is filtered is damaged. That allows other parts of the mind to process information that is normally filtered out of the person's consciousness.

"It is fascinating stuff and there are scientists who believe extrasensory perception is real."

"ESP?" Jace interrupted.

"Yes — that's what we're talking about here," the doctor tried to sound reassuring. "There is a large population, scientists included, that believes it exists, even though the medical profession is skeptical because they can't prove it using traditional scientific methods."

"Parapsychology," Charlotte added.

"Correct. Psychologists call it parapsychology, or

psi for short. Several try to study it, but getting research dollars for it is difficult. A few pay for their studies out of their own pockets."

"So now what? I'm a mind reader?" The sarcasm and frustration were obvious, letting the doctor know Jace was not too happy with her explanation.

"We'll treat the headaches with meditation, and that could have a calming effect on your heightened senses too. As in the other cases I mentioned, these sensations may very well go away on their own."

"Or they may not," Jace tersely countered.

"I could order more tests — a CT scan, MRI, x-ray, ultrasounds — but nothing justifies doing them. The CT scan and the x-ray would give your head unnecessary doses of radiation. Besides, they're expensive. I doubt your insurance will pay for them. Nowadays, they want justification to approve the test before agreeing to cover it.

"There's not much more I can do," Dr. de Havilland added after an awkward silence. "I expect your symptoms will subside, and you'll be back to normal in a week or two."

On that note of hope, Jace and Charlotte rose from their seats to leave.

"One more thing — if it turns out you need help to get through this, you might talk with a psychologist who specializes in parapsychology. You'll be able to find someone close by and they'll be more than happy — excited — to talk to you. A good place to start is the A.R.E."

Chapter 15: A.R.E.

While Jace thought the headaches were getting better in the last day, he looked forward to starting his meditation therapy. As soon as he and Charlotte returned home from Dr. de Havilland's office, he took one of the pain pills to ease the headache and quiet his mind, retreated to his study, and read the information the doctor had given him.

Charlotte seized the opportunity to use the internet to research the A.R.E. If you've lived in the Tidewater region for very long, you've heard of Edgar Cayce's Association for Research and Enlightenment. Its headquarters is on the north end of the Virginia Beach resort area and overlooks the Atlantic Ocean. Visiting the center is one of those things Charlotte always wanted to do, but never took the time for it. It thrilled her to find Cayce had founded Atlantic University, dedicated to personal transformation, on the same property. Together they provided all the resources and expertise the Wests needed to understand and cope with what Jace was experiencing. They were incredible resources, so close to home. It was a bonus to Charlotte to find the Association's programs offered massage, meditation and relaxation therapy — services of immediate benefit to Jace.

She found him napping in the study. Although excited to tell him what she discovered, she decided not to bother him. Rest was what he needed most. The headaches and cacophony of extra sensations hadn't allowed him to get much sleep. Charlotte went back to her home office, picked up her phone, and dialed the number for the A.R.E.

Chapter 16: The Return

J ace had been away from work for two weeks and was becoming antsy. There was only so much relaxing and meditating he could do, and he felt Charlotte needed a break from him. He was unsure he was ready to be in a busy, noisy environment with more than one other person around, but he was doing very well calming his senses. He was looking forward to getting back into the real world, and truth be told, he was curious to see how he functioned around other people with his extrasensory abilities. Jace wasn't ready, however, to take the plunge and call it ESP.

Dr. de Havilland was right. With the meditation, he had been able to control the headaches, and it had been only a few days since he saw her. Something she got wrong, at least so far, was that his enhanced abilities to sense things had not diminished. He was successful in ignoring them, though, relegating the 'extras' to background noise in his head. And Charlotte told him she read of others who have learned to turn their extrasensory perceptions on and off at will.

Lightning-strike victims usually suffer from debilitating injuries. Even though Jace only suffered headaches, he was expecting the worst. When he told his team he'd be taking time off, the prognosis seemed bleaker. But things were getting better, not worse, so he phoned his assistant to let everyone know he would be returning on Monday. It would be 15 days since the accident, and he decided it was a good day to resume his normal routine. *Time to move on.*

Jace founded West Clean Energy. He used his Civil and Environmental Engineering degree to design waste treatment facilities for large corporations and was quickly bored with traditional environmental engineering. So, he formed his own consulting firm to help people transition from using fossil fuels to other sources of energy. He figured it made sense to not pollute in the first place rather than trying to clean your waste after you created it. His company grew rapidly, helping homeowners go 'off-grid' and larger companies use less oil, gas, and coal.

His executive team started to consider how to proceed without him and was thankful to find he was coming back. They couldn't wait to hear his story; a firsthand account of being struck by lightning would be a very interesting thing to hear.

Jace arrived earlier than usual, hoping to settle in before the start of the day was crushed by well-wishers and curious coworkers. He made it from his car to the office without being stopped to talk by anyone, but most of his team shows up early and they knew he was there. Soon enough, they meandered into his office to greet him and learn what happened.

"What in the heck did you do?" Jane was the first to walk in, joking and giving him a hug. Before he could answer, folks began welcoming him and helping themselves to his guest chairs, getting comfortable to listen to his tale.

The engineering division's new student intern leaned into his office and greeted Jace as she did every morning. He appreciated her bright smile and cheery hello. It was a great way to start the day. Having been out for a couple weeks, he realized that he missed it.

"Good morning, boss!" Millicent called. This day she added a little extra, "I'm glad you're here."

"Thanks, Mil. So am I," Jace called back, as the room chuckled.

"I want to hear too," she said.

And with that, the storytelling had begun. The part about being a 'mind reader' was left untold.

Chapter 17: The Introduction

Charlotte's first call to the A.R.E. was to an outreach manager. She wasn't sure how to begin, or even know who, or what service to request, so she started bluntly. One thing that attracted Jace to her was her straightforwardness. A genuinely friendly person, she was smart, funny, and was always straight to the point. Because of the smile on her face and her pleasant manner, folks hardly ever took offense.

"We think my husband has developed ESP and we'd like to talk to someone about it. We — um — don't understand what's going on and we need...," Charlotte searched for the right word.

"Enlightenment," the outreach manager suggested.

"Haha! Yes, that's an excellent way to put it." Charlotte laughed, and so did the woman on the other end of the phone.

"Tell me what's happening," she said in a reassuring way. And Charlotte started from the beginning.

After an hour of talking as though they were close friends, the women invited the Wests to visit her at the A.R.E. Virginia Beach headquarters. They would tour the campus, talk to members of the faculty, and then they could decide their next steps.

◆ ◆ ◆

Jace and Charlotte were on the grounds the day after the phone call. The beach facility is a favorite of summer tourists enjoying guided tours and daily classes, but April, the outreach manager, treated the Wests to a personal tour, massages, and a class on meditation. Jace was thankful for the instruction—something he could use regularly to ease his headaches and calm his senses. But the open discussion they had with April regarding parapsychology is what they needed.

"What Jace is experiencing isn't crazy or magical," April started. "In fact, it's normal."

"Normal?" Jace interrupted.

"I don't mean to say getting struck by lightning and developing clairvoyance is common, but Edgar Cayce believed, and most other parapsychologists agree, that everyone has psychic abilities. All of us are born with them, but most people don't work to develop those skills, so they dull as we grow. Only the lucky few recognize their gifts and can overcome the barriers everyday life throws at us that keep people from sharpening those talents."

"I read intuitions, gut instincts, and déjà vu are

manifestations of our undeveloped psychic abilities," Charlotte said.

"Absolutely, we've all experienced those things. In some folks, those feelings are extraordinarily strong. Most legitimate psychics work hard over many years to learn about themselves and to enhance their natural skills. At A.R.E., we help people do that."

"So, what happened to me? Is there a logical explanation?" Jace was an engineer and had been struggling with suddenly becoming psychic. His world was grounded in science and reality, and his perception of ESP was not.

"There are perfectly rational explanations. It occurs enough that scientists have hypothesized what happens in a brain that suddenly unlocks clairvoyance."

"Think of the brain as though it's a radio. The radio receives electromagnetic waves we humans can't sense. That information is swirling around us all the time and is invisible. The radio searches for information on different wave frequencies and finds it when tuned to the right channel. The brain is just a receiver. It has functions that tune-in parts of our reality but filters out others. If something happens to it — like a lightning strike — that realigns its tuner, it can receive signals that have always been out there, but never had access to."

"Jace, your brain has access to signals that have always been there, but like most people's brains, it has been filtering them out of your consciousness."

"The neurologist touched on that," Charlotte added. "She said the massive electrical current could have resulted in a flood of neurotransmitters opening up new channels of communication. Or the lightning damaged the section of the brain that filters signals and it now allows more information into Jace's consciousness."

"That's right. The lightning changed Jace's brain, so it's receiving information out there that most of us are not aware of."

"That makes sense to me," Jace admitted, "but I'm going to have to chew on it for a while."

"Consider this. There are lots of examples of this in nature. Dogs have a heightened sense of smell. They find drugs, sniff out explosives, and even detect cancer in people. But we can't do that. Hawks see their prey from a mile away, but there's no way we can see a mouse from a hundred feet away. It's well-documented animals sense a storm approaching or an imminent earthquake and take cover while we humans are oblivious. Why is it hard to believe we can extend our senses? It's easy for me to accept," April concluded.

"We're here to help you. Call me, and I'll connect you with the resources you need."

Jace and Charlotte had a sense of relief after their day-long experience with April, and understood more about Jace's condition by the end of the day. They felt less apprehensive moving forward with the aftereffects of the accident. Before they left, they scheduled an evaluation of Jace by a parapsychologist at Atlantic University.

Chapter 18: The Kalashnikovs

After talking with Bilal, Mohammad logged in to their message page to find the issue they had discussed. As an added measure of privacy, both utilized Virtual Private Networks to use the internet. They were confident in their security measures — simple and inexpensive, yet effective. Splitting their communications between disposable phones and VPNs made them satisfied no one would learn details of their plans.

Bilal's message told Mohammad that it was difficult to obtain weapons for the assault. The common criminal in America has easy access to guns through their black market connections. But the law-abiding citizen in Virginia must buy firearms from dealers authorized by the government to sell them. And each buyer has to pass a background check before purchasing. He decided he couldn't buy the weapons they needed. He didn't have the contacts that criminals do, and his brothers could not buy them legally. Besides, Mohammad insisted on using

AK-47s in their strike. The AK is the jihadist's iconic rifle of choice, and attacking Americans on their own soil with it would be as symbolic as the attack itself.

The AK-47, designed by Soviet General Mikhail Kalashnikov, is known for its ease of use, durability, and potency in combat. There are many versions, manufactured by dozens of nations, making it one of the most widely available and inexpensive weapons on Earth. On television, Americans have seen jihadists use Kalashnikovs to kill non-believers across the Middle East, Africa, and Europe. Now, Mohammad would let them see AKs kill Americans in their homeland, at the apex of their Navy.

Bilal felt sure someone willing to tell authorities would notice any attempt by him to get AK-47s in Virginia. American bias against Middle Eastern-looking men is strong. Even criminals would hesitate to sell them guns.

Mohammad understood this to be true and knew a simple solution. Much of Mexico's gun violence is fueled by guns flowing into the country from the U.S. So, weapons, including AK-47s, are easy to buy near the border. There, Mexicans and Americans alike ask no questions when selling them. Another trusted lieutenant, Abdulaziz, would purchase Kalashnikovs in Texas and have them ready for Mohammad to transport to Virginia when he travelled there in October.

It was a simple thing for Abdulaziz to pay a Mexican in Juárez to buy one AK-47 at a time. If the man didn't know someone who was selling, it was no more difficult than looking at advertisements in the newspaper. They were readily available on either side of the border, and a Latino buying a gun in Texas is no more unusual than a white man doing the same. Abdulaziz paid the man handsomely to acquire six Kalashnikov rifles, four large magazines for each, six semiautomatic handguns with extra magazines, and enough ammunition to fill them all.

He instructed his man to six buy duffel bags in which to carry the guns and hide the cache in the house at an address off Interstate 10 near Las Cruces, New Mexico.

Chapter 19: Naval Station Norfolk

Bilal instructed Haider and Owais to surveil the main gates to Naval Station Norfolk. The largest naval base in the world is home to the U.S. Navy's Atlantic Fleet. It is akin to a small city, servicing 75 ships, including six nuclear aircraft carriers, seven nuclear submarines, and 134 aircraft. Thousands of sailors and their families live on base or nearby, and thousands more civilians work there. The gates allowing access are extremely busy, especially at the beginning and end of every workday.

They took turns watching each gate to determine the times of the heaviest traffic flow, and to note the attentiveness of the guards. Do they wave vehicles through to ease congestion, or do they carefully check identification? The task was arduous. Support activities sprawl beyond its secure fence line, and there are no places to park or stop to observe the gates without being noticed. They devised a complicated plan to watch the busiest gates. At times, they joined the queue of cars waiting to enter but pulled out of the line before the guards noticed. Other times, Haider or Owais walked along Hampton Boulevard, giving them the opportunity to eye the guards as they worked, and then passed by as though they were headed elsewhere. People going to work are creatures of habit. They wake up at the same time every morning, follow the same routine to dress and have breakfast, and then drive to work. Knowing this, the two shifted their surveillance by 20 minutes each day so that the same commuters in traffic at the same point each day wouldn't notice the same guys walking past the gate or pulling out of queue just before they get to the gate. The 'twins' used different cars when they could. Each had their own, and they used Bilal's too. Sometimes they borrowed Kent Green's car using an excuse that theirs were not available. Bilal's girlfriend, Millicent, had a sporty sedan, but neither Haider nor Owais had the nerve to ask her to use it. The American woman had a strong will, and neither of them knew how to talk to her without drawing her ire.

The Navy doesn't publish the comings and goings of their ships to and from Naval Station Norfolk. An observant party, though, can deduce what vessels are in port and when they leave or arrive. The local news does a good job documenting the human-interest stories associated with homecomings and departures. A carrier battle group, with six thousand sailors, has a huge emotional and economic impact on the community. So, if you watch the news or read the paper, you know when a carrier arrives home and when it departs. It's hard to miss if you are paying attention. Not to mention that taking a drive on a nice day to the City of Hampton and back over the Hampton Roads Bridge-Tunnel gives an observer an excellent chance to see what ships are in port. And on any summer day during tourist season, a harbor cruise will give whoever is on the tour an up-close look at the ships and submarines docked there. Bilal knew what targets were available.

Chapter 20: Dr. Allo

J ace was thankful to be at work with his friends and coworkers, but regretted he didn't take more time off explore his extrasensory perception. April from the A.R.E. connected him with Dr. Ike Allo, a Ph.D. and expert in parapsychology who was interested in helping him discover his potential.

Jace didn't see the doctor until after he returned to the office, and he was having trouble focusing on his job. He spent most of his time pondering what he was learning about himself.

The literal meaning of clairvoyance is 'clear vision,' but the term has become an umbrella for all the extended senses. There are people who see, hear, smell, feel, and taste things that most others cannot. This is what he had experienced since his accident, particularly his senses of hearing and smell.

But even before he went back to work, he found he could block out the extra odors and sounds he was experiencing.

Dr. Allo explained that to Jace, "Folks do it all the time. They adapt to their surroundings and soon don't notice certain things around them they did before. People who live downwind of paper plants grow accustomed to the rotten eggs odor that the plants exhaust into the air. People who live near airport runways don't notice the roar of jet engines.

"It's natural, and automatic, for humans to block out information they don't need. How many times have you driven past a big road sign and not even know what it said?" he asked.

"A lot. Charlotte says I'm absent-minded."

"Your eyes see the sign, but your brain filters out the message. Chances are, if the sign is the only one on a lonely stretch of road, you'll read it and take note. If it's a sign in a sea of other signs, you subconsciously filter out information to help you concentrate on the task at hand — driving the car. Sometimes absent-mindedness is your brain focusing on what is important at the moment.

"What's cool, though, is when you learn to turn that ability on and off."

"Yeah, I've been doing that in the office a little. At first, it was driving me crazy. I could smell the burning coffee on the other side of the building. I heard cell phones dinging way down the hallway and conversations everywhere. Eventually, it just tuned out and I focused more on what I was doing. But if I want to, I'll listen for my desk phone to ring when I'm out on the floor. Jane, our office manager, has figured out that I have become overly sensitive to some things and she likes to play a game with me. She'll be in her office down the hall and call to ask me to guess what she's having for lunch. I can smell it and usually get it right, but I also sense what she's thinking. It freaks her out."

Dr. Allo was most intrigued with Jace's ability to sense the thoughts and feelings of others around him. The doctor was excited to evaluate the extent of his telepathy and empathy, and ultimately help him use his new gifts.

"Tell me how you handle that — sensing what others are thinking. How strong is it?"

"It's the same as with the smells and sounds. In the beginning, it was a bombardment — everything was coming at me. That had a lot to do with my headaches. When I was home, the meditation helped, and I could block things out that I didn't want in my head."

"And at work?"

"I thought I made a huge mistake going back. The cacophony of sounds and feelings rushing in and out of my head was almost overwhelming."

"What did you do?"

"I focused on what was in front of me. Lots of friends greeted me when I first got back, and they wanted me to tell them what happened, so I focused on their faces and responded to their questions. I broke out into a sweat trying to stay sane."

"You were hearing their thoughts?"

"Yes. Some folks noticed I was struggling, and they helped clear my office. Jane shut my door, so I used meditation to calm myself."

"But you controlled the rush of information?"

"Yeah, just like the odors and sounds, I tuned out the extra sensations. That was more difficult. I had to focus to discern what was real and what wasn't."

"Remember, it's all real," Dr. Allo needed to make the distinction. "What you are sensing is real. The communication channel just differs from what you're used to."

"So, you've been able to filter things out — the extraneous stuff you don't need?"

"A lot, but it still takes effort. I now know what thoughts sound like if you know what I mean."

"I do."

"Actual words coming through my ears have a clarity to them. Thoughts are clear too, but they're in the background. I hear them, but they have sort of a different texture."

"That's consistent with what others report."

"Have you tried honing in on one person, blocking everything else out except that one person's thoughts?

"No, not at work. Most of my effort is trying to block it out.

"But at home?"

"Charlotte and I have been playing games. She imagines a thing or a word, and I tell her what's on her mind."

"How often are you right?"

"Every time."

"Wow — 100% of the time? She never stumps you?"

"Yes — 100%. It's easy. Now she reads to herself —

a passage in a book — and I repeat it back to her."

Dr. Allo raised an eyebrow and stared at Jace for just a moment. *It's not supposed to be that way — not for a beginner.*

"This is telepathy. The mentalists you see on the television talent shows — they are telepaths. The good ones that make you wonder how they do it; they are reading the thoughts of others. They are the ones who have honed their skills and added slick showmanship to entertain and make money with their gifts. Have you noticed that some of these acts include a mentalist and their partner?"

"Yeah?"

"Sometimes they do that for show, but telepaths can develop a strong connection with one person. If their partner goes into the audience and connects with the subject, such as touching them, then the telepath's connection with the person can be much greater."

"I have that with Charlotte. We can be an act!"

"Haha!" The doctor chuckled. "Well, let's hold off on the television appearances for a while until we get a better understanding of what you are dealing with!"

"I'd like to run tests with you over the course of the next weeks and months. We'd start by playing the same games you and Charlotte play, but with a little more control. I expect those tests will point us to more complicated ones, and then we'll explore new areas to see how broad and deep your abilities are. It sounds as though you are dealing with the extra communications you are receiving. That's a good thing, but you have to control it consciously. We don't want your brain to filter out stuff you need to know."

"Okay, let's go. When do we start?" Jace wanted to get in front of this thing.

"Let's start right away and continue to meet as often as possible, daily for now. Is that doable?"

"Daily?" Jace didn't expect that, *but what the hell.* "Sure. I can manage that."

Chapter 21: The Beginning

"**O**kay, we'll start with a simple test," Dr. Allo explained when Jace arrived for their next session. "This time of year, we have lots of people touring the center and taking classes. We asked for volunteers today and selected a few to help in our tests. All are tourists from out of town."

"I've instructed them on what to do. They will sit at the table across from you and hold a placard in their hands. Facing them on the placard is a word that is the name of a color. The side of the card facing you will be blank. Their task is to focus on the word, and your job is to tell us what it is. Three different people will run the same exercise, one at a time."

"Do you understand the exercise?"

"Yes."

"Okay. Send in our first helper." A woman, about 40-ish, walked in and took her place. Her hair was blond, pulled back into a ponytail, and she had gotten a lot of sun. *Oh yeah — definitely a tourist*, Jace mused. The cards were lying face down on the table.

"There is a microphone in front of you, and a video camera aimed at the placard. I'm going to step out and watch from next door, and we will tally the results as we go." Jace suddenly had butterflies. *Here we go.*

Dr. Allo exited the room and then said over a speaker, "Miss, shuffle the cards to your content, please. Don't let Mr. West see them."

The woman shuffled the small stack and then said, "Ready."

"Okay — look at the first card and concentrate on the word. Jace, focus on her, and receive her thought."

As instructed, the helper read the card to herself. *Blue. The word is blue. Blue*, she began to repeat herself, but Jace interrupted.

"The word is blue," Jace stated confidently. The woman was rattled but remembered to follow her instructions. She laid down the card with 'blue' on it and picked up the next card. It surprised her. She wasn't expecting 'chartreuse.'

"Chartreuse?" Jace spoke before the lady could focus. "I don't even know what color that is."

Instinctively, she said to herself, *it's a yellow-green*.

"Oh — yellow-green, right." The woman froze for a moment. Her instinct was to leave, but then she realized; *This is why we came here. This is cool.*

"Sorry."

"That's okay." She gathered herself and continued

with the test.

"We'll have to kick this up a notch or two," Dr. Allo said to April in the observation room. April wanted to stay involved with the Wests, so she volunteered to be the person tabulating the results.

"Holy cow," she said staring at the video feed. She had seen nothing like that before.

The doctor completed all three tests as planned, interested to see how Jace did with the other two helpers. Jace was embarrassed by how he started with the blond lady. He realized he made her feel uncomfortable, so he made sure he stayed within the bounds of the test with the others.

When the blond-haired, sun-tanned woman found her family waiting for her in the center's garden, her daughter excitedly asked how it went. "It was cool, but I'm freaked right now," she told her family as she rubbed the goosebumps on her arms and looked back toward the old building she was just in. "He read my mind. He knew everything I was thinking."

Dr. Allo reviewed the results with Jace, "I have a feeling I don't have to tell you how you did."

"I got them all right," Jace said, "they were very clear in my head."

"Obviously, I started with something too simple. There is a standard test used to measure telepathy using what we call Zener cards. Dr. Karl Zener, a perceptual psychologist, developed the experiment. He and his colleague at Duke University conducted extensive research over years, testing subjects with these cards. The test is similar to what we did today, but it uses five different shapes instead of the names of colors. For establishing a baseline — to compare your results with others — we'll do the Zener exam tomorrow. Then we'll move on to other things."

Dr. Allo had years of experience mentoring and teaching people how to develop their clairvoyance, but he had seen no one like Jace West. The ease and clarity with which he sensed others' thoughts and feelings were beyond anyone he had ever seen. Most psychics take years of practice and learning to understand and apply their abilities to real life. Jace did it naturally, as though he had been doing it his whole life.

After Jace left, Dr. Allo looked at April, "He has an open window to the energy fields around him that others simply do not have. I'm amazed."

Chapter 22: Scoping

Bilal liked Millicent more than he could admit. She would not be met with approval if he were to bring her home to meet his family in Saudi Arabia. Well-educated and free-willed, she did not hesitate to express herself. She would wind up being punished, or even killed in his culture. He convinced himself his relationship with her was beneficial for his mission. Being seen with her helped him blend into American society. America's culture was so diverse that he and she together did not stand out and made him look more normal. So what if he enjoyed being with her, as long as it increased the likelihood of mission success?

If they were still together, that's how he would present it to Mohammad when he arrived. He may not need her by then, but she may prove useful.

But today, he thought, he would enjoy his American girlfriend while he familiarized himself with Norfolk. There were things he needed to know: where large groups of people congregate and when, what roads are busy at certain times of the day, and where he can go without drawing attention. He asked her to show him around the city and spend the entire Saturday with him.

Millicent wanted to eat lunch at that famous smokehouse at Waterside.

"Okay, what we're going to do is park at Waterside, then stroll over to Nauticus," Milli explained her plans for the day. "I haven't been there in years and I've never toured Wisconsin, so I want to do that."

"Wisconsin is the huge battleship downtown?"

"Right — most of it is closed-off, but parts are still open for tours, and I'd love to see it. It's an awesome ship and they don't build them like that anymore. Warships are cool."

"Okay." *That's exactly what I want to see.*

"Then we'll stroll back through Town Point Park and eat at Waterside. I'm dying for barbeque and an ice-cold beer."

"Town Point Park — that's where they have large gatherings."

"Yeah, they have wine and beer festivals and outdoor concerts — all sorts of events. We just missed Harborfest — that's huge."

"Yes, we missed it." *The timing wasn't right.*

"We'll figure out what to do after lunch while we're eating."

"Let's go to the mall and I'll buy you something."

"Well, a girl won't pass on that offer."

He wanted the opportunity to walk MacArthur Center Mall to see where shoppers gather and where there are easy entrances and exits. There is no better way to do that than with a woman, strolling as a couple spending the afternoon together.

"Man, that was good! I ate too much." Milli said as they were finishing their lunch. "I need to walk. Are you okay with walking a few blocks to the mall? The breeze blowing off the water will be refreshing."

"Perfect — I could use a walk too."

"Great. We'll pass through Seldon Arcade. I love browsing as I walk through there."

"An arcade?"

"It's a marketplace for small businesses. There're lots of cool little shops to check out. Then we'll cut through MacArthur Square — a small park right across the street from the mall."

As the couple passed the light rail station in the square, Bilal suggested it would be fun to ride the length of the line.

"That's a wonderful idea," Milli agreed. "I've never done that. It's not long, and not many people ride it unless there's a big event going on. Like people in Virginia Beach will park at Newtown Road and ride The Tide to Harborfest, or whatever is going on downtown."

"But the train isn't normally busy?"

"No."

That might be useful.

"What is the MacArthur Memorial?" he asked as

they walked past the stately building.

"That's where General Douglas MacArthur and his wife are buried, and there's a museum there."

"Have you been there?"

"Yes — I love American history. It was my favorite subject in school. My dad took me to most of the military history museums in the area."

"Douglas MacArthur — he was a war hero?"

"In World War II."

"Do many people visit there?"

"Um, a lot of tourists go there during the summer — older folks — baby boomers whose parents were in World War II. Lots of students have field trips there during the school year too."

"Have you been to the mall before?" Milli was curious.

"Not really — I went to a store to buy clothes, but never looked around."

"When we get there, let's find some coffee and hang out at the main court for a while. My feet are hurting."

"Mine too. That sounds nice." Bilal enjoyed the coffee in America. A Starbucks shop was a favorite place to be, even back home.

Bilal straightened his back and stuck out his chest when he was with Milli in public. He noticed other men eye the attractive woman, and it made him proud she was with him. He also saw that no one noticed him much. They were a typical couple enjoying the day together and no one cared.

Millicent was glad to have alone-time with him.

Haider and Owais were always in the house when she wanted to be with him. *Those two are annoying as hell. Don't they have something else to do?* Today she had him to herself, and she intended to get to know him better.

"So, tell me about Saudi Arabia. Where did you grow up?" She prompted over their coffee.

"Well, I was born in Mecca. Mecca is Islam's holiest city. It is the birthplace of the Prophet Mohammad, the founder of Islam. The ancient city centers on the Great Mosque to which millions of Muslims pilgrimage every year. Mecca has transformed into a beautiful and modern city around the ancient center."

"It sounds wonderful. I'd love to visit there sometime."

"Saudi law allows only Muslims to enter Mecca. My family moved from Mecca to the capital of Riyadh. Riyadh is much bigger and is where my father's construction business grew. It is a large, modern, busy city, and the climate is much better than in Mecca. It gets even cooler in the wintertime."

"Is that what you plan to do once you get your degree? Work for your father?"

"Yes, I am preparing to take over the business when he retires."

"Am I allowed to visit Riyadh?"

"Yes, Riyadh is an exceptionally metropolitan city. There is an American community there, but I don't think you'd like it in Saudi Arabia. The sexes are segregated. Women are restricted to family activities. Large gatherings such as Harborfest are only for men."

"Nope, definitely not for me," Millicent added with a little defiance in her tone, and pangs of disappointment in her heart.

Chapter 23: Kent

Kent Green grew up in Portsmouth, Virginia. Portsmouth is on the western bank of the Elizabeth River, opposite Norfolk on the eastern side. Like sections of downtown Norfolk, Olde Towne Portsmouth is a historic seaport with beautiful old homes and well-kept streets. Kent was not from these affluent parts of the city. Kent's life was in the working-class neighborhoods south of Interstate 264. His mom and dad worked hard and maintained a proper home with a neatly groomed yard for him and his siblings. Dad died relatively young from cancer, probably caused by exposure to something at work. There was no recourse for the family — no one to stand up for them to manipulate the system. It was part of life. Mom had to continue the burden of earning a living and raising the family on her own. The kids tried to help as much as they could, but their mother insisted that the best help they could give her was to do well in school and go to college.

Kent witnessed many of the neighborhood kids fall to the allure of the local gang, dealing drugs and stealing for easy money. His parents taught him right from wrong and the value of hard work. It outraged him that his so-called friends preyed on their own people. He heeded his mother's plea to excel in school and to live an honest life. He graduated from I.C. Norcom High School with a 4.2 Grade Point Average and earned a full scholarship to the local university.

It hurt him, though, that so many of his classmates were not prepared to do more than deal drugs or take low-wage jobs. Single mothers, weighted with all the responsibilities of providing for the family, struggled to raise the children. Absent were the fathers to help discipline them and instill values expected by a lawful society. Kent lamented; they were going to wind up in prison, toiling in dead-end jobs, or shot dead by fools just like them.

From what he could see, white people live in the wealthier parts of town and own businesses and have careers that allow for comfortable living. The kids go to decent schools and attend college, or their parents give them decent jobs. The neighborhoods like his were mostly black, where people struggle day-to-day to make ends meet. *It's always been that way*, he thought. *It's just not fair.* Kent considered his parents — decent, hard-working people, but unable to break into the comfortable middle class because the system doesn't work that way. *It's not right.*

Kent's disillusionment allowed him to be susceptible to the divisive rhetoric on television, the news, and on the internet. Racism was alive in America. It was just more subtle than it was during the civil rights movement of the 1960s. Now, instead of toiling on the plantations of the South before the Civil War, black people are slaves in inner-cities, laboring at jobs that white people control. Whites rule today as they have since Africans arrived in the New World.

Some websites play well to that narrative and take advantage of it. They draw people in — people like Kent — and tell them what to think. Once the disillusioned believe what they read and see, the masters behind the websites influence the Kents of the world. They instruct them to send money, how to vote, and almost always reveal to them the one true religion in the eyes of God.

Kent's cynicism led him to one of Mohammad's subtle, but persuasive websites extolling the virtues of Islam with a sense of belonging. His site was the light attracting the unknowing into something dangerous. Mohammad nurtured a few into his web of jihadists to be active soldiers in his holy war. Others were merely 'useful fools' to be used to carry out seemingly benign tasks to further his jihad and then discarded.

Chapter 24: Empathic

D r. Allo ran the Zener test just as he did the simple exercise with the names of colors. He took advantage of the large number of tourists in the center and offered them opportunities to take part in actual telepathic exercises. There were more volunteers than needed, so he tried to pick a few diverse sets of 'subjects' for Jace.

As expected, Jace named the Zener shapes with relative ease, but there were individuals that he had a harder time reading. To investigate what it was about certain individuals that caused him to struggle, Dr. Allo performed more tests than usual.

"Some folks are scatter-brained — they're less focused than most people," Jace said. "I don't think it's one type of person; they just weren't concentrating. The teenaged boy — his mind was everywhere but the wavy lines on the card. If he's that way in school, I imagine his grades are probably not very good."

"Interesting. Do you feel it was deliberate? Did he mean to fool you?"

"I didn't consider that. He could have been intentionally scattering his thoughts. Did you ask him to?"

"No, but it's a great idea. I want to try it. Can a person purposely defeat you? That would be fascinating to find out."

"Well, the kid had Attention Deficit Disorder or was really clever."

"There was an older woman in the third set of testers. Your answers came considerably slower with her than with other subjects."

"Yeah, she looked at the cards and saw the shapes, but it's as if they didn't quite make it into her consciousness. I worried she may have dementia."

"Maybe so, but there are psychics who use their abilities to communicate with people who cannot do so otherwise. They talk telepathically with folks with dementia, autism, and stroke victims. That is another compelling area to explore. There are so many things we can do. There is still much to do."

"How are you doing at work? Is it getting easier blocking out others' thoughts?"

"Definitely. Everything is back to normal. People tune out without me trying now. It just happens."

"But sometimes emotions hit me unexpectedly — usually coming from someone nearby. I walked by Abe's office the other day and got a rush of anxiety. I put my hand on his shoulder and asked him if he was okay. He told me all was fine, but I could feel he was torn up. He had a fight with his wife."

"Why do you say that?"

"He was replaying it in his head, and I could sense the sorrow."

"I've believed for a while you are an empath, Jace. Some people are sensitive to emotion; they empathize with others. But empaths physically feel other people's emotions. That is what you are describing."

"But most of the time things are as they were before the accident."

"I'm not surprised to hear that. The brain is amazing. It lost control for a few short weeks, but it learned what was happening and regained command. What is awesome is your brain is allowing us to consciously open and close these new communication windows."

Chapter 25: Charlotte

Charlotte West looked forward to getting into a routine after the accident. She worked from home to stay with Jace. Not that he needed her to take care of him, but she wanted to be there just in case. He was struck by lightning, for goodness' sake. The workload in the U.S. Attorney's Office was heavy. Taking two weeks off was tough, but her laptop and iPhone allowed her to work her cases. A few meetings in downtown Norfolk were the only times she left Jace alone for more than an hour.

With Jace returning to work, she was free to get back to her colleagues in the World Trade Center. The distinctive building on Norfolk's waterfront overlooks Town Point Park and the Elizabeth River, and she found the setting, and the camaraderie with her fellow prosecutors professionally inspiring.

Charlotte's father was in law enforcement. He started as a beat cop and retired as the deputy chief in command of the detective division. Since she was a little girl, she aspired to be like her dad, sleuthing mysteries and busting criminals. When she was older, and with a nudge from her parents, she decided to be a lawyer, prosecuting the bad guys and sending them to jail. Charlotte majored in Government in college, and then graduated with honors from the University of Virginia School of Law. She began as an intern with the U.S. Attorney in Richmond and later clerked in the Norfolk office. Landing an appointment as an Assistant U.S. Attorney was her dream come true.

Working with local law enforcement and the FBI to fight organized crime was her responsibility. Nowadays that meant breaking up gangs that import drugs, sell firearms, and traffic humans. Charlotte discovered her purpose in life: putting human scum who steal children and young women to sell, behind bars. She loved piecing a case together with the evidence presented by the investigators and was in her element in the courtroom. Defense attorneys were never pleased to find that she would be their adversary. Charlotte could not respect lawyers who defended the amoral, soulless men that she prosecuted, and that made their jobs much more difficult.

She was hungry for her next court date, but another assignment loomed that would take her away from the courthouse. The boss had agreed to put it on hold for a few months while she finished her caseload, but it was time to get it going. The job offered new and exciting opportunities and would expand her base of experience in ways she couldn't imagine.

Chapter 26: Grace

The September 11th attacks on the U.S. homeland in 2001 were the precipitating events that caused many young people in America to join the military and fight terrorism. As a little girl, Grace Madson saw her older brother enlist in the Navy, determined to be a SEAL. When she was twelve, he lost his life fighting the Global War on Terrorism in Afghanistan. Grace had always looked up to her big brother, and his patriotism and valor in combat inspired her to join the fight.

In college, she decided the FBI was her calling. Being a woman disqualified her from the SEAL teams, and women in other combat units filled support roles rather than shooting bad guys. But the FBI's top priority is protecting the United States from terrorist attacks. As a Special Agent, she would be on the front lines. She'd pass the physical and academic tests and stand shoulder-to-shoulder with her male counterparts, investigating and responding to terror threats.

Grace finally entered the fray when the agency assigned her to the Joint Terrorism Task Force in the Norfolk field office. She felt close to her brother in more than one way. She kept warm memories of family vacations in Virginia Beach, spending time with him while he was stationed at Little Creek and Dam Neck. And now, she was there carrying his legacy.

The opportunity to work with a diverse group of investigators and specialists energized Grace. There were over 200 JTTFs around the country, coordinated by a national task force at FBI headquarters. Each included professionals from local and federal law enforcement and intelligence agencies. This impressive network of intelligence-gathering and sharing was the first line of defense against terrorism. Grace loved the military significance of the region. She loved the beach; she loved the dedication and professionalism of the people, and she had a deep passion for its mission. It was where she wanted to be.

She considered it a priority to contact each person on the task force as soon as they joined. She was not their leader, but since it was an FBI coordinated effort, she felt obligated to take a leadership role. Each team member had a full-time job in their agency, and she embraced the importance of creating familiarity among its disparate teammates. The JTTF does this with joint training exercises, but she made a point of developing personal relationships with every colleague.

So, she scheduled an appointment with a task force teammate she had yet to meet. On a recent summer day, she drove to Norfolk to have lunch with the newly added Assistant U.S. Attorney. She heard this prosecutor was tenaciously tough on gangster thugs and hoped she would bring that dedication to tracking down and putting away terrorists.

That lunch at a sandwich shop in Seldon Arcade, just a block down Main Street from the World Trade Center, began a relationship that would have a profound impact on Grace's life — an impact that no one would see coming.

Chapter 27: PRISM

"The right of the people to be secure in their persons, houses, papers, and effects, against unreasonable searches and seizures, shall not be violated, and no Warrants shall issue, but upon probable cause, supported by Oath or affirmation, and particularly describing the place to be searched, and the persons or things to be seized."

The Fourth Amendment to the Constitution of the United States refers to the American citizens' right to privacy. It guarantees that government will not unlawfully seize their homes and belongings and not search their persons and their personal records without reasonable cause and approval to do so. The county's reaction to the September 11th attacks, and the mind-boggling advancements of surveillance technology leave the amendment in danger. The FBI and other intelligence agencies must walk a remarkably fine line between discovering and preventing terrorist activity and Americans' constitutional rights.

Edward Snowden, the former CIA contractor

wanted by the U.S. Government for espionage, revealed to the public that the Government collects vast amounts of data regarding people's use of their phones and the internet. The investigation into intelligence agencies' spying on the Trump presidential campaign showed something even more startling to the average American. U.S. intelligence records all telephone calls and text messages in the country every day for potential analysis in terrorism investigations. They save the communications for 30 days and then overwrite them with new ones. The Government can also determine the websites visited by every single person in the country. This sweeping electronic surveillance program was code-named PRISM by the National Security Agency, and the NSA added several other highly secret programs to its massive intelligence-gathering arsenal since.

The Foreign Intelligence Surveillance Act, the Patriot Act, and the Protect America Act allow for such surveillance and data gathering, but the libertarian-minded argue these laws violate the Constitution. Regardless, with the proper approvals required by the FISA and Patriot Act, an analyst or FBI Special Agent can listen to any call, view any text message and see what internet websites anyone in the United States visit.

As a member of the Joint Terrorism Task Force, Special Agent Grace Madson had access to these awesome tools to combat terrorism. She understood, as every agent did, that she cannot abuse the power to invade the privacy of normal U.S. citizens and that protection of their constitutional rights starts with them. After all, they took an oath to uphold the Constitution.

The number of transmissions between people in the greater Norfolk area and countries in the Middle East and Europe that harbor known terrorists shocked Grace when she first started on the task force. It was tempting to listen to a random sample of these phone calls, but impossible to hear them all. Surely these calls would provide leads to extremist activities or to those that fund them. But Grace could not do that. Doing so would violate the law and the Fourth Amendment. She would have to have a reason to apply this tool in an active investigation to tap-in to any phone call or read a text. Every Special Agent in counterintelligence and anti-terrorism believed they would expose dark, illicit, and dangerous activity if they could just listen in.

Until she had a specific reason to target a certain individual and tap that goldmine of data and information, Grace had to rely on more traditional methods of intelligence gathering and chasing down leads, including tips from observant citizens.

I like this woman, Grace thought as she and Assistant U.S. Attorney Charlotte West chatted during lunch. *What an impressive addition to the team.*

"So, what are you working on now?" Charlotte asked.

"There was that case a while back where an engineer at Norfolk Naval Shipyard tried to sell drawings of the design of the new class aircraft carrier to who he thought was an operative of Egypt. The Egyptian was actually an agent from our office."

"I remember that." Charlotte knew the case. One of her Norfolk colleagues was the prosecutor.

"Well, we're still looking into his motive. He was born in Saudi Arabia and raised in Egypt. On the surface it looks like he was loyal to Egypt and attempted to transfer the technology to the Egyptians, but for a price. He wanted money. We're pulling strings to see if it goes deeper. He was giving the undercover agent tips on how to sink the ship. Was he part of a bigger terrorist plot? We want to make sure we know."

"Do you have other cases? How big is the caseload?"

"Yes, we're always running leads to ground. We get lots of tips of suspicious activity. With such a large military presence and NATO military headquarters near the naval base, our area is ripe with potential targets. We have close connections with the Naval Criminal Investigative Service and base security units."

"So, what's my role with the task force? Are you prosecuting any cases?"

"We're not prosecuting any suspects now. We'll use your experience and expertise to advise the team in what we need to do to build solid indictments against individuals we suspect in subversive activities. You'll also be regularly engaged in chasing leads and piecing investigations together."

"Oh, that sounds fun."

"Based on what you've told me about yourself, I thought you'd enjoy that part of the job."

"Well, I'm ready to start." Charlotte felt better about her new assignment. It promised to be fulfilling, and just as important as getting gangbangers off the streets.

"Good. Let's meet tomorrow at my place and I'll brief you on our current investigations."

Chapter 28: First Encounter

Charlotte hung around the office until she finished or grew tired of what she was doing at the end of the workday. An assignment never ended until the trial was over, and the scum were in prison. That only meant she could put the file aside and devote more time to the next case in the queue. The conclusion of the day was sometimes hard to pinpoint. The easier days were in court. When the judge dismissed the proceedings for the afternoon, she drove home rather than to the office. Invariably prepared and confident in her strategy, she had no reason to go back to her desk.

Jace had a passion for the company he built, working into the evening, inspired by its mission and by the people around him. But since the accident, he left work early. He had complete trust in his management team, so clearing his calendar to meet with Dr. Allo was an easy thing. They knew he was seeing a doctor, but he neglected to explain for what, and they didn't ask.

So, he got home before Charlotte. It was Friday, and they typically had no interest in cooking by the week's end. Takeout from one of their favorite nearby restaurants was the norm, but he hoped that his wife was up to going out to eat. A steakhouse at the MacArthur Center mall in Norfolk served especially delicious barbeque ribs that he had in mind for dinner all day. He called Charlotte before she left work and they made a date for 6:30 p.m. That gave her extra time without having to rush, and it gave him time to drive to Norfolk.

Jace was always early for whatever appointment he had, and he was early for his date with Charlotte. After finding a place to park, he wandered into the mall. Most people pass through the main court and he figured he'd catch his date on her way to meet him.

"Boss!" Jace heard someone call out but gave it no regard. It was another sound in a sea of voices and the bustle of a Friday evening in MacArthur Center. "Jace!" got his attention, and he turned to see Millicent coming down the escalator near where he was standing.

"Mil! Haven't we seen enough of each other today?" he joked.

"Hi," she greeted him with her usual big smile that he grew to look forward to each morning. "This is a nice surprise. Don't you live in Virginia Beach?"

"I do, but my wife works a few blocks from here and we're meeting for dinner." Jace could feel Mil's genuine warmth, a benefit, he thought, of this new 'gift' of his. He felt it every day. *What a pleasant young person.* But there was another impression. A fore-boding crept in around him, and he was strangely apprehensive. The sudden change in emotion was confusing and caused him to pause.

"This is my boyfriend," Millicent said as Bilal stepped closer. He had stayed a few steps behind Milli as she said 'hello' to her boss. "Bilal, this is the owner of the company I work for, Jace West."

"A pleasure, sir," Bilal said and extended his hand.

Jace hesitated for a second or two before he could regain his bearings and then shook Bilal's hand. The chill enveloped his consciousness as their hands clasped, in stark contrast to the warmth from Mil. *What the hell?* The shock of the darkness paralyzed him.

"Jace?" Millicent brought him back to awareness.

"Um — hello. Sorry, my mind wandered for a second there. Nice to meet you." Jace was relieved when Bilal loosened his grip and the handshake ended, but the darkness lingered.

Charlotte walked up to the three of them and broke an awkward silence. "Hello everyone," she approached the group and looked to Jace for introductions. He took the cue and introduced his favorite intern and her boyfriend and then declared they needed to run.

"I'm starving and don't want to miss our reservation."

Charlotte exchanged pleasantries with the couple and followed Jace's lead.

"What's going on with you?" She asked when they were out of earshot. She could tell by his distant look and his quickened pace that he was in a hurry to leave. "Isn't that the friendly intern you told me about — the one that wishes you 'good morning?'"

"Yeah, that's Mil."

"So why are we rushing away?"

"That dude."

"Bilal?"

"Yes. Something is wrong about him."

"What do you mean? Is this a clairvoyant thing or a Jace thing?" Charlotte knew him better than he knew himself. As an introvert, he avoided social situations, and running into Mil outside of work with someone he didn't know would have made him uncomfortable. At this point in his life, though, those minor annoyances rarely bothered him.

"I need to talk to Ike tomorrow."

"It's the weekend. Can't you wait until your session Monday?"

"No. I don't know. Maybe."

"Tell me what's happening," Charlotte insisted.

"I've never felt that and don't what it means."

"What?"

"Bilal — I sensed darkness — something ominous. At first, it was good seeing Mil, but there was something unusual. Then she introduced him. We shook hands, and a coldness came over me. It was strong. I've never experienced that with anyone. It was — unsettling."

"Weird." Charlotte was unsure what to make of it.

"Yeah, give Dr. Allo a call — or text him."

"I'll text him when we get to the table and ask him to call me tomorrow."

"That man is strange," Bilal said as they walked away from their chance meeting with Jace.

"No, he is a sincerely nice, very calm person, but he acted strangely, though."

"He doesn't like me."

"Oh, no. Jace is under a lot of stress. He's still recovering from a frightening accident, and it's the end of a long week. He was just tired." Millicent made an excuse for Jace, trying to sound convincing, but she could see he did not care for Bilal. She had never seen him act that way.

Chapter 29: JTTF

Southeastern Virginia includes the seven cities that loosely define Hampton Roads. With 1.5 million people, it is by far the largest metropolitan area of the Commonwealth. Urban Norfolk is at its geographical center, Virginia Beach is to the east, Chesapeake to the south, Portsmouth and Suffolk to the west, and Hampton and Newport News are north, across the Chesapeake Bay.

The FBI's Norfolk field office is in an industrial park in suburban Chesapeake — an anomaly that isn't unusual to the residents in the homogenous Hampton Roads. Thousands of commuters cross city lines every day, without noticing, in different directions, traveling to their places of work or leisure and entertainment. For Charlotte, it was a short, 15-minute scoot through the Downtown Tunnel and south on Interstate 464 to the FBI building, and Grace.

Grace described the JTTF caseload to Charlotte. "As I mentioned at lunch, there are no current investigations where we are building a case to prosecute any individuals. There are plenty of leads and strings to pull to make sure they don't lead to terrorists. If they do, we'll open a case and investigate with urgency. We have 16 military bases in our region, NATO, and a ton of large public gatherings from beer fests at Town Point Park to music festivals at the beach. Someone with a grudge against the U.S. or the military has their choice of targets."

"How many leads are you working?"

"Forty-eight at the moment." Grace explained as she handed copies of the dossiers to Charlotte. "A lot of them we work with the NCIS. The regional command that provides security for the Navy bases forwards suspicious activity to them, and they inform the FBI. But we have Army, Air Force, Marines, and Coast Guard commands in the area too, not to mention local police departments — and tips from citizens. Lots of them are impossible to run down because they lack details."

"Glancing through these files, it looks as though a bunch give very little to go on."

"Yep — we do the best we can. Agents assigned to counterintelligence are helping with some of these. We share the load when we don't yet know if we are dealing with an intelligence threat or a terror threat.

"I also noticed that a few of them come from Washington?" Charlotte posed the statement as a question.

"The national task force will get hits through its intelligence network and pass them to us. It's common for NSA to identify something suspicious and ask us to check it out. Those we investigate first."

"Tell me where to start. My calendar is clear."

"Please read through the files and become familiar with what we're doing and offer any thoughts you have — legal questions or guidance. And if you have any ideas about pulling a thread, call me. I also need your advice. I'm accessing the NSA's electronic surveillance metadata."

"Yikes," Charlotte knew what was coming. "Do you want to open that can of worms?"

"Yes. FBI uses it frequently in anti-terrorism and counterintelligence. It's a vital tool. You wouldn't believe the number of phone communications between Hampton Roads and known Al Qaeda regions all over the world. I'm going to analyze the metadata for patterns and relationships. If I'm able to do that, we might find terrorist threats and their targets here at home."

"Let me brush up on FISA and the Patriot Act," Charlotte said, "but I'm sure you're okay looking for patterns and cross links. I'll evaluate further when you target individuals' records."

Grace ended the meeting excited to get started. "I'll do preliminary queries in the database and show you what I have in a day or two."

Chapter 30: Evil

"Thanks for calling back." Jace had texted Dr. Allo the night before, after he and Charlotte sat down at the restaurant. "Something strange occurred yesterday that I want to ask you about. It was unsettling, and I hope you can explain what it means."

"What was it?" Ike had been mentoring Jace for more than a month and was extremely interested in his psychic experiences. Jace's clairvoyance was unmatched in Ike Allo's personal observation, and working with him had been the highlight of Ike's career.

"I met someone who turned me dark, and cold I sensed deep down."

"Details, please. Explain what happened minute by minute, second by second." Ike expected this day to come. With the depth of development that Jace had achieved in such a short time, it was inevitable. Ike was excited to learn more from Jace, as he was every session they've had. Jace described his encounter with Millicent and Bilal second by second as the doctor asked.

"When you shook this man's hand, what did you see?"

"See?"

"In your mind's eye or with your physical eyes."

"I don't know."

"Concentrate on what you observed when you shook hands. What were you looking at?"

"I saw him extend his hand. I could see my hand take his. That's when I felt the rush of coldness."

"In that split second, what did you see?"

"I remember looking up to look him in the eye as I always do when I greet someone…"

"And?"

Jace focused, replaying the handshake in his mind. "All I remember is darkness, as though I blacked out for a second."

"Did you look at his face?"

"Yes. I recall seeing his face, but everything was mostly dark — sort of green or black."

"You are describing colors now. Is that what you saw — colors?"

"I see it now that I'm focused on the encounter. I'm seeing greenish-black wisps around his head. I didn't see that when it was happening. Does that make sense?"

"Yes. It makes perfect sense. You see what happened in your mind now that you are in a safer environment. You are calm — not in a state of shock and confusion as you were when it happened. Your brain saw the colors, but your conscious self was too overwhelmed, too inexperienced to understand."

"Are we talking auras? Am I seeing auras?" Jace asked with consternation. He had learned so much in the sessions with Ike in the last four weeks. He thought he understood what he could do and how to control it. *What the hell is this?*

"Maybe. Or it could just be the way your brain is manifesting the dark feeling you had. You are so new at this that sometimes you just don't know what your brain is telling you. Over time, you'll learn to interpret things as you see or hear or feel them. When we started, I told you things like this would happen. We expected this."

"I'm want to know what this darkness means. What do the green and black wisps mean?"

"I'll tell you, but first realize that you will understand the meaning of these things with practice. Eventually, you'll learn what the energy around you means, however it's manifested."

"Okay, so tell me what it means." Jace was growing impatient.

"First, tell me what you think it means."

"What I felt was ominous, as though Bilal is bad, like he's..."

"Go ahead."

"Evil."

"In parapsychology, we believe that sensing cold, or seeing black is an indicator of evil," Ike confirmed what Jace didn't want to reveal. "The greenish-black is more difficult to explain. Green can mean many things, and you must pay attention to the shade of green. Sometimes green feels evil, but transitions to something more positive. Red can mean good at first, but transitions to evil. Dark blues show religiousness."

"And red and dark blue make a dark green," Jace thought out loud.

Ike and Jace both let that linger. Neither knew what it meant.

"It'll take a lot of experience and skill to interpret what you sense, Jace."

"What did he say?" Charlotte heard Jace's end of the conversion with Dr. Allo but wanted to know what the doctor said.

"Ike said I was right. What I sensed probably means Bilal is not a good person."

"You used the word, 'evil.'"

"Yes, that's what I sensed, and Ike confirmed darkness, cold, black means evil."

"You saw colors? Are you seeing auras?"

"He's not sure that I saw an aura. It's just the way my brain communicated the feeling to my consciousness."

"Have you seen colors before?"

"No, it may not be auras at all. Ike and I will discuss it on Monday."

"But Bilal is evil. What the heck does that mean?"

"I don't know." Jace was tired of his new gift. *The gift that keeps on giving.*

Charlotte could sense the frustration and wanted to leave him to his thoughts. *He just needs time to think through things...*

"Maybe we should invite Mil and Bilal to dinner," she blurted, surprising even herself. She had a pit in her stomach and worried about Millicent. She wasn't about to let that sweet person get into something unaware — something dangerous. And Charlotte doesn't hold back, especially when someone could get hurt.

"What?!" That was the last thing Jace expected.

"We're inviting 'Mil-n-Bil' to dinner. We're going to sort this out — this feeling."

"I am not inviting them to dinner," Jace was adamant. "I barely know them. It would be awkward as hell. I'm not doing that," he added for emphasis, but he knew it was already too late; she had decided.

"Millicent might be in trouble and not know it."

"Mil-n-Bil? Really?"

Charlotte smirked. "Give me her phone number. I'll handle it."

Chapter 31: The Pattern

Grace drove to the World Trade Center to meet with Charlotte in her office. It wasn't the first time she'd been in the building. She'd worked with Assistant U.S. Attorneys on plenty of federal cases. She had done some queries into the NSA database and needed to show Charlotte her progress.

"My first selector," she slipped into NSA jargon, "was for phone calls in the last 12 months between Hampton Roads cities and countries known to have an Al Qaeda presence. That was too broad. So, I narrowed the selectors to the past six months and Afghanistan, Pakistan, Iran, Iraq, Syria, Yemen, and Saudi Arabia."

"By the way," she interrupted herself, "did you hear where we established strong connections between that Saudi pilot trainee who shot up Pensacola and AQAP — Al Qaeda on the Arabian Peninsula?"

"Yes, I saw it in the news."

"The media says we got the data from the shooter's iPhone, but there was no way to unlock the phone. The analysts pieced together his conversations with Al Qaeda using PRISM — the very telephonic surveillance data that we are using. They also found anti-American and jihadist material on 21 more trainees' internet accounts. We sent those 'friendlies' home and suspended the pilot training program. I wish someone had done that before one of them killed three American servicemen." Grace added righteousness to the discussion they were about to have.

"So, what did you find?" Charlotte prompted her to continue.

"There are still a ton of calls, but I found patterns, even non-patterns that may be telling."

"Show me."

"First off, you'll see a lot of calls and texts from this cell phone number. Most of the calls originate from Norfolk, a few from Virginia Beach, and are to the same number in Saudi Arabia. The calls vary in length from a few minutes to an hour or more, and they occur at varying times of the day. On the surface, this could be suspicious. But if you think about it…"

"It looks like a student to me, calling home," Charlotte finished Grace's idea.

"Right, we might want to watch that one, but we won't bother with it now."

"Here's an example where the pattern is suspicious. There are four calls from one phone number, each to Saudi Arabia at the same time of day, a month apart, from the same cell tower in Norfolk.

The calls each last around a minute."

"That doesn't sound like a homesick student calling home to mom."

"Nope. I'll dig on that one. Do we have probable cause to listen to the content?"

"Under NSA targeting and minimization rules, you need to be at least 51% sure your target is foreign. This minimizes the chance of surveilling a U.S. citizen without a warrant, violating their constitutional rights. I'd be more comfortable if you dig deeper before targeting that individual."

"Yep, I'm with you."

Grace discovered several patterns in telephonic communications from the Norfolk region to terrorist-active countries. None rose to the bar to justify potentially targeting a citizen. Both she and Charlotte were encouraged, though, by the tack Grace was taking. She very well could develop serious threats from her study of the metadata. They agreed to meet in the next few days to look at what leads she develops.

Chapter 32: Preparation

"**T**his is stupid. I do not want to do this," Jace told Charlotte.

"Just give me Mil's phone number," she pressed. "I'll be cool about it. You don't trust me?"

"Of course, I do." Jace snapped back out of frustration. He trusted her more than anyone. She knew that. "It will be out of the blue; it's weird. You met her for a second."

"I'm going to explain that I felt impolite running off the way we did, and I want to make up for it, and I enjoy getting to know your coworkers. It'll be fine. I am very charming."

Jace gave it one last try. He lost the argument, but at least Charlotte knew how uncomfortable he was with the whole thing. What he didn't say was that he's afraid of what he'll feel and how he'll react when he sees Bilal. He had no idea how to handle it. And she wants to invite evil into their home? *What could possibly go wrong?*

"Don't fret. Talk to Dr. Allo, explain what we're doing, and Ike will tell you how to handle Bilal."

"What, you're reading my mind now?"

"I know what you're thinking. I'm worried too, but you'll get through it. We need to do this."

"What exactly are you expecting me to do? Grab Bilal's hand and go into a trance?" He was only half-joking. He didn't know what to do and what she was expecting to get out of the dinner.

"Well, yeah. What else?" She smirked the smirk that Jace could never resist. "Now, get me the phone number. I'll set it up for next week, so you can plan this out with Ike."

"Let's do it in a restaurant."

"Okay. We'll do it at that Grill 21 place on West 21st Street that you like." She was way ahead of him.

Jace found his call sheet in his briefcase, looked up Millicent's phone number, and gave it to his wife.

Jace was anxious to talk more about his encounter with Bilal in his Monday session with Dr. Allo. He explained the upcoming dinner Charlotte planned to arrange with Millicent, but more importantly, Bilal.

"So, what do I do?"

"This will be your first try at a deliberate reading of a stranger outside of the controlled environment at the center. This is new to you. My advice is to not do it, but I understand what Charlotte wants to do. It is most important to be calm. Be ready to control your own emotions, no matter what you are feeling from him. Meditate at home before the dinner or have a drink or do whatever you need to relax. As long as you do that, you'll be fine. Have a clear head to focus on Bilal, and then interpret what you see, hear and sense. Be confident that nothing dangerous will happen. It's just a reading."

"How do I get through an entire dinner with this guy?"

"Look at it as an opportunity to gather information. Control your emotions and use the time you have with him to understand who Bilal is. Ask questions. Engage in small talk. Include Millicent in the discussion and try to read what he is thinking when she is talking. It's no different from meeting someone for the first time and having a conversation to get to know each other. You just have an extra way of receiving messages from people."

"Charlotte will help with the small talk."

"Good. It doesn't matter who does the talking. What matters is that you focus on him and be open to receiving his thoughts and feelings. Cover as many subjects as you can. Different things will trigger him in different ways. His immediate reactions will tell you his true thoughts, even if he tries to disguise them in his outward interactions with the group."

"Should I try to touch him — like the handshake?"

"Expect to shake his hand right off, so prepare yourself to feel the same thing you did the last encounter. Anticipate and look forward to it. Use it as an opportunity. If you need to, work-in a pat on the shoulder or something. But I don't think you need physical contact to get a reading. You sensed him approaching last time. Remember the ominous feeling before you even knew he was there?"

"Yes, I do."

"As soon as possible after dinner, write down everything that happened. Discuss it with Charlotte in the car on the way home. Getting it on paper will help you understand what's going on with him."

Chapter 33: The Dinner

"**O**h my gosh, you don't have to do that!" Millicent told Charlotte.

"I'd love to do it. I like to meet all of Jace's coworkers, and I felt so awful rushing off the other night." Although she had an ulterior motive, she meant what she said. "Jace has a favorite hamburger place, Grill 21 on West 21st Street near West Ghent, and I thought we'd eat there."

"Oh, great! That's just a few blocks from where I live. Bilal lives close by too."

"Perfect, then. It's a date." Charlotte spoke with authority to settle the issue. "Make sure Bilal comes. We want to make it up to him too."

"We'll both be there," Millicent assured her.

The dinner was set for the coming Friday evening at six o'clock.

"Are you going to be ready?" Charlotte double-checked with Jace that morning.

"Yep, I've got this. Ike has been preparing me all

week. He even had volunteers come in and let me practice on them."

"Tourists again?"

"Yeah. Each of them thought of an event in their past to evoke different emotions so I could read feelings other than a tourist relaxing at the beach. I'm ready, although I'm going to take Ike's advice tonight."

"What's that?"

"He suggested that I have a drink before dinner to help me relax. I'd like to get there early and have a beer."

"Well, that sounds good. I'll join you."

***

When Millicent and Bilal arrived at the restaurant, she noticed Jace and Charlotte sitting at their table. Charlotte saw them and motioned for them to come over. She purposely placed herself between the couple and Jace so she could greet them both before he did.

The women welcomed each other with a hug. Jace stood back to allow them to say hello and Bilal did the same. Even though Jace felt prepared for this encounter, he was edgy. As he and Charlotte had planned, he did not acknowledge Bilal until it was his turn to greet him. On Dr. Allo's advice, they thought it would help him stay calm and maintain control of the reading.

After Charlotte shook Bilal's hand, Jace looked at Millicent. "Hi Mil. It's good to see you guys." He then stepped toward Bilal and looked him in the eye as he extended his hand. At that moment he was well prepared and confident and knew what to expect. The two men smiled at each other as they clasped hands. Jace slightly pumped his arm to signal a more prolonged handshake than when they previously met.

"I'm glad we have this chance to meet again," Jace told him.

"Yes, me too. Thank you for inviting me," Bilal replied in a gentlemanly way.

"Let's sit," Jace said to the group as he released Bilal's hand.

Charlotte sneaked a glance at Jace while they took their seats and studied his face for telltale signs, but saw none. She was dying to find out what he sensed, but she was a master of hiding her emotions. It served her well inside — and outside — the courtroom.

She opened with small talk. "I hope we weren't rude in ordering beer before you got here. We arrived early, and this Imperial Stout looked too good to wait."

"Oh yeah, that's good. It's from the brewery around the corner. I don't blame you!" Millicent naturally engaged in the banter.

"Bilal," Charlotte started the undercover interrogation right away, "you have a lovely accent. Where are you from?"

"Saudi Arabia, I'm here on a student visa studying engineering."

"Where in Saudi Arabia? I know a little about

your country." In fact, several years ago Charlotte had researched the kingdom in an investigation of a suspected terrorist associated with Al Qaeda.

"My family is in Riyadh. My father runs a construction company there."

"I've seen photos of Riyadh. There are some beautiful buildings there. That's a huge city, isn't it?"

"Yes, it's very metropolitan. There are many cultural sections. It is an interesting place to explore. If I may, how do you know my country?"

She hoped she would prompt a question like that. She wanted him to react when she told him, "I'm an Assistant U.S. Attorney and researched Saudi Arabia for a case I was working."

That piqued Millicent's interest. "Assistant U.S. Attorney? That means you are a federal prosecutor, right?"

"Yes, that's right."

"Oh, I want to talk more on that. My mom is an attorney too, and I'm thinking about law school after I graduate."

"Why would a federal prosecutor study Saudi Arabia?" Bilal wasn't ready for the discussion to move to another topic.

Charlotte looked at him and smiled. "We were preparing to prosecute a terrorist with ties there. The case never went to trial," she tried to close the subject. She got a reaction from him and hoped it gave Jace something to read.

Charlotte and Millicent clearly liked each other. Strong, influential women like her mother inspired

Millicent, and she thought Charlotte would be another mentor for her, and Charlotte loved talking to ambitious young women. But as much as she wanted to gab with her new friend, she remained focused on the dinner's aim, and kept Bilal involved in the conversation. He was a gentleman throughout the evening, but she knew she had struck some nerves. Jace did his part too, and was comfortable discussing his studies with him, especially since he was pursuing a Civil Engineering degree — the same that Jace had earned in school.

Charlotte couldn't wait to hear what Jace had sensed. When the four of them finished eating and the evening grew later than they expected, she shot a look at Jace, and he signaled their server to bring him the check. Charlotte used the opportunity to start the pleasantries to end the dinner and promised Millicent they'd talk again soon. The couples walked themselves to the door of the restaurant and said goodbye.

Chapter 34: Disdain

"**M**y boss's wife called me to invite us to dinner Friday." Millicent phoned Bilal as soon as she hung up with Charlotte.

"Dinner? Why?" Bilal limited his participation in American culture to what he planned and controlled. He especially didn't like it when a woman was so forward to interject herself into his life. It annoyed him when Milli made plans for him, but she was around by his choice. She had a purpose.

"She's so nice and thoughtful. Charlotte felt bad that she had to run off in a hurry the other night without talking with us. She said it was rude and wants to make up for it."

"That is unnecessary." Bilal kept his composure, but it irritated him.

"Oh, it will be fun! I really like Jace, and Charlotte sounds so nice."

"He doesn't care for me. Perhaps it is a bad idea to meet with them." He was searching for a reason to decline the offer.

"Don't be silly. That's not the case. Pick me up at my place at 5:45. Dinner is at six. It's just a few blocks away on West 21st Street." Milli knew how to close the discussion to get what she wanted. Bilal could feel his muscles tense and his face warm. He bit his lip as his irritation grew to anger, but he didn't want to show it to her, so he agreed to go.

Millicent and Bilal arrived at Grill 21 at 6:00 p.m. Early in their relationship, she had instructed him how gentlemen treat ladies in America. She noted there were certain norms he was not accustomed to when it came to girls, and she pointed them out. One lesson was that the man holds the door for his date and allows her to enter a room first. That was another annoyance that he accepted, and he did it as they entered the restaurant.

Millicent noticed Charlotte right away, motioning them to the table. Charlotte stood out and was easy to spot. She pulled her long blond hair into a ponytail, and her tailored, navy blue pantsuit revealed her femininity but gave her a distinctly professional style. She projected an easy-going strength that impressed Millicent.

An American indulgence Bilal enjoyed is how women display their beauty in public. And he saw Charlotte too. He followed Milli, but was not pleased that he allowed these women to manipulate him. He resented having to take part in the meal, but at least they were a pleasant sight.

Bilal watched as Milli hugged Charlotte. He didn't

understand the display of affection between people who have barely met. It was one of many things he had to tolerate living in the U.S. Then the woman extended her hand to greet him with a handshake. If he were home, this act would be highly offensive, but he hid his displeasure and shook her hand.

As gentlemen do in western culture, he and Jace deferred to the ladies to finish their greetings, and then the men faced each other. Jace surprised Bilal when he stepped toward him and looked him square in the eyes. Millicent's boss seemed uninterested in meeting him the last time they met. Now he was keen to shake his hand.

Charlotte again annoyed Bilal, starting the conversation by directing questions to him. He understood that is the way here, but it was challenging to accept. *Women should not speak unless spoken to,* but he would engage in the discussion as politely as he could.

Millicent thought it gracious of Charlotte to make him feel welcome and at ease by asking about his home. Bilal, too, was more comfortable when he could contribute by talking about something familiar, but his mood quickly turned dark. *She is part of the arrogant U.S. Government. Infidel. She calls my brothers who fight the jihad, terrorists.*

Bilal struggled to contain his disdain as the dinner trudged into the evening and was relieved to see the Wests call for the check and end his charade.

Chapter 35: The Reading

Millicent had more vigor in her step than normal and a smile on her face. She enjoyed talking with Charlotte and was excited to continue to build that relationship. She knew her mother and Charlotte would be fond of each other, and she was already planning a girls' night out for the three of them.

"Did you have a good time?" she asked Bilal as they walked to the car after dinner. "I had an amazing evening."

That gave him an easy way to avoid the question. "I could tell you liked talking with Mrs. West."

"It was nice of her to include you in the conversation. She tried to make you more comfortable."

"Yes, I appreciate that." Bilal attempted to hide his genuine feelings, but couldn't resist, "I'm not accustomed to women speaking to me that way. That is not acceptable in Saudi Arabia."

"Well — it's different here," Millicent, unsure how to respond to Bilal, let the topic drop.

"Tell me," Charlotte demanded as soon as they were out of earshot of Millicent and Bilal. "Start with the handshake."

"Ike did a great job preparing me. I was in control the entire way."

"I saw no reactions from you. You were the same old, steady Jace. What did you get from Bilal?" she prodded again.

"There was no icy darkness like before — at first. The warmth between you and Mil distracted me from him. I focused on you two. Then, when I turned my attention to him, the sensation shifted from warm to cool. I looked him in the eye and at once felt agitation — bothered, unsettled, as though he didn't want to be there."

Charlotte left work earlier in the day to meet Jace, so they could go to the restaurant together. The plan was that she would drive home from dinner so Jace could focus on recalling the reading. They got into the car and continued the discussion.

"What was he thinking?"

"Let me run through it from the start. I didn't hear clear thoughts as I have with you and the kids. I ran into that during testing with Ike. Sometimes I had the impression the people were just absent-minded and couldn't focus, and other times they were good at covering their emotions. Some of those strong silent types, who always look calm and in control, do that by suppressing their intentions. Anyway, Bilal is one of those people who is well-practiced in hiding who he is. It's not as though he intentionally blocked me. He's an accomplished actor, consumed with his character's identity, and he disguises his own. But there were a few moments when he revealed himself."

"Okay, get back to it. What did you sense?" Charlotte clued Jace to keep going.

"As I said, when I first focused on Bilal, he was agitated and bothered. I tried to be more deliberate and hold the handshake longer than normal without seeming odd. The coldness was different when we touched, but it was there. Previously, it enveloped me — like shock and awe. This time it ran up my arm before everything turned cool. And then there it was again— a sensation of dark green. I can't say I saw color. It's hard to explain — but it haunted me. I don't know..."

Charlotte waited a moment, "keep going."

"When you started talking and directed questions to him, is when it became telling."

"Yeah?"

"Until that point, I only sensed the general bad vibes. When you quizzed him, I read specific thoughts. Did you notice anything when you asked where he was from?"

"He paused. I assumed I startled him, like he wasn't expecting a question right off the bat, and it took him a moment to gain his composure — which was particularly good. He was composed and polite throughout."

"That was his first slip. When you talked, he had

a strong, negative reaction. He regarded you with condescension."

"Really?"

"That's when he said it."

"What?"

"'Should not speak unless spoken to.' It pissed him off that you spoke to him."

Charlotte paused. "That makes sense. Islam is the Saudi state religion. Women are second-class citizens, according to Islamic law. Bilal is studying in America, but he's still a Saudi man."

"It gets more interesting, Char. When you said you are an Assistant U.S. Attorney and prosecuting a terrorist, he lost control."

"He didn't show it."

"He was angry and emitted a powerful wave of coldness, and colors emerged. When the coldness hit, the shadowy green formed around his face. Then it transitioned into a deep blue and pulsated between the blue and the blackish-green. But that's not the most interesting part. When you said 'terrorist' it prompted the words, 'arrogant,' and 'infidel.' And he said, 'my bothers that fight the jihad.'"

"What?" Charlotte considered those words, and the color drained from her face. "That's not interesting. It's scary," she said in a chilled whisper. "Do you know what that means?"

"Jihad is a holy war."

"Yes, and he associated terrorists — his 'brothers' — with holy war."

The trip home fell silent as Charlotte and Jace digested what they just discussed. After a long break, she nudged him to continue.

"What else? That was early in the dinner."

"There was contempt the entire time, and he was relieved when we signaled for the check. I read no more thoughts, but there's something more. When I asked him when he would finish his degree, I felt avoidance and sadness from him. Strange — I didn't feel that at all except for that one instant."

"Let's run through this again when we get home. You're meeting with Dr. Allo tomorrow, right?"

"Yes, he wants to know how it went. Maybe you should go with me," Jace suggested. "He'll get a more complete picture."

The mood in the car turned ominous. Things took an unexpected turn. Charlotte worried Millicent may be in danger of domestic violence or other common crime, but now, the potential danger was on a different level. She had a terrible feeling about Bilal.

Chapter 36: Darkness

Saturday morning Charlotte and Jace drove to Atlantic University for their conference with Dr. Allo. They felt sure that they understood Jace's reading and hoped Ike would shed more light. Ike was pining to hear from his mentee. He worried that Jace using his telepathy in an uncontrolled setting on a potentially hostile subject may be dangerous. Without guidance, it was too soon for him to be a practicing clairvoyant in public.

Jace detailed the evening's brush with Bilal, and Ike was relieved. From what he understood, Jace did well and interpreted important aspects of the encounter. Something Ike had not yet evaluated in him is the ability of telepaths to communicate with their subjects without speaking. He feared Jace would unintentionally connect with Bilal and transpose Jace's own thoughts into his consciousness. Ike avoided mentioning it. He thought the suggestion that it might happen could have prompted it to occur. He knew Jace wasn't ready for that.

"Jace, I agree with your interpretation of the reading. You and Charlotte have drawn logical conclusions," Ike said. "But you missed one thing."

"What's that?" They were hungry for his feedback.

"The dark blue you sensed from Bilal. You have a good idea of what he was feeling and saying in his head, but you haven't addressed the blue you noted at that point."

"Right. I just assumed it was part of the green-black."

"No. If you see colors, you need to pay attention to every detail, every shade. All of it means something. When you observed the dark blue, what did Bilal say to himself?"

"He was angry," Jace replayed it again in his head. "I sensed the cold. I noticed the green-black around his head."

"What did Charlotte say that caused it?"

"She said she was an Assistant U.S. Attorney."

"What else?"

"And she was prosecuting a terrorist."

"That's when you heard him," Ike prompted for more.

"He called her an infidel and was angry she labeled his brothers in jihad terrorists."

"That is when you saw the dark blue."

"Yes."

"We talked about colors after the first time you experienced Bilal. Do you remember what I told you blue means?"

"Yes, I do now. Dark blue means someone is religious." Jace recalled what he thought back then. "Red usually transitions from a good impression to an evil one. Red and dark blue make a dark green. I remember pondering that and not knowing what it meant. Now I know."

Charlotte's job in the courtroom is to lay details bare and make sure everyone understands them. She had to talk it through — more for herself than for Jace and Ike.

"Bilal is from Saudi Arabia. Officially, we don't label it a terrorist harboring nation, but their conservative form of Islam produces jihadists. Jihad is an Islamic holy war. He called me an infidel, the target of jihads, and referred to terrorists as his brothers. The dark blue means Bilal is religious. And he is Muslim. The cold, green-black denotes evil. It makes sense now. Bilal is angry. He's evil. He is a pious Muslim who considers himself a jihadist — someone we call a terrorist. He's an Islamic extremist. The question is — what is he doing in Norfolk, Virginia?"

Chapter 37: The Puzzle

Grace Madson called Charlotte to set up another meeting in Norfolk. It was time to show her what she had been doing with the PRISM data since they last talked. She had gotten stuck on that one pattern of calls they had discussed earlier. She tried to move on to other leads, but it was too fishy for her to focus on anything else.

"Remember that one pattern that looked interesting? The one with the four, one-minute phone calls at the same time every month?" she reminded Charlotte.

"Yes—the potential target."

"I focused on that one. I couldn't help it." Charlotte could tell Grace was on to something.

"Did you find anything more?"

"I did. It gets more suspicious. I only found those four telephone calls, but I looked for the same pattern in the data set. I selected only six months of data. In those six months, I found our pattern of four calls from the same phone number. I also found two other calls from a different phone number, at the same time as the other four, to the same phone number in Saudi Arabia."

"That's interesting," Charlotte waited to hear more.

"I went back and pulled the last 12 months of data. I found two more phone calls made from the second number, in the same pattern." Grace's cadence hastened with tension.

"Okay — we have two sets of four calls. Whoever it is, made all eight calls at the same time of the month to the same cell phone in Saudi Arabia..."

"And all calls lasted about a minute, give or take," Grace finished Charlotte's thought.

"So, it sounds like we are on to something." Charlotte sensed the excitement Grace was feeling.

"That's not all. There is a third number. Four calls, same time, calling the same number. Every call emanated from the same cell tower."

"Damn," Charlotte said out loud.

"One more thing," Grace calmed herself, "I cannot find any other calls made in the last 12 months from those three phone numbers." She gave Charlotte time to let that sink in.

Charlotte summed up her thoughts. "It sounds to me we have someone in Norfolk calling Saudi Arabia once a month at a prearranged time. They only talk for a minute." Grace waited to see if Charlotte drew the same conclusion that she had. "And the person is using burner phones. Why would they do that?"

"That's what I want to know," Grace said, satisfied they were thinking the same way.

Charlotte's mind was racing. Were pieces of a puzzle falling into place, or was it a coincidence? "Grace?"

"Yes?"

"What cell tower in Norfolk?"

"West 24th Street. It's in Park Place."

"West 24th Street?" Charlotte's pulse quickened. She turned to her computer and found Grill 21 on the map — on West 21st Street. "Where on 24th Street?"

"It's right there." Grace pointed to the cell tower on the map, close to the restaurant.

Charlotte thought back. Millicent said that both she and Bilal lived a few blocks from there.

"What is it?" Grace realized Charlotte had something on her mind.

"What if I told you I know who's making those phone calls?"

"The first thing that comes to mind is to ask if it's a non-U.S. citizen because I want to listen to those calls. But how would you know?"

"It's..." Charlotte hesitated. She decided it might not be a good time to say, 'Well, my husband's a psychic, and...' "it's just a hunch."

That disappointed Grace. *Hunches aren't good enough.* But she still wanted to find out what Charlotte was thinking.

Chapter 38: Recruitment

Mohammad's family fortune and connections throughout the Arab world served him well in his mission to build a jihadist cell in America. He had no desire to affiliate with Al Qaeda, or any other jihadi network. His objective to execute a strike against the infidels on American soil required complete dedication and secrecy. Focused on winning the chaotic war and gaining control of Yemen, AQAP lost interest in international confrontations. Besides, this was his operation, and the scrutiny of the United States intelligence agencies and military that Al Qaeda brings with it was something to avoid.

Mohammad needed help, though. He required true believers who could gain legal entry into the United States to gather information on their targets and plan the strikes. The operatives also had to execute their plans when ordered to do so, and be willing to become martyrs for their cause.

Mohammad made it a practice to attend mosques in his home city of Riyadh and in cities on the Arabian Peninsula and in Northern Africa. As a tall man with a full, thick beard and a deliberate nature, he commanded respect from fellow Muslim men. His impressive appearance and university education drew young men to join his intellectual discussion groups in which he espoused the virtues of Wahhabism. Many had already attended madrassas, funded by Saudis, that teach this ultraconservative version of Islam.

After months of careful mentorship, he secretly offered the most promising of his cadre of followers opportunities in his jihad. Three of his recruits were from his hometown, where he had the most influence. These three were well-educated, from privileged families, and were the core of his cell that would plan and coordinate the strike in America. The ability to win student visas and enter American universities was a key consideration of their selection for this role.

Mohammad also chose two Yemenis for his jihad. They had no education and were not so privileged, and demanded a different, more covert way to enter the United States. These two were intensely dedicated and ready to become martyrs for Allah. Experienced fighters, they grew tired of the never-ending, and seemingly pointless warfare in their country. They had seen their comrades die from missiles fired from American drones and were keen for a chance to harm the U.S.

Mohammad had to train his recruits from Riyadh but not draw attention to them. He could tell them what target to choose, how to observe it, and how to plot an assault against it. But it was better to have professional fighters teach them to be soldiers. One reason he picked the Yemenis, Abu and Fadel, was that they had ties to a training camp inside Yemen. It was easy enough to secure entry for Bilal, Haider, and Owais into the camp 50 miles west of the coastal city of Al Mukalla. For two weeks out of the months-long process of applying to colleges and for visas, they trained in the mountainous region of Yemen to learn how to kill. Their friends and families knew only of their pilgrimage to Mecca with Bilal's family friend, who had become a mentor to the boys.

Mohammad felt it necessary to command the attack on the ground with his soldiers. He had no plans to martyr himself. It was imperative that he remain behind in this life to sponsor more jihadi actions. But he needed to be at the center of the storm to witness firsthand his strike and exult in the death and chaos and pain that he wrought.

Afterward, he required a way to leave the U.S. There would be no need to exfiltrate the others.

Chapter 39: The August Call

The time had come for Bilal's August call to Mohammad. Planning for the strike had been advancing satisfactorily since the jihadists in Norfolk were no longer preoccupied with school. It seemed to Haider and Owais that attending classes and achieving acceptable grades was irrelevant to their cause. Bilal reminded them that they had to stay in good academic standing so they could legally remain in the country and not draw attention to themselves. Besides, he told them, Mohammad may abort their planned attack, and they had to be ready to develop alternative plans for another day.

As Bilal had grown accustomed, Mohammad answered after one ring, "My friend, salam alaykum."

"Wa alaykum as-salam, my brother."

"How are the plans for the visit proceeding?" Mohammad asked, as he usually does, to start the conversation.

"All is well. We have a few activities planned. The

details are progressing nicely."

"Will they be to my liking?" The question was a reminder to Bilal.

Mohammad had given him instructions to pick targets to strike against the U.S. military to send the message to American citizens that the holy war can be brought to their doorstep. Muslim brothers had already done that. Since Mohammad's idol, Osama bin Laden, killed over 3,000 souls on September 11th, there had been over 100 jihadi attacks on the U.S. A couple were successful, but most were not. Some are well known, such as the infamous shoe bomber who tried to bring down a flight from Paris to Miami but failed to light the fuse of the bomb hidden in his shoe. A more successful attack was the Fort Hood shooting in Texas by an army major. A follower of former Yemeni Al Qaeda leader Anwar al-Awlaki, he shouted "Allahu Akbar," while gunning down 13 fellow servicemen and wounding 32 more. But Mohammad knew that the memories of those strikes faded quickly in the American psyche. His intent was to shock Americans with the fury of the holy war and let them know they are not safe in their large, comfortable homes. They cannot wage an unholy war against Islam, secure in their home-land thousands of miles away.

"Yes, brother. There are several options. We are ripe with opportunity. I look forward to review-ing them with you." Bilal was excited to get Mo-hammad's approval of his plan of attack, but their rules for maintaining security prevented him from disclosing details. They became leery of discussing specifics on their message board. They knew there were talented analysts who could defeat their measures and did not want to chance detection. Disclosure of specific targets and approaches of attack had to wait until his arrival in Norfolk. Mohammad decided to come 30 days before the strike to give them time to finalize and rehearse before actual execution.

"How are my other brothers?" The reference was to Haider and Owais. He trusted Bilal with no apprehension, but the other two, while trustworthy, were less reliable than he desired.

"They are doing fine. I have no worries." Bilal lied. Lately, they seemed less focused on the mission and more focused on American women. It served no purpose for him to express that to Mohammad, who might see it as a failure of Bilal's.

It was time for Mohammad to end the call. "Thank you, my friend. Alhamdulillah," (*praise God*).

"Yes, my brother. Until next month, Alhamdulillah."

The target opportunities were plentiful. So much so that Bilal had trouble choosing which to hit. The ideal target would be a military one associated directly with attacks on Muslims in the Middle East. American culture glorifies the U.S. Navy SEALs who have killed thousands of jihadis, including Osama bin Laden, and they are stationed at the Navy base at Little Creek in Virginia Beach. The Navy base in

Norfolk is home to the aircraft carriers that bring the jets that rain bombs on their brothers. Oceana in Virginia Beach is the base for those jets and their pilots. Those would be ideal objectives in Bilal's mind, but they are hard targets — encircled with iron fences and vehicle barriers and defended by guards with weapons. Not that he would shy from a fight, but the goal is to shock America by killing hundreds of people. An assault on a Navy base gate won't do that. A comrade recently tried a direct assault on the jet base in Corpus Christi, Texas, with no success. A female sailor — a woman infidel — stopped him by triggering the traffic barrier that blocked his truck from entering the base and allowing other guards to shoot him.

There are other, softer targets with little or no security that would offer no resistance and allow his jihadists to shoot at will. Targets with thousands gathered in one place, preferably military men and their families, would allow for maximum casualties. Bilal imagined that killing hundreds of American military people would satisfy Mohammad's thirst for revenge — and full media coverage around the world. Bilal favored soft targets with military significance — perhaps the impressive battleship, now a museum berthed in downtown Norfolk, or the memorial museum to a U.S. war hero.

But he had finally settled on a few. All of them could result in many dead Americans and allow for his fellow jihadis to flee so they may live to strike again. *Mohammad will be pleased.*

Chapter 40: Sharing

Charlotte was driving home to Virginia Beach when her iPhone beeped. She used to enjoy downloading songs to change the ringtone to suit her moods, but ever since Jace thought it might be funny to change it, she's stayed with something short and professional. Some of her coworkers still occasionally called her 'Mary' to rib her about 'Mary Had a Little Lamb' playing from her phone during a meeting with her boss, the U.S. Attorney for the Eastern District. It was embarrassing, but she still laughed when she thought about it. Jace knew not to pull that again. And a simple beep-beep-beep-beep would not evoke more mocking from her co-workers.

Charlotte synced her phone with her car's audio system, so she heard Grace's voice in stereo when she answered.

"Hey, I pulled July's data from PRISM to update our dataset. I did it today, so we have some August data too."

"Since you're calling me, I'm guessing you found something."

"I found two more calls to 'Bossman.'" They figured the caller in Norfolk must be checking in with his superior each month, so they started calling the Saudi end of the phone calls Bossman and the Norfolk end 'Minion.'

"With a new burner phone?" Charlotte guessed.

"Yes, and the last one was yesterday."

"Both from Park Place?"

"You got it. When are we going to talk about listening to those calls?" Grace was becoming impatient. She could do it herself by requesting the recordings, as long as she followed the targeting and minimization rules set by the NSA. The recordings aren't available indefinitely. Every day, algorithms automatically overwrite 30-day-old calls with new ones, so they needed to move soon to preserve for future use those that are still available.

"Let's meet tomorrow." Charlotte wanted to talk too. "Can you come to my place again? Nine o'clock?"

"Yeah. See you then."

Charlotte understood delaying the legal decision to listen to Minion and Bossman could mean they were losing valuable evidence of a potential terror attack in Norfolk, or anywhere in the U.S. Her partner was being professional and cautious, deferring the judgment to her. As a Special Agent, Grace could decide herself there was at least a 51% chance that

Minion was a foreign national. That would give her the power to surveil. The NSA targeting and minimization rules safeguard Americans' constitutional right to privacy, but give intelligence agencies the tools required to battle terrorism. To protect the homeland, agents must move quickly to tap into terrorist communications without having to wait for the courts to approve warrants. Even though the calls were suspicious, especially since Minion used prepaid phones, Charlotte wished they had one more piece of information to support what is essentially a wiretap without a warrant.

She knew in her gut that Bilal was Minion, but her husband's telepathic reading of him would not stand up in court as a legitimate intelligence source. Not that she expected to have to defend it in court, but it was the principle — the standard — that was important. Besides, Minion might be one pissed-off American if he found out the government was listening to his telephone conversations because he made monthly wellness checks to a loved one living in Saudi Arabia.

The meeting had an increased sense of urgency and she decided to confide in Grace. They were teammates in this thing, and if they didn't make the right decisions, they might allow an attack to happen that could cause the death of citizens whose rights they were trying to protect.

"What can we do to justify surveilling Minion's phone calls?" Grace got straight to it.

"We're on the verge. We need a little more to be

comfortable that we're doing the right thing."

"You don't think the disposable phone thing is enough?"

"No. That's suspicious and reason for us to listen in, but even if Minion is up to something nefarious, if he is a U.S. citizen, we need a warrant. Would you expect a judge to grant one because we suspect the guy uses burner phones?"

"I know they won't — I've tried. Just because criminals use burners, does not mean your average, everyday, paranoid American doesn't."

Grace finally asked the question she had been hoping her friend would offer the answer without having to ask. "So, what's that hunch of yours?"

"I've avoided telling you. I don't know how you'll react, or what you'll think of me."

"What? You are an intelligent, consummate professional and have an impeccable reputation. That's why I was excited to learn you were appointed to the JTTF. Now, what's up? There's nothing wrong with having hunches."

"I have a good idea who Minion is. He's a Saudi national living in Park Place."

"Why do you suspect he's Minion, other than he's a Saudi?" That was the question Charlotte was not looking forward to answering.

"My husband, Jace, and I had dinner with him around a week ago."

"Yeah?" Grace urged her to continue.

"Jace has an intern at work. Millicent is her name. We ran into Millicent and her boyfriend in the mall and then made a dinner date to get to know them better. The boyfriend's name is Bilal, from Saudi Arabia, and he lives in Park Place."

"Because this guy's a Saudi doesn't mean he's a terrorist. There's more, right?"

"Yep."

"Come on, out with it."

"Both Jace and I have concluded that Bilal is an Islamic extremist. We engaged in small talk with him throughout the dinner. He became contemptuous toward me when I said I was an Assistant U.S. Attorney and angry when I told him I had investigated a suspected terrorist in AQAP. He called me an infidel and was angry that I called one of his brothers in jihad a terrorist."

"Well damn, that's a lot more than a hunch. Why hold that back? That's enough to target him. I don't understand."

"What you don't understand," Charlotte began, "is that Bilal's facade was gentlemanly and respectful. He said those things to me in his head. He kept his negative reactions and words to himself. He didn't say them out loud."

"Uh…"

"My husband has a unique ability — a proven ability to hear what people are thinking, to sense what they are feeling. He is clairvoyant, and his abilities are quite demonstratable and verifiable."

Grace didn't know what to say, so she said nothing.

"We have told no one," Charlotte felt the need to

add, "well, except for the few folks who are helping him use the gift."

Chapter 41: Targets

In his mind, Bilal narrowed his list to a few soft targets associated with the U.S. military. He was still considering a couple with no obvious military connections, but on which strikes could cause hundreds of deaths. Surely, any sizeable crowd in the area will include military families. He wished he could discuss details with Mohammad and learn his target preference, but that had to wait. The safest thing to do would be to plan several strikes and choose the best one to present to Mohammad. If he didn't like it, he'd have more from which to choose.

He gathered his brothers in his study in the house in Park Place to solicit their recommendations. Up to this point, a hot sunny day in August, the three of them had scouted several places and collected intelligence on each. It was amazing to him how much useful information they could discern from the internet. Google Maps, local news sites, and the Navy's own websites provided a wealth of intelligence. Combined with their physical surveillance — sometimes with remote hidden cameras — they had the information needed to plan attacks. It was time to make detailed preparations as the occasion for the assault was approaching.

Bilal explained his preference for soft targets, but wanted a last review of hard military objectives before deciding to discount them.

"Tell me what you learned from your surveillance of the carrier navy base," Bilal started.

"It is not a suitable target," Owais offered. "It is an exceptionally large base. Thousands of sailors and civilians work there each day, spread throughout the facility."

Haider continued. "The gates are hardened. There are vehicle barriers that rise from the pavement when triggered by the guards. This happened to our brother in Texas. He failed to get onto the base and they killed him before he could kill even one American."

"If we defeat their security at the gates, there would be two more layers of armed guards between us and the ships," Owais added. "There are sentries on the piers, and each ship posts security on its gangway. And none of that includes the response triggered if we force our way through the gates. There is no way for a small force to get close to a target of meaning. We would die without accomplishing our mission."

"That is what I concluded," Bilal validated his team's assessment. "What of the bases at Little Creek and Oceana?"

"Owais and I agree the same conditions exist

there. They are considerable in area with no concentration of sailors and workers, and we would encounter similar security measures."

Owais then offered information of which Bilal was unaware. "We checked Dam Neck too." Haider shot a look at him, but it was too late.

"We had excluded that base from our surveillance." Bilal's terse statement was clearly a directive to explain themselves.

Haider left his comrade to answer. "We had finished our reconnaissance at the Oceana jet base that day. Dam Neck is next to Oceana but is on the ocean. We thought we should check it out."

"What did you discover?" Bilal forced the words through tight lips, trying not to show his irritation.

"Nothing different." Owais was reluctant to say what happened, and Haider remained silent.

What they did not tell Bilal is that they were careless. As they approached the Dam Neck gate, they realized too late they had no opportunity to exit. Trees bordered the road, and there was an elaborate arrangement of concrete barriers before the entrance. They didn't realize a line of cars had queued behind them. Owais was behind the wheel and could do nothing except pull forward to the gate. Both began to sweat, and unsure of what to do, their eyes darted from each other to the guard. Owais hoped the guard would be lazy and just wave them through, as sentries sometimes do. But they had no such luck. The guard motioned for the driver to stop and to roll down his window. When Owais opened the driver's window, the woman in green camos and a sidearm on her hip waited for the two men to present their Common Access Cards — the universal identification that gains access to U.S. military installations. Five or six seconds passed before Haider realized what she was expecting. They saw this interaction with gate guards from afar hundreds of times.

"I am sorry. We are lost," Haider shouted from the passenger seat.

Flustered, Owais rapidly stuttered, "Yes, we are hoping to find the beach."

"This isn't the way to the beach, sir. You need to turn around."

"Yes, of course," both jihadis were quick to comply. The guard used proper protocol. She radioed dispatch to let them know she was closing the gate and escorting an unauthorized vehicle in a turnaround. Deeply relieved, the two drove away believing they had talked themselves out of a problematic situation. But the sentry had other thoughts. She reported that she thought the turnaround was an attempted incursion by foreign nationals, and she included the incident in her shift turnover.

Bilal suspected there was more to their story. Their Google Maps research dissuaded them from attempting direct observation. Dam Neck Road leads straight to the base with nothing else on the road nearby. There's no place to surveil without raising suspicion, so they had excluded it from their list of potential targets. He was reluctant to pursue the matter, so he avoided discussing it further.

"What about the shipyards?" Bilal asked. He knew the answer but wanted to make sure he wasn't missing something. There are several in the region, and most service U.S. Navy ships.

"Norfolk Naval Shipyard in Portsmouth is just as hard, maybe harder than the naval base. They have the same layers of armed security and it is very large." Haider explained.

"The big shipyard in Newport News is the same," Owais said. "Those are the only two that work on the nuclear aircraft carriers."

"The smaller shipyards only have a few of hundred people working at once. The facilities are old and do not have modern security features. Breaching the gates might be easier, but we would still have to contend with ships' sentries. To me," Haider concluded, "the prizes at these small yards are not worth the sacrifice."

"So, we agree to eliminate these military targets?" Bilal asked, and his cohorts agreed. "What are your favorite soft targets?"

Haider spoke first. "There is a beer festival at the Town Point Park in October that thousands of people attend. The Elizabeth River borders the park on the west and the rest of it is fenced in, leaving them nowhere to run. If we attack from the north, east, and south we will kill many Americans, and then disappear into the city to live and fight another day."

"Yes, I like that target. What about the battleship museum? When I toured it with Millicent, there were a lot of people on the ship and in the Nauticus museum next to it."

"I think we should include it in our planning," Haider said. "It will not be so crowded when the tourist season ends, but we can think about that."

"Include the MacArthur Center mall as well," Owais suggested. "We'll have a few easy approaches to enter and exit. Many people shop on a Saturday. The problem is, it is big and has many places to run and hide."

"That will be something to mitigate during planning," Bilal said. "I agree we should consider the mall. Haider, what did you find out about the Scope arena?"

"The arena holds 10,000 people and a few large events are scheduled for the fall and winter. There are three places to enter before an event, but there are several exits all around the arena. It would be difficult to go undetected while entering Scope, but once inside there would be people all around us to shoot, and then we'd exit and disperse."

"Good, choose the best times to strike," Bilal directed, but Haider had another suggestion.

"There is a better target on the same property — Chrysler Hall. It is a smaller building with less security and would be easier and faster to penetrate. There will be 2,500 people at the theater, and we could strike, empty our magazines, and leave before the police react."

Bilal liked it. "That's an excellent idea. We have enough viable targets to consider. Are there others to mention before moving forward with the planning?" Haider and Owais were content, and especially liked striking and dispersing, rather than martyring themselves. It would allow them to strike the Americans again, they reasoned.

It was time to get to begin their work, so Bilal clarified assignments. "Haider, develop two assault plans focusing on Scope or Chrysler Hall. Owais, you do the same for Town Point Park and the MacArthur Center. I'll develop a plan for the Nauticus-Wisconsin museum, and I have another target in mind. That gives us plenty of work to do. Have preliminary plans ready to discuss in a week."

But Owais had one last idea. "Should we consider simultaneous attacks around the city to create chaos?" he wondered out loud. "It may confuse the police in their response."

"That is something to contemplate. There will be five of us," Bilal pondered. "That could be a very smart idea."

Chapter 42: Doubt

"I'm not sure what to say," Grace said. She took a few moments to digest what Charlotte just told her — that she thinks this Saudi in Park Place is a terrorist because her husband read his mind.

"Well, you understand why I said nothing." Charlotte's retort was almost one of annoyance, but she understood Grace's reaction and was not expecting a positive response.

Charlotte knew Jace like no other person did. They had that bond soulmates have that enabled them to trust each other without question. It didn't cross her mind to doubt his sincerity and legitimacy. Besides, his clairvoyance played out in a way in which they discovered it together. Grace didn't have the benefit of that experience, and she was stuck between her respect for Charlotte and believing something that had no validity in their professional lives.

"So, now what? I don't know what to do with this."

"First, accept that Bilal is an Islamic extremist.

Once you do, we figure out how to tag him as Minion so we can target him for surveillance and find out if he is up to something."

"Presuming I believe you and we investigate this dude, and it turns out to be the wrong guy, then we've wasted valuable time."

"If he is plotting an attack right here under our noses, and we do nothing, then we will allow people to die." Charlotte countered Grace's apprehension. "I don't mean to argue with you. Let's decide together what to do."

"I don't know..." Grace let her thoughts fade. She started the conversation excited to determine how to listen to Minion's phone calls. Now, she felt as though the effort may be derailed.

"Would it help for you to talk to Jace? He will quickly convince you what we are saying is legit." Charlotte offered the meeting more to mend the schism she may have caused between the two of them. She hoped Grace would accept Jace's reading of Bilal, and they could get back on Minion's trail with no loss of trust. At first, Grace considered talking with him would serve no purpose. Whether or not she believed him had no bearing on how to proceed legally. But she wanted to have faith in her friend.

"Let's do it. Sooner the better."

Charlotte picked up her cell phone and called him. "Jace, I need you to meet me for coffee this morning. Can you come now?"

Jace had gotten out of a long staff meeting and hoped to catch up on unread emails when his cell rang. He saw on caller-ID that it was his wife. It was unusual for them to talk during the workday, so he answered it as soon as he realized it was her.

"Hey," he said, more curious than as a greeting.

"Jace, I need you to meet me for coffee this morning." She didn't greet him as she normally does when she calls. She was direct as always, but more businesslike.

"Okay." This was strange, and he wondered what was going on.

"Can you come now?"

"Ah, yeah. I'll be there in 20 minutes."

"Thanks. See ya."

That's weird. Something's up. He couldn't remember Charlotte ever calling him at work and wanting to see him. *She must not be alone. Otherwise, she wouldn't have been so terse.*

Chapter 43: The Drop In

Millicent knew better than to drop in on Bilal unexpectedly. She realized early in their relationship that he always had to be in control. He only did what she wanted to do if it suited him, or if he knew she would be particularly upset if he didn't. And he did not take surprises well, even little ones. One day she stopped by the house between classes to say hello and he became noticeably irritated with her. Bilal was always calm and respectful and did not like to show his emotions. If you didn't know him, you may not recognize his annoyance, but Millicent learned what his barely pressed lips and narrowed eyes meant. At first, she was suspicious that he was entertaining someone else, but after a few quick glances around, she realized he was alone. Of course, Haider and Owais were in the living room with that video game they were always playing.

So Milli was hesitant to drop in at Park Place on a Friday afternoon, knowing the reception she would receive may not be a warm one. It was hot and sunny as it is every August day in Hampton Roads, and she left work early to spend the rest of it at the shore with girlfriends. The plan was to meet at her place in West Ghent, then head to Virginia Beach. They'd be at the resort strip in 25 minutes. Unfortunately, Milli had left her beach bag at Bilal's house. Bilal had promised her they'd go to the oceanfront last Saturday, but he insisted on taking a midday harbor cruise instead. While Milli had fun checking out the ships at the Navy base, it was not the beach. She had carried her tote with her beach things, including her favorite swimsuit, into the house. When he told her he had changed his mind and they weren't going to the strip, her ever-present smile left her face and she focused on not getting angry, forgetting her bag in the study. Now it was time for a girls' trip, and she needed it. She called Bilal from work to tell him she was coming by, but he didn't answer his phone, so she texted him. He didn't respond to that either, and it wasn't the first time he ignored her calls. He had explained to her that when he's busy, he doesn't like her to disturb him. Well, Millicent needed her gear, and she was going to get it. She'd be in and out in 30 seconds. *His Saudi ass needs to learn a thing or two about American women,* she thought. As she sat at her desk, her lips pursed. She was perturbed. *You do NOT ignore my phone calls.*

It wasn't a long drive from West Clean Energy to Park Place. It was long enough, though, to give Millicent 15 minutes to stew. By the time she got there, she had transitioned from perturbed to pissed. She parked in the street, shut the car door harder than she needed to, and with a furrowed brow and clenched jaw, closed the distance to the front porch in just a few seconds.

Without hesitating, she opened the door and stepped into the hall. Bilal insisted on keeping the doors locked, but Haider and Owais never bothered. She left her tote just inside the study. That was Bilal's space, and Milli felt more comfortable leaving her things there than somewhere else. Her aim at this point was to get in and out as fast as possible and not speak to anyone inside the house.

Millicent slid open the pocket door to the study with a solid thud. Focused on the floor where she put her bag, she didn't notice if anyone was in the room.

"What are you doing?!" a surprised Bilal shouted at her. Millicent recoiled with shock as she raised her head to see him, glaring at her with cold eyes. He, Haider, and Owais were sitting around the table. She had never heard him raise his voice before, and besides startling her, his anger was scary. For a few moments, the fright left her unable to speak.

Stunned, the Saudis froze for a second or two. When they regained their composure, they scrambled to close their laptops and gather papers they had spread around them. Millicent's stare was naturally drawn to what they were trying to hide.

Bilal broke the silence. "What do you want?" he said as though he were scolding an unruly child.

"I want my bag," she spoke with a stern reply. She was not the type of person to allow someone to bully her. *No one talks to me that way*. She found the bag, picked it up, and defiantly walked out. If she had let her anger get the best of her, she might have stormed away, slamming the door behind her. But her parents taught her to be better than that, to control her emotions and handle herself with dignity. When she was in her car, she let herself vent. "Asshole," she whispered through her clenched teeth.

Bilal rose from his chair and hurried to the window. He watched as Millicent walked to her car. Satisfied that she was not returning, he turned to his compatriots. "What did she see?"

"I don't think she saw anything," Haider answered, "but I was picking up my notes and maps and not looking at her."

Owais said the same, "I don't know what she saw."

"Even if she did, it was just words and maps. She was too far away to read any of it," Haider said with confidence.

"Haider is right. Even if she could read them, they were exposed for only a second. She had no time to make any sense of it. We were planning our trip to the zoo!" Owais laughed at his own joke and Haider chuckled too.

Bilal was not amused. Once again, the lack of seriousness from his comrades angered him, but he kept his cool. "Did she hear anything?"

"I am sure she did not," one of them said.

"Definitely not. We were at a pause in the conversation when she entered the room," the other added.

"Your woman should learn her place," Owais admonished Bilal. Haider looked at Owais in disbelief. The day will come, he thought, Owais would get them into trouble with his boldness.

Chapter 44: The Incursion

It is not an uncommon thing for spies to drive onto naval installations in Hampton Roads. Sometimes guards are not attentive and wave drivers, who don't have access to the base, through the gate. Once they get past the sentry, intruders can ride around, take photos, and see what they desire.

Late in 2019, the United States expelled two Chinese diplomats, one suspected of being an intelligence officer, for doing just that. As reported in the press, the diplomats, with their wives along for the ride, drove onto a sensitive military base in Virginia. The Navy speculated they were testing security measures at the base that houses special operations forces. Most people are aware the Navy SEALs are those forces, based at Little Creek. Those who pay closer attention know that Dam Neck is the home to the elite team that doesn't officially exist — SEAL Team Six.

It was at this same base Haider and Owais found

themselves stuck in the queue at the main gate, unable to turn off or turn around. They had no choice but to drive to the sentry and feign ignorance. Their excuse they gave the guard was that they were going to the beach and got lost. The diplomats' excuse was that they were sightseeing — and got lost.

The difference between the Chinese incursion and the Haider / Owais incursion is that the diplomats' intent was to test security measures. When the guard instructed them to turn around, they just kept driving into the facility, prompting a security response. The Chinese, of course, had immunity and the Navy released them. Haider and Owais had the good sense to execute their turnaround as ordered and were relieved when they thought they had gotten away with their mistake. What they didn't realize, and what Bilal could not know, is the guard reported their blunder as a potential attempted intrusion by foreign nationals. She explained the two, Middle Eastern-looking men spoke with Arabic-sounding accents and appeared nervous when she talked with them. She had no reason to detain them, so she ordered the turnaround and recorded their vehicle description and license plate number.

As they did with the Chinese incursion, the command in charge of security for the Navy bases reported the incident to other commands in the region for their awareness. They also forwarded the latest foray, by the nervous, Middle Eastern men, to the NCIS for investigation.

Chapter 45: The Demonstration

Mid-morning traffic was light. Jace caught all green lights, so the drive from the Central Business District to downtown Norfolk took only a few minutes. He parked in the Town Point Garage and walked across the street to Charlotte's building. He found Charlotte with another, younger woman in the café off the lobby on the first floor. They already had their coffee in hand and his wife had his favorite waiting for him.

"Jace, this is Grace Madson." Charlotte introduced her husband. "She's a Special Agent with the FBI. We're working together on the Joint Terrorism Task Force. I told you about that."

"Yes, hi." He extended his hand, and they greeted each other.

As Charlotte does, she got straight to the point. "I told Grace about your reading of Bilal."

Surprised he could only muster an, "Ahhhhh," as though the doctor was holding a tongue depressor in his mouth.

"We need to convince her we're right about Bilal."

"Okay. How are we going to do that?" Jace did not like where this was going.

"You're going to read her mind."

"Oh no, I don't want to do that." He was fine in the controlled environment with Ike at the center. His subjects had volunteered and understood what they were getting into. They were there for fun. Using his clairvoyance on normal, everyday people made him uncomfortable. Besides experimenting with Charlotte and Jane, he'd only done it once with intention — on Bilal.

"This is important. How do you want to do it?" She had already made up her mind, and once again, he had no choice, and he realized that. "Do it here, or in my office?"

"Let's do it like you and I did when this first started. Grace can read a passage and I'll repeat it back to her. That will be the easier, less intrusive way."

Before he could say, 'in your office,' Charlotte grabbed a menu from the center of the table and gave it to Grace. "Grace, pick anything on the menu. Read it to yourself, and Jace will tell us what you are reading."

"It isn't always that easy...," he tried to interject, but Charlotte focused on one thing.

"Go ahead, Grace," Charlotte urged her, cutting off Jace.

"Really? This is weird." Grace reacted with some hesitancy.

"Just go ahead. Focus on the menu and this will be over in a minute." Charlotte's goal at this point was to amaze Grace, so there was no question in her mind about Charlotte's credibility. It was important to her personally and professionally.

Grace opened the breakfast menu of the café and began perusing the selections. "Hmm — nah. What else?" She was considering what to read, as though she were ordering.

"Grace!" Charlotte implored. "We're not eating. Just pick something."

"Okay, I'm reading. Okay, here we go." *I do not like them, Sam-I-am. I do not like green eggs and ham.* Instead of reading a menu item, she quoted one of her favorite Dr. Seuss books as a child. She said it again in her head, enjoying herself because it brought back warm memories. *I do not like them, Sam-I-am. I do not like green eggs and ham. Ha — read that!* She thought with a malicious smirk on her face.

Charlotte noticed the grin and then looked at Jace. The wide smile on his face surprised her. "Uh, okay, what's going on?"

Jace turned to her and said, "Grace called me Sam." Grace's smirk disappeared, and her eyes opened wider.

"What?" Charlotte asked. "Just say what she was reading, Jace."

"Unless they have Dr. Seuss on the menu, Grace didn't read it. 'I do not like them, Sam-I-am. I do not like green eggs and ham.' Ha — I just did!" Jace repeated out loud what Grace said to herself and responded to her little taunt, too. Grace's intelligence made it easier to hear her thoughts. Her logical and inquisitive mind, much like Charlotte's, gave her a natural ability to focus and think. This made the telepathic communication clear for Jace.

Charlotte knew from the look on Grace's face that he got it exactly right. The playfulness left Grace's face. Her eyes were wide, and she looked almost angrily at Jace. There was a long, awkward pause. Neither Jace nor Charlotte said anything. Grace didn't appear to be in the mood to chat at that moment. Charlotte gave Jace a 'what did you do?' look.

He could sense Grace's anxiety from realizing he read her mind. He apologized to her. "I'm sorry. I didn't mean to be rude."

"No. No, you're fine. No need to apologize." He caught her unprepared. "I was not expecting such...," she searched for the right word, "accuracy. You quoted me word for word. I thought I was being clever and cute. That was — unnerving."

Charlotte knew that this one small demonstration was enough to convince Grace of the efficacy of the Bilal theory. She also wanted to arm Grace with all the information available. "Let's go upstairs and talk — the three of us."

Once they settled in her office, Charlotte closed the door. Her demeanor had softened, but was back-to-business. "Grace, I need you to be comfortable moving forward. We will tell you all about Jace's situation and what we did with Bilal, and why. We'll answer any questions you have. First, though, do you have any doubt about Jace? Do you need more evidence?"

"No, I'm good. There is no way he could have guessed what I was thinking. No way that could have been a trick. I'm still a little flustered," she admitted.

"You'll feel better when we explain it all. Let's get this done now. We can take as much time as you want."

"But then we need to figure out how to use what we know to connect Bilal to Minion."

Chapter 46: The Crossing

When Max Lopez arrived at the Hotel Ciudad Juárez, he found the man named Mohammad waiting for him as they had arranged. The foreigner paid him the $10,000 to guide the men to Las Cruces. Max gave the payment to his cousin, Luis, and Luis then drove him and his guests to the border.

There are stretches along the Mexico — U.S. border where no fences or barriers exist. The long distances and treacherous conditions make those places too dangerous for Max to try crossing. Instead, he devised a strategy that included help from friends on both sides.

Luis drove the crossers to a section protected only by vehicle barriers. It was a hot and dusty ride that took over two hours, but it was a convenient place to enter the United States, and relatively safe if you knew how to do it. Max had done it many times. He learned when to cross and had several trails from which to choose that were easy to hike. Max's secret weapons were his friends who lived in El Paso. The day before the trek, he shared his plan with them, and when it was time, they established contact with long-range, two-way radios. His network warned him when U.S. CBP was near his crossing site. When given the all-clear, he and his party slipped through the vehicle barrier and set out on foot towards a rendezvous point with one of his partners.

Max liked to cross close to dusk — a time when CBP Border Patrol has shift changes, and the sun is low in the sky. His adversaries are good at detecting recent crossings on the dirt road along the border, so he carefully swept their footprints away with a switch of brush. He couldn't be too careful, so he tried to erase any sign of people for 30 feet off the road. Luis did the same on the Mexican side. Depending on where his helpers established their point of rendezvous, the hike might be as little as two or three miles and take around an hour with a quick pace.

This trip came with special instructions that no one besides Max could accompany the travelers. So, he arranged for his cohorts to park a four-wheel-drive SUV at the meeting place and then remain at a distance until the crossers were safely in the vehicle. They reached it with ease. The CBP had no idea of the illegal entry, and the evening hike was without incident. Once in the comfort of the SUV and on their way, Max radioed his friends their job for the day was done. He would pay them for their troubles after he dropped his passengers off in Las Cruces.

Max knew that the most dangerous part of the trip was ahead of them. Avoiding Border Patrol and the short hike to the vehicle was comparatively easy. Driving the highways patrolled by CBP, State Police, and local sheriffs is the leg of the journey of which he had the least control. To his advantage, he learned how to navigate the crosshatch of county roads and the occasional unmarked dirt trails in the desert that seemed to lead to nowhere. It was one reason he preferred to travel at night. It's difficult for law enforcement to see the people inside moving vehicles, so they are less likely to have cause to stop them. He picked his way to Interstate 10 and drove east to their destination — an address given to him by Mohammad.

The secluded desert location made the house tough to find. It was in one of those neighborhoods you didn't know existed unless you had been there. But Max found the place using the GPS device left for him in the SUV and was relieved when they arrived safely. Not much of the evening had passed, so he planned to reunite with his friends, stay the night, and have a late, home-cooked meal.

A white truck had already parked near the rear of the house, so he pulled up behind it. Light splashed from the windows, so he surmised that someone was there to greet the group. He decided that there was no reason for him to linger as he might when guiding his friends. Glad to be rid of the foreigners, he stayed in the car and kept the engine running, expecting to drive away as soon as his guests unloaded. But their leader invited him to stay.

"Please come in for a refreshment before you leave," Mohammad offered.

"No thank you, Señor, I have friends to meet." Max wanted to go.

"Please," the man insisted as he opened the driver's door.

Max obliged and turned off the ignition. He got out, and they walked towards the back of the house. After a few steps, Mohammad turned to him and thoughtfully thanked him for a successful journey. Before Max could respond, he pulled a pistol from under his shirt, drew the weapon to Max's forehead, and squeezed the trigger. Abu and Fadel instantly grabbed the fallen husband and father, and dragged him to the SUV. Over in a second, Max was dead before he understood what was happening.

Chapter 47: A Clue

Grace had been focused on Minion's calls to Bossman and struggling to find a principled reason to listen to them. After her meeting with Charlotte and Jace, she took a day away from Minion to catch up on other business. Investigators from various agencies had been running down leads provided to the JTTF. Part of her job was to read the reports and maintain an awareness of what has been happening in the region. One recent report forwarded to the task force by the NCIS caught her eye and prompted her to pick up the phone and dial Charlotte's number.

"Hey, do you have Bilal's street address?" Grace asked.

"No, Millicent never mentioned it. Why?"

"There is an interesting report here from NCIS. Security at Dam Neck reported a suspected incursion attempt a while back. The guard said two nervous, Middle Eastern-looking guys drove up to the gate. They acted surprised and gave a story about looking for the beach."

"How does that connect with Bilal?"

"It doesn't — yet. But the guard recorded the license plate number of their car. NCIS ran the plate and tracked it to a name and address. The address is in Park Place."

"Now that is interesting." Intrigued, Charlotte asked, "Did you run it?"

"Yes. It's a rental. I didn't call the owner to see who's on the lease. There's no need to raise suspicions at this point."

"Yeah, that's a good idea. I need to find out where Bilal lives. What about the name? Who is the car registered to?"

"Owais al Omani is on the registration. I'll do a background check on him."

Charlotte called Jace right away. "Do you have Bilal's address?"

"No, I wouldn't unless Millicent listed him as an emergency contact, and I know she didn't do that."

"That's what I expected. It was a long shot. Thought I'd try." She didn't expect it to be that easy. "I'll figure out how to get it."

"Well, it would be strange if I asked her for her boyfriend's address."

"No, you're right. Don't do that. I'll work something out." Charlotte had a plan. She just needed to think through it.

Chapter 48: The Lunch

Millicent's afternoon at the beach was just what she needed. The girlfriends hadn't been to the shore since last summer, and it seemed like forever. The young women met at her apartment, greeting each other with beaming smiles and heartfelt hugs, excited to be together again. They loaded into Millicent's BMW, a high school graduation gift from her parents. They bought the car used, but it was exactly what she wanted, and loved how cute she looked in it. Once they pointed east on Interstate 264 — a straight shot to the resort area — the months without seeing each other melted away. Millicent forgot about Bilal and how he disrespected her. Who needs him? I've got my girls.

The afternoon bled into the evening and the friends didn't want their renewed camaraderie to end. They ate dinner at one of the seafood places on the resort strip and shared aspirations for after college. While the others in the group had specific career plans, Millicent was undecided. The world presented so many choices. But her friends' enthusiasm inspired her, and she couldn't help but think of Charlotte and share with the girls her experience with the Assistant U.S. Attorney. They agreed the opportunity was too exciting to pass up and decided Mil should contact her new mentor on Monday to set up a meeting. And so, she promised she would.

As Charlotte planned the tack to take to learn Bilal's address, her iPhone beeped, and seeing 'Mil' on the screen prompted a warm smile. Charlotte liked her and hoped to build a genuine friendship beyond the current situation. Unfortunately, pulling the Bilal string had to come first.

"Hi Mil, I was just thinking of you," she answered the phone with sincerity.

"Hello!" Millicent sang into the phone, with an upbeat, "Hopefully pleasing thoughts!" Charlotte remembered what Jace said about Mil's pleasant, almost bubbly demeanor that put him in a good mood every morning.

"Absolutely! I was thinking we need to get together. We had fun chatting at the restaurant the other night and talked about doing it again."

"That's why I'm calling. I'd love to set something up and pick your brain about being a federal prosecutor."

"Let's do it. Is tomorrow good?"

That surprised Mil. She assumed it would be difficult to fit into her schedule. "Yeah, that's great. What time?"

"We'll have a long lunch. Meet me in front of the World Trade Center and I'll show you around, then we'll walk down the street to a place that makes delicious sandwiches."

Charlotte looked forward to seeing Mil but was torn. She wished it were purely a personal meeting. There was sadness and guilt that she had to use Mil to get to Bilal. *Maybe it'll all work out.*

As they sat down to eat, she opened the door to the discussion right away. "So, how's it going with Bilal?" It was an innocent enough question to start some small talk.

"Oh, that relationship has run its course." Millicent decided she was done with him, but hadn't told him yet.

"Sorry, I wasn't expecting that." Charlotte had to press to learn where he lives, but this fresh revelation added a twist that needed more thought. "Do you mind me asking why? What happened?"

"Oh no, you're fine. Our cultures don't mix. He's respectful on the outside — most of the time — but in Saudi Arabia women are supposed to be quiet sheep, and I know he thinks that way about me. I'm over it."

Charlotte was relieved. She started this thing with Jace reading Bilal because she cared for Mil's safety, and was glad she was ending it. *It will work to everyone's benefit — except maybe his.*

She still required more information, so she probed gently. "So, how'd he take it?"

"Ah — well, I haven't talked to him yet. I sort of left in a hurry the last time we were together, and he hasn't called me, and I haven't called him."

"Yikes. Did you guys have a fight?"

"Not really. He snapped at me, I took off, and we haven't spoken since so..." Mil let the conclusion hang, and then added, "I guess I should call him."

Asking more at that point would be a miscue, Charlotte decided, so she changed the subject, but she'd have to steer the discussion back to him later in the lunch.

"How's the job going with that cranky old boss of yours?"

"It's good. I love my cranky old boss," she laughed. "But I'm thinking engineering isn't as exciting as prosecuting bad guys."

The turn in the conversation was welcome to Charlotte. It provided a moment to strategize.

Lunch went by quickly. The two women chatted like a younger sister was catching up with her older sibling who had been away. An hour and a half slipped by as though it were 15 minutes. Charlotte suggested that they both had to get on with the rest of their afternoons, but before they parted, they made another lunchtime appointment for the same day the next week. Regardless of the satisfaction of a budding friendship she felt at that moment, she had to put back on her task force hat.

"One more thing," Charlotte said as they rose to leave. "I'm curious. How are you going to handle Bilal? See him, phone him, text him, or ghost him?" Both laughed.

"I won't text or ghost him. That's not right."

"True, but I prefer you to be safe. Not that I expect he'll do anything bad, it's just that I've seen a lot in my career. When you do what I do for as long as I have, you become careful and aware. May I make a suggestion?"

"Please do."

"I suggest you tell him face-to-face. That way he receives the message in no uncertain terms. And let me go with you." Charlotte laid it out there as smoothly as she could.

"Go with me?"

"Yes. I'll stay in the car, so it won't be weird, but will be seconds away. I've done this for clients before, and know it sounds paranoid — sorry."

"No, that's fine. Knowing you'll be there to have my back is comforting. That's a good idea."

"Okay. If you want to break it off, you should do it soon. The sooner the better. I'll be there whenever you need me. I can do it tomorrow if that's what you decide."

"Tomorrow sounds good. I'll call him in the morning to tell him I'm dropping by and then call you."

Charlotte had her plan. Not only would she have Bilal's address, but she'd also be able to check out the house.

Chapter 49: The First Connection

Millicent didn't expect that. Charlotte offering to go with her to Bilal's seemed unnecessary. She broke up with guys before and never felt the need for physical backup. But she trusted Charlotte's judgment. Bilal was from a different culture where men dominate the women and may react negatively to getting dumped. She's right, Mil thought, I'm glad she's coming with me.

As soon as Millicent left from lunch, Charlotte called Grace. "I'm going to Bilal's house tomorrow."

"You're what?" Grace heard what she said but loudly expressed her dismay. Just walking up to a potential terrorist's residence and asking questions wasn't a good strategy. Especially when you have no training. *She must be teasing me,* "What do you mean?"

"Millicent and I had a long talk. She plans to break

up with Bilal, so I offered to tag along. I'll be in the car while she goes into the house. We'll have the street address soon."

"I want to go."

"Yes, I imagined you would. Mil will call me to tell me when. Then I'll call you. You can follow us."

Foreign students travel home to visit family during summer break. Those who don't, usually take classes hoping to graduate early, or they get jobs to help pay expenses. The three Saudis living in Park Place did none of those things. They did not lack money and graduating was not their goal. They had something more righteous planned and had said their goodbyes before they left Saudi Arabia. Their families were told they'd be spending the summer sightseeing and enjoying the beach.

Planning had become meticulous in the last week. Each jihadi had two attacks to plan from which they would choose the ultimate target. Mohammad demanded assaults with high probabilities of success and mass casualties. Bilal, Haider, and Owais fretted over details such as how to get to the target without raising suspicions, what time of day to attack, how to prevent or respond to resistance, and how to escape. Escaping was not in Mohammad's plans. He expected the fighters to martyr themselves — to die. To him, it was an important part of the symbolism of bringing the jihad to

American soil. Bilal was pondering how best to present plans to him that included the jihadis' survival when Milli called. Although he preferred not to pick up, he answered the phone. They hadn't talked in days and he wanted to placate her.

"Hi, do you mind if I come over for a few minutes?"

"I'm busy at the moment." He did not desire the distraction of a visit, but chose not to anger her, so he used a conciliatory approach. "Can it be later?"

"Sure. I'm at work, so I'll stop by afterward. Is 4:30 good?"

"Yes, that will be fine." Bilal wanted to hang up and get back to work, and he supposed he would need a rest by then, anyway.

Millicent phoned Charlotte to give her the update. They decided she would pick Charlotte up at the World Trade Center, and she offered the Park Place address without being asked. *Finally, we're making headway,* Charlotte said to herself as she dialed Grace's number. "218 West 30th Street. Sound familiar?"

"That is the address of Owais al Omani, the nervous intruder at Dam Neck," unwittingly giving him a nickname. Charlotte heard the satisfaction in Grace's reaction. "Millicent gave you the address?"

"Yes. I am now at least 57 and a half percent positive that Minion is a foreign national. Pull the calls."

"You are funny," Grace snickered at the jab at the NSA targeting rule. "So, you think that is enough?"

"No question. We have unusual calls from burner

phones coming from the West 24th Street cell tower. We've placed Owais the Nervous Intruder on West 30th in the same neighborhood, and he lives with a known Saudi national. That's sufficient to conclude that the Minion calls are likely not from a U.S. citizen. We only require a 51% probability. That's a loose standard."

"We're still backing her up at 4:30, right?"

"Absolutely," Charlotte was adamant. "We'll make sure she's safe and get a look at the place too. Be out in front of my building in your car and then follow us. Mil is picking me up there in a BMW sedan."

Chapter 50:
Identification

The only Minion telephone call Grace retrieved from PRISM was from August. The others were overwritten by the billions of calls recorded each month by the NSA. At first, the content of the conversation disappointed her. There was nothing in it that was actionable. Nothing gave them a solid target or date of a terror attack. There was no indicator of an attack at all, except for the context of the metadata and Jace West's telepathic reading.

The morning after they provided cover for Millicent's breakup, Charlotte set out to see Grace. She found it difficult to contain her excitement, knowing they may be on the verge of a breakthrough, expecting to listen to the call for herself and to identify Bilal as Minion. Grace played it for her as soon as she arrived.

"My friend, salam alaykum."

"Wa alaykum as-salam, my brother."

"I think that's Bilal," Charlotte whispered quickly,

trying not to talk over the recording.

"How are the plans for the visit proceeding?"

"All is well. We have a few activities planned. The details are progressing well."

"Will they be to my liking?"

"Yes, brother. There are many options. We are ripe with opportunity. I look forward to reviewing them with you."

"How are my other brothers? Are they doing well?"

"They are doing well. I have no worries."

"Thank you, my friend. Alhamdulillah."

"Yes, my brother. Until next time, Alhamdulillah."

"That's it," Grace said. "So, are you positive it's him?"

"I need to listen to it again, but the second voice sounded like him. Was that Minion?"

"Yeah, that was the Norfolk end. So, what do you think?"

"It's not a home run, but we've learned a few things. It sounds as though Bossman may come here."

"And he asked about his other brothers. To me, that means there's at least three here in Norfolk — Bilal, Owais, and a third."

"Assuming they are terrorists, it appears they are planning multiple attacks," Charlotte said. "What do we do now?"

"We start an official investigation. I already tagged Minion's and Bossman's phone numbers.

PRISM will catch and save every call they make on U.S. soil. We'll surveil the house and find who else is living there. All of them must have personal cell phones, and once we determine what those numbers are, I'll develop contact chains. Obviously, we need to be sure that Bilal is Minion. Can you say that?"

"Not 100%." Charlotte was disappointed. She was not confident enough the Norfolk side of the conversation was him. She only talked to him that one evening at Grill 21.

"Should we bring Millicent in to ID him?"

Exposing Mil to this clandestine investigation was not something she wanted, but it was important to be sure of Minion's identity. After listening to the recording again, Charlotte decided, "We have to. Let me talk to her," and she picked up her phone and touched Mil's number.

"Hey! What's up?" she answered with her same warm demeanor.

"Well, first off, how are you doing?"

"Good, I'm just glad that's over," referring to the breakup.

"I could tell you were relieved afterward."

"Yeah, that relationship was going nowhere. I am happy to move on."

"Mil, I um," Charlotte struggled to find the right words — something typically not a problem for her, but she valued the friendship they had developed, and what she was about to ask could ruin it. "Remember I told you I was a member of the FBI's Joint

Terrorism Task Force?"

"Yes."

"I'm with a Special Agent now. Her name is Grace Madson, and she played a recording for me a few minutes ago. I'd like you to hear it."

"Um, okay." Millicent was cautious, but curious, "why?"

"We'll explain it when we see you, but you will do us a big favor. Is today in my office doable? After you get out of work?"

"I'll be there."

That gave Charlotte and Grace time to plan their surveillance of the house on West 30th Street.

After she introduced Millicent to Grace, Charlotte got to the point.

"Before we start, you must understand you cannot reveal what we do here today to anyone. We can proceed only if you agree to keep what we discuss and what you hear confidential."

"Okay," Mil was uncertain, but intrigued.

"One more thing. If you violate this agreement, the federal government could prosecute you. Please indicate you are clear on that."

"Um, I understand." That made the situation sound more serious, but she trusted Charlotte.

"Good, let's start. We get metadata from a database the National Security Agency maintains. It provides information on cell phone and internet usage in the U.S. Grace noticed an odd pattern of calls to Saudi Arabia that originate from Park Place in Norfolk. We have a recording of the most recent call and it is important that you listen to it."

"Saudi Arabia? Is it Bilal?" Mil made the obvious connection.

Charlotte was careful with her words, "That's what we want you to tell us. I've listened to it and think it is Bilal, but I'm not positive."

"Does this mean he's a terrorist?"

"All it means is these calls are unusual. Grace noticed them during normal reviews of the metadata. Listen to the recording and let us know if one of the men talking is Bilal, or not. Then we'll decide what to do next."

"Are you ready for me to start, Mil?" Grace spoke for the first time, taking a cue from Charlotte.

Millicent nodded, so Grace clicked play on her laptop. When she heard Minion's voice, it was obvious by the look on her face — she recognized him. "That is definitely Bilal."

"The second guy that speaks?" Grace had to make sure.

"Yes, it sounds like he's talking with Mohammad."

Both the Assistant U.S. Attorney and the FBI Special Agent cocked their heads and glanced at each other at the unexpected revelation.

"Mohammad? You know the other person?" Grace asked with the anticipation they were going to learn more than they hoped.

"No, I don't know him, but Bilal is wound up

about him visiting from Saudi Arabia."

"Wound up?"

"He would get evasive, and when I tried asking him about it, he became irritated with me."

"Who is he to Bilal? Are they related?" Grace focused on extracting as much information from this new, unexpected source. She looked at Charlotte as if to seek her permission to continue, and Charlotte returned an almost imperceivable nod.

"No, they're not. Bilal told me Mohammad is his mentor. He's coming from Saudi Arabia to check on their progress. I don't know what that means. He wouldn't tell me."

"You said he was coming to check 'their' progress. Who are they?"

"I assumed he meant Haider and Owais, his friends. They live in the house with him."

Charlotte interjected, "Do you mind answering these questions, Mil? Are you still good with this?"

"Yeah, I'm fine." She felt empowered by the two strong, accomplished women in the room with her and wanted to keep going.

Grace continued, "Haider and Owais — what are their last names?"

"That never came up. I didn't talk to them much. They're just immature college boys if you ask me."

"When is Mohammad coming to visit?"

"In October during fall break. Bilal is sending Kent to pick him up."

"Kent? Who's Kent?"

"Kent Green — he's a nice guy. I see him around

campus, and he and Bilal are friends. I think they met at mosque."

"So, Kent is a Muslim? Is he from Saudi Arabia too?"

"No, he's from Portsmouth. He's all wired about racism and white privilege and he somehow connected with the mosque near school. Now he's converting to Islam. I never asked, but I assumed that's where they met."

"You said Kent is picking him up. Where?"

"I'm not supposed to know he is meeting Mohammad. He just let it drop one day when we were hanging out at the house. He mentioned a long drive and then Bilal quickly changed the subject. I got the message it was none of my business."

"This might be hard to answer, but in the context of this conversation, is there anything else you think may be of interest?" Grace asked the catch-all question, providing the opening for any fresh revelations from Millicent.

"Ummm — nothing that comes to mind," Mil said with a slight shrug, still unsure of what information was relevant.

Grace needed one last thing. "Before you go, will you give us Bilal's telephone number?"

"Sure, but don't you have it?"

"We believe he uses a different phone to contact Mohammad. We need to find out who else he talks to."

After the interview, Charlotte walked Millicent

to the lobby. "I can't tell you how helpful you've been. We are very grateful."

"I want to help. If you have more questions, please ask."

"Thanks. Remember, do not mention this to anyone. This is important."

"I won't."

"Are we still on for lunch next week?"

"Yes! I'm so looking forward to it."

Back in the office, Grace was excited. "Wow — that was a lot more than I expected. Millicent was so helpful. We know Bossman's name, when he's visiting, and that he's driving in from somewhere far away. And best of all..."

"We have Bilal's phone number," Charlotte finished the sentence.

"Now I can build a contact chain from PRISM. That may be a goldmine."

Chapter 51:
Lincoln's Dream

After several weeks, the mentoring between Jace and Dr. Allo had transitioned from daily to weekly. Ike had seen the wear on him of exercising his extrasensory perception and suggested they ease the training. Everyone experiences moments as though they are in sensory overload, and Jace's heightened senses exacerbated the problem. His life was back to how it was before the accident, except for their daily sessions. Ike decided it was important for him to relax, and guessed that by shifting to once a week, his new reality would become normal.

The breadth of Jace's capabilities amazed the doctor, and he was confident weekly exercises would continue to train his brain to recognize alternative paths of communication. It was reasonable to him to expect Jace could develop cognition to match that of Edgar Cayce. Cayce was known for his ability to give different types of psychic readings. He provided thousands of them in which he read what other people were thinking; he could see what others observed; foresee future events, and describe past episodes. With training and self-awareness, Jace might do the same.

Ike's work with him turned from measuring and strengthening his telepathy and empathy, which came easily and naturally, to exploring precognition. Developing and practicing precognitive skills is not as simple as using flashcards like the Zener test for clairvoyance. The effort was slower and more difficult to comprehend.

"Cayce believed we all have precognitive experiences, but we don't recognize them as seeing the future," Ike explained. "His readings suggest an explanation for déjà vu. All of us have had a sudden awareness that we've already had the exact experience that just occurred. At times it gives me goosebumps—it's uncanny."

"Definitely creepy."

"Cayce offered that our dreams sometimes foreshadow things yet to happen. When we have a déjà vu event, we are recalling the dream that foretold what we had just experienced. Folks rarely remember their dreams, so we don't associate the déjà vu occurrence with them. But what really happened is we witnessed the future."

"And that's why you want me to keep a dream journal."

"Right. Are you aware of the legend regarding Abe Lincoln's death?"

"No—tell me."

"After Lincoln died, his friend Ward Hill Lamon recalled Abe had dreamed of a corpse lying in state. He asked a soldier standing guard, 'Who is dead in the White House?' The soldier replied it was the President, and an assassin killed him. Ten days later, John Wilkes Booth shot Lincoln at Ford's Theater."

"Foreknowledge doesn't just happen in dreams," Ike continued. "Most folks will recognize what we call 'flash precognition.' People suddenly have these vivid, spontaneous visions of things that are about to happen. There's the story about the guy who was boarding an airline flight and had an intense fore-boding the plane would crash. He left the aircraft, and sure enough, the flight later crashed."

"I've heard stories like that."

"Gut feelings may be a form of flash precognition. Sometimes you have a strong sense about some-thing, but can't logically explain it. Pay attention to those instincts. They could portend what is to come."

"Most experiences of foretelling are dreams or flash visions. Parapsychologists maintain that 85% involve people close to the clairvoyant, and the events typically take place within a short time — minutes or hours."

Jace found the discussion interesting but was skeptical he could learn to see the future. "I don't re-member experiencing any of those things since the accident. They just happen. I'm not sure what I can do to develop precognition."

"That's okay. I'd like you to keep the dream journal, and record any déjà vu and gut feeling occurrences, too. You'll find that by remaining open to the idea these are precognitive events, and reasoning through them by writing them down, your ability to sense future experiences will become clearer."

"I also want you to try focused meditation."

"Is that different from what I've been doing?" Jace had been using meditation techniques he learned at A.R.E. since the first time he and Charlotte visited.

"No, it's no different, except you concentrate on one person when you meditate. You don't have to do it for long, but do it often — maybe once a day. I'm hoping it brings the individual closer to your conscientiousness. That focus may spawn visions of things about to happen."

"I get it. I know where you're going with this," Jace understood.

Chapter 52: Revelations

Understandably, Millicent was curious about the Bilal-Mohammad phone call and the FBI's interest in it. She looked forward to lunch with Charlotte, hoping to learn more about that than anything else. The days dragged on until their date the next week.

Mil picked a restaurant on East Main Street and the two met there for an early meal, expecting a lengthy chat as they dined.

Charlotte waited impatiently to see her, too. Although she wanted to cultivate a mentor-mentee friendship with Mil, she could not divert her attention from Bilal and the potential danger he presented. The conversation easily slipped to the topic center in their minds.

Charlotte started with an apology. "I'm sorry I involved you in the phone call. It was important to identify who was initiating it in Norfolk. After I realized it might be Bilal, I thought of you."

"That's fine. Glad I helped. Honestly, I'm dying to learn more. I have so many questions."

"I figured you might. There's not a lot I'm allowed

to share but ask and I'll tell you what I can."

"Well, what shocks me most is that you have a recording of a random phone call from Bilal. How? Why? What's going on?"

"Those are questions I can answer." Charlotte's lips parted into a slight grin, pleased she could be honest with her. "Until Edward Snowden leaked it to the public, it was top-secret, but now it's out there and I'll tell you what we did. The NSA has an electronic surveillance program called PRISM. There are several more sibling programs that provide different signal intelligence, but we refer to them all as PRISM, even though it's not technically correct. Anyway, as we explained the other day, part of Grace's job is to review metadata provided by those programs."

"Metadata?"

"Yes. It's data about the billions of digital phone calls made in the United States every day. It tells us who is calling what numbers, when the calls are made and how long they last. Data like that. Grace noticed calls originating in Norfolk and connecting to the same cell phone in Saudi Arabia. A pattern to those calls caught her eye. Without telling you details, Grace and I established justification under federal law to listen to the conversations. A sibling program to PRISM provided the recording to us."

"The government listens to all of our phone calls?" Mil was in disbelief.

"No, it's not that way. But the NSA records them and saves them for a short period. If a government investigator establishes justification to listen to a call, then the recording is accessed by the agent. That can only be done if we are reasonably sure the person we want to listen to is not a U.S. citizen. To listen to conversations between U.S. citizens is against the law. The government created PRISM, and the other programs like it, to track communication of suspected foreign terrorists."

"Why Bilal?"

"Grace noticed a pattern in the metadata. I can't say more. We didn't know it was him until I heard his voice and thought it might be." Charlotte did not want to go further, but Mil was still too curious.

"The FBI thinks he's a terrorist?" She was going where Charlotte didn't want to go.

"Please understand, I cannot answer that question. Remember, though, it was the unusual pattern in the metadata that made us want to listen to the phone call. What we heard doesn't point to him being a terrorist." Charlotte avoided saying the entire truth; yes, they think Bilal is a terrorist based partly on a psychic reading by none other than Mil's own boss. That is something not easily explained.

Charlotte added, "But you understand the diligence of people like Grace, following these flimsy leads that typically go nowhere, keeps us safe. The FBI has thwarted many terrorist attacks since 9/11 doing this kind of investigative work."

"Let me ask you, Mil." Charlotte had questions of her own. "In hindsight, is there something he did or said that was unusual?"

"Such as?" Mil had already been replaying her relationship with Bilal in her head.

"Like visiting the same place multiple times or fixating on one thing."

"We spent most of our time in downtown Norfolk. He was extremely interested in the Wisconsin museum at Nauticus."

"Did he seem overly curious about anything?"

"Not really. He wondered about The Tide and suggested we ride the line, and asked questions about the MacArthur Memorial. I know he's been on at least two Harbor Cruises." Mil's eyes became wider with the realization things may not have been as they seemed. "He wanted to take a tour cruise after promising me he'd take me to the beach. He snapped a lot of photos of the fleet at the base. It was no big deal to me because I'm a Navy geek."

Charlotte listened closely to what Mil told her and took mental notes. She would write them for Grace later, but her profession demanded she remember key pieces of information, especially when she performed in the courtroom. "Anything else?"

Millicent paused, recalling the first day she had Bilal to herself. It was a Saturday, and they strolled through downtown. She saw things differently now — from a fresh perspective — and felt uneasy. "I thought nothing of it, but looking back, he focused on how many people would be in the places he asked about. Like Town Point Park — he knew it was a place with large crowds, and he wondered if MacArthur Memorial gets a lot of people. He wanted to go to the mall. There were tons of people there."

"He was using me."

"Not necessarily," Charlotte tried to comfort her.

"Bastard was using me." Millicent's face turned cold, jaw slightly clenched, and nostrils flared.

"It's all good. You are being a great help."

Millicent was a happy and trusting person, always aiming to raise the spirits of those around her. But at that moment she realized she was betrayed by this man she thought was her boyfriend — with whom she spent so much time. The hurt, and embarrassment of being played without realizing it, made her want to slump in her chair, hide her face, and cry. Millicent, though, was a proud, young woman who loved her country — the one her dad served for 20 years. She would not allow herself to shrivel away in the face of a foreign terrorist looking to do harm.

With tears of sadness, embarrassment, and anger welling in her eyes, Mil straightened her spine, lifted her chin, and firmly told Charlotte, "I need you to keep me involved in this."

Chapter 53: Surveillance

"I just talked with Mil. She told me things about Bilal that you'll want to hear." Charlotte called Grace right after lunch. Even though there was little evidence that he was anything other than a student from Saudi Arabia, she felt in her bones he was planning a terror attack. An urgency had crept into her psyche that she could not shake. From this moment forward, the clock was ticking.

"What did she say?"

"She told me he scoped where large numbers of people congregate. He's checked out Nauticus and Wisconsin, Town Point Park, MacArthur Memorial, and MacArthur Mall. He wants to ride The Tide, and he took cruises past the Navy base, twice that she knows. Mil thinks Bilal was using her to probe Norfolk."

"Well," Grace validated what Charlotte was thinking, "those are excellent targets for an attack. Just think of the carnage if gunmen opened up at an event like Harborfest — or if they planted bombs around Town Point Park."

"It would be worse than the 1996 Centennial Park bombing in Atlanta." Charlotte's stomach was in knots. She was in unfamiliar territory. As an Assistant U.S. Attorney, she prosecuted felons who had already committed crimes. As a member of the JTTF, she was waist-deep in attempting to foil an attack on Americans that had yet to occur. She rarely failed in court. She never thought about it because she was extraordinarily good at what she did. But failure now would have dire consequences, and it haunted her.

"Can you stop by? We'll review what we know so far."

"Yeah. I'm walking back to my place, but I'll head out as quickly as I can." Charlotte picked up her pace. She felt an urgent need to get this case moving.

Charlotte's phone beeped while she was still walking back to the office. It was Millicent.

"What's up, Mil?"

"I remembered something else."

"What is it?"

"Friday my girlfriends and I took the afternoon off to go to the oceanfront. I had left my beach stuff at Bilal's, so I dropped by unannounced to run in the house and get my bag. I was in a hurry, so I let myself in and opened his study door — that's where I left it — and I walked in on Bilal, Haider and Owais huddled around the table. Bilal got angry at me and yelled. That was the last straw, and I decided it was past time to break up with him. But the three of them acted like 12-year boys caught looking at porn by their mother. They scrambled to hide what they had on their laptops, and they had papers lying around that they gathered-up. They were up to something and tried to hide it when I entered the room."

"Did you see anything?"

"No, they covered it up so quickly, except I saw one laptop had a map on it — like Google maps."

"Did you see what was on the map?"

"No, I only saw it for a second."

"Did you hear anything?"

"No, nothing."

"Okay, thanks. That's excellent information. Mil, I should have said this earlier. You realize you cannot contact Bilal, right? He can't know that we are interested in him. And you need to stay away for your own safety. You understand that, right?"

"Yes, absolutely," Millicent assured Charlotte.

"If he contacts you, or tries to, call me right away. Just play it cool as though you don't want to talk and then call me."

"Okay. That will be no problem," Mil said with a timid laugh.

"How is it going with surveilling the Park Place house?" Charlotte asked as soon as she stepped into

Grace's office.

Grace didn't bother to say hello either. Their relationship evolved past greeting each other with the normal pleasantries. "My boss doesn't think we have enough to justify 24/7 surveillance. Everyone is working other cases, so it's just you and me, and a favor from one or two others here and there." Charlotte understood. Even if they told their bosses of the psychic reading of Bilal, it would not be enough to warrant more than cautious attention. "But we're learning things."

"Like what?"

"Well, to start, I planted a camera outside the house. We can't watch it all the time, but it records everything that happens. I put it inside a vehicle parked across the street."

"What have you seen so far?"

"Random comings and goings. Three Middle Eastern males come and go several times a day, including late into the evening. I presume they are Bilal Khalil, Owais al Omani, and Haider Khan."

"I can identify Bilal. If you shoot me stills of the other two, I'll ask Mil to ID them."

"There is a fourth. A young, black male. He visits regularly. He doesn't stay long — an hour at most. That must be Kent Green."

"Forward me that one too."

"I want to see where they're going. They don't keep regular hours, as you would expect if they had jobs or classes. Starting tonight, I'm watching the house and tailing the first person who comes out."

"Good, that should give us an idea of what they are doing. Can I go with you?"

"No. There's something else for you to do."

"Sure. Tell me what you want me to do."

"PRISM tells us everything anyone does on the internet. We see emails, websites, all of it. I've asked our cyber guys to download all activity from the IP address at the Park Place house in the last month. They gave me a file that includes metadata, email content, and URLs of the sites they visited. I thought we both should start looking at it."

"Cool, I can do that." Charlotte wanted to dive-in and get the investigation moving.

"One thing, though. The guys told me they detected the intermittent use of a Virtual Private Network. That means that whatever they did on the internet using their VPN is invisible to us. IT says there are ways to defeat an individual IP on a VPN, but we don't have access to that horsepower."

"So," Charlotte surmised, "what PRISM gives us may be benign and not tell us much."

"Maybe so, but we still need to look at it."

"Did Bilal's phone number Mil gave us reveal anything interesting?"

"Nothing jumps out at me. I developed a primary contact chain from his phone data, but he made very few calls. Most were to or from Mil's number. A few were to Saudi Arabia — probably to family, I'm guessing. I tagged his phone for retention, and they have recorded several calls. Can you help listen to those?

"Yes. Just tell me when."

"The data from his phone included the numbers of Kent Green, Owais al Omani, and Haider Khan. I'll develop contact chains for those, and I'll need your help to listen to those calls too."

"Okay, sooner the better."

Grace sighed, "it doesn't sound like much."

"Yeah." Charlotte felt the same way. "But we'll piece this together. We need to find out where they are going and what they're doing. Then we'll have a better idea of what their plan is."

"We still have a lot of work to do. Know what I wish?" Grace offered with a weary smirk.

"What?" Charlotte smiled at the look on Grace's face.

"I wish we could get Jace in the same room with Bilal for an hour."

"Ha! Wouldn't that be nice. Bilal would tell us exactly what he was up to without knowing it." Charlotte let out a laugh.

"There's no way to do that without tipping our hat, huh?" Grace half-joked, but Charlotte could tell she was more serious than not.

"I don't see how we could do that, Grace."

"I know." But she left Charlotte unconvinced.

Chapter 54: Tails

Grace knew from reviewing the video footage that her targets on West 30th Street probably wouldn't leave the residence until late morning. She parked behind a car several houses down the street and watched the house in real-time from her surveillance camera. It wasn't long before someone emerged from the house. Millicent had identified Haider, Owais, and Kent from the pictures that Charlotte had shown her, so she knew that the first person to tail was Haider.

He got into his late-model Nissan — the kind of car normal, middle-class Saudis drive — and headed away from where she had parked. She followed him as he made his way to Monticello Ave and south toward downtown. After a short drive, he pulled into the parking garage under the Scope plaza. Parking in that garage at that time of day was easy, especially when there were no events at the venues above, so she could monitor Haider while maintaining her distance. They both parked and proceeded on foot up the stairwell to the plaza.

Haider emerged on Monticello and stopped. Facing the square, he raised his phone and snapped a photo. The sudden halt caused her to reveal herself to him as she rounded a corner, but he was too focused to notice her. With Chrysler in front of him and Scope to his left, he ambled to the fountain in the center of the square, and he sat on the fountain's perimeter. Facing the arena, he swept his camera slowly across the courtyard. Grace realized he was making a video and quickened her pace to maneuver to the other side of the fountain where she was behind him.

He then turned his focus on Chrysler Hall, taking videos from different perspectives from the front and sides of the building. The rectangular fountain covers a large part of the plaza and provided easy cover for her as she moved in the opposite direction as Haider, staying behind him and out of his line of sight. She could have easily been a businesswoman on an early lunch break, enjoying a peaceful stroll in the square.

When he finished, he had video recorded 360 degrees around the venues, including views of the surrounding streets. In the age of the smartphone, everyone has a camera with them all the time, and it's not unusual to see someone taking photos wherever they are. Even so, Grace thought it was brazen of him to take such extensive video at one location in the middle of the day. On the other hand, the place was virtually empty. There was no one to find it curious.

Haider finished his outing with lunch at a deli a

few blocks away and then returned to the house.

Grace decided that she had enough in-person surveillance for the day and was looking forward to sharing what she saw with Charlotte. But, when Haider pulled up to the house, Owais was leaving, so she took advantage of the opportunity. He drove in the opposite direction on West 30th than did Haider, but turned south, once again towards downtown. She followed him into the parking garage directly across Main Street from Charlotte's building. She parked in a space reserved for visitors to the U.S. Attorney's Office and followed him on foot. He crossed Main Street using the familiar red-brick pedestrian crosswalk to the World Trade Center that she had used many times before and then crossed Waterside Drive to Town Point Park. Owais strolled through the park recording his surroundings, including streets and access points. The large open spaces, plenty of trees and benches, and other features allowed her to blend in with the others who were enjoying their lunchtime in the sun. No one noticed the Middle E astern man surveying the area.

Instead of following Owais when he left, Grace called Charlotte. "Hey, I'm downstairs. Can I come up?"

"Yeah — sure," Charlotte wanted to talk with her but hadn't expected her to show up at her door.

Charlotte's door was open, so Grace gave a quick knock on the doorframe and then sat at her table.

"Hey. What brings you here unannounced?" Charlotte was glad to see her partner, but knew there had to be a reason for her to be downtown.

"Oh, I was just practicing my personal surveillance skills."

"Hm — let me guess. Haider."

"I tailed both him and Owais the Nervous Intruder."

"That sounds like a good day's work. And there's still half a day to go." Both started the conversation with some levity.

"You'll never guess where Owais wound up," Grace prompted with a bit of sarcasm.

"Well, since you were following him and just popped in here, I'd guess Town Point Park."

"Yep, and he took extensive photos and videos of the park and surrounding areas."

"That validates that Town Point Park is the objective. They would hit it during an upcoming event when thousands of people are there."

"Right," Grace agreed. "We need to find the schedule of events. The question is, when? Will it be from mid-October on, or sooner than that?"

"I think it's safe to say that Mohammad is coming to direct the attack. He wouldn't come here after the attack. There's no reason to, and it would be too dangerous for him."

"I agree, but there is a twist I haven't mentioned to you yet. I tailed Haider earlier this morning."

"Okay?"

"He scoped-out Scope." A slight grin curled Grace's lips at her unintended play-on-words, but her mood was less playful than a moment ago. "And Chrysler Hall; he took videos and photos of the entire plaza and vicinity. It looks as though we are dealing with more than one target."

Charlotte's stomach turned with the unwelcome thought of multiple attacks. She let slip the first thing that came to her mind, "Crap."

After a pause, Grace reviewed the facts. "It appears we have three targets: Scope, Chrysler Hall, and Town Point Park. If they are planning simultaneous attacks, they have to occur when the three venues have events at the same time. We can nail down a date pretty definitively if that's the case. If there is no such date, then we have a single attack with three potential targets and multiple dates."

"From what Mil told us, there may be more targets—the mall, the MacArthur Memorial, Nauticus, The Tide," Charlotte added in a serious mood.

"Don't rule out the Navy bases. We know they checked out the naval station and Dam Neck." Grace sighed, "We've got some digging to do. I need to tail Bilal, and their internet searches may help us. What have you found there?"

"Nothing that we don't already know, but their internet activity is very suspicious for innocent

Saudi college students. There are a few innocuous emails, but guess what — they looked at maps of Norfolk and Virginia Beach dozens of times. Foolishly, they used Google Maps. The thing about Google Maps is that every place you click has detailed coordinates included in the URL. We can see exactly what they were viewing on the map, or at least what they clicked on."

"They've looked at Naval Station Norfolk, Oceana, Little Creek, Dam Neck, Norfolk Naval Shipyard, Town Point Park, Scope, the mall, ODU, and even the Virginia Aquarium and the Virginia Zoo; plus normal places like restaurants and other businesses."

"That doesn't give us a definite target, but it's more evidence that they are targeting either Navy bases or public gathering places," Grace concluded. "The circumstantial evidence is mounting. The clues are there. We just need to find them."

"Places they only looked at once or twice," Charlotte speculated, "we can eliminate from the list. In fact, it's reasonable to assume they are narrowing their list to those spots they've Googled the most, and most recently.

"Absolutely. Will you list the places they researched in the last two weeks and rank them from highest number of looks to lowest?"

"I'll do it today. I can tell you, though, using that criteria, they've abandoned the military targets."

"That makes sense to me. Attacking a soft target with virtually no security versus attacking a Navy base with armed security seems like a simple decision."

"I'll count the hits. I'm curious to know what it tells us."

"We have phone calls to listen to, too. Before I left the office to tail the boys, I did more of Bilal's but there was nothing useful. Maybe this afternoon I'll peek into what Haider and Owais are talking about while you compile the internet hit-count."

"Okay. Let's talk before we go home for the day." Charlotte wrapped up the conversation, feeling confident they could follow the trail Bilal and his friends were leaving them.

Chapter 55: Near East Café

"Call Jace. I need him to take me to lunch tomorrow," Charlotte heard Grace say as soon as she answered her phone.

"Ah, okay — why?"

"Haider and Owais will have lunch at Near East Café on West 21st Street."

"Yeah?" Charlotte had a feeling what she had in mind but had to ask. "What are you thinking?"

"They've never seen him and don't know who he is, so why not get up-close and personal with them and see what Jace can hear? They won't even notice us."

"Are you sure that's a good idea? You've been watching them. What if they recognize you?"

"They haven't seen me. And I can't ask an untrained civilian to observe FBI persons of interest by himself."

"A psychic observation is kind of unconventional, anyway. It's not like this would be by the book."

"I know, but we need to get ahead of their game. I want to wait outside until they enter the restaurant and then follow them in as a couple. Hopefully, we'll get a table next to theirs and Jace can do his thing. If he picks up something useful, it will be worth it. If he gets nothing, then no harm done."

"He's still new at this. He may read nothing."

"What he did with me was impressive. Let's just try."

"All right, I'll call him right now." Charlotte agreed with little push back. She was too curious to find what Jace could learn.

Jace met Grace in Charlotte's office mid-morning the next day. From a phone call between Haider and Owais, she learned they planned to meet at the café at one o'clock to eat, and prepare to meet with Bilal later that afternoon. That was an opportunity that was too good to pass up. The plan was simple, but Grace wanted to cover as much detail as possible to prepare for the surveillance. They decided what to order from the online menu, so it appeared to others in the café they were familiar with the place. Charlotte found a pocket notebook for Jace to use to write whatever he felt he needed to record.

They arrived at 12:30 and parked on the street across from the café to wait for their subjects to arrive. Near 1:00 p.m., the Saudis walked into the restaurant. Grace and Jace hurried across the street and followed them inside. Haider sat at a table in the storefront window while Owais was standing at the counter. Jace knew what to do, looked at Grace with a nod, and sat at a table close to Haider's, leaving her to order the food.

While Arabic is the official language in Saudi Arabia, English is the language of business. So, Saudis are taught English in school starting at age six, and many families, particularly middle and upper-class, teach it at home earlier than that. Grace found it curious that the Saudi men spoke to each other in English, not realizing it was natural to them, and it was their preference when immersed in the English-speaking culture of the U.S. Her misgiving was that they think and speak in Arabic making the lunch-time observation a wasted effort. She was relieved to hear English when she got to the table and sat with Jace.

She saw Jace focused on the dialog drifting from the Saudi's table, so she placed his lunch in front of him and quietly ate her own. Grace heard what sounded like small talk and hoped he was hearing something more substantial. When the discussion turned more pointed, she reached for her own notebook to take notes and saw he already had his open, with pen in hand.

Haider and Owais were careful with their words. Their conversation would seem unremarkable to an unaware third party, but Grace's frame of reference gave her an advantage unknown to the two men.

"Today we eliminate candidates," Haider said. "I

have detailed videos of my locations for both the afternoon and in the evening. They will be useful in helping us decide, I believe."

"Yes. I have the same for my two assignments."

"I assume you have one that is your recommendation?"

"Yes. Given the details of my research, the choice for the greatest success is obvious. Timing may be an issue that ultimately decides, however."

"Agreed. I have a much-favored plan, and timing is the key as well. I intend to advocate for one evening that gives us several advantages."

Grace noticed Jace was keeping notes. *That's a good sign*, she thought.

"I have heard nothing from Bilal regarding his responsibilities," Owais spoke with a hint of cynicism. "Has he told you what he is thinking?"

"No, he's told me nothing. Maybe he will tell us today."

"Haider?" Owais asked with some angst. "Are you looking forward to the end of this?"

After a lengthy pause, he answered, "That depends on the ending."

With that, the conversation stopped. Grace looked to Jace, but he was still writing in his notebook. When he stopped taking notes, he put down his pen. She could see sadness in his eyes and his forehead was moist with perspiration. Preferring not to disturb the anonymity of her table, she remained silent, and watched as Jace held his fork for the first time and picked at his plate. That reminded her of how tasty the shawarma was, and she made a mental note to come back to this place when she could relax and enjoy the cooking. *When this is all over, I'll bring Charlotte and Jace.*

Chapter 56: Details

The car ride back to Charlotte's was quiet, and only a few minutes' drive. Jace and Grace took the time to reflect on what they just observed. When the two arrived, their contrasting demeanors confused Charlotte. Grace controlled excitement, while Jace was subdued.

"How did it go?" Charlotte asked with anticipation. She expected Grace to call immediately after lunch, so it surprised her to see them in the office.

Grace glanced at Charlotte with a tightened lip, signaling some uncertainty, "It went well."

As they sat at the table, Charlotte eyed Jace as he opened his pocket notebook, then looked at Grace as she did the same. "Who's going to start?"

"Besides the small talk, they had a brief talk about what they've been planning. I overheard most of it," Grace started. "What I heard confirms what we already know. They are preparing multiple attacks. It sounds as though each of the three had two targets to scope and they will narrow their list to the preferred places and times."

"So, six targets," Charlotte stated.

"Yes. They didn't say six, but that's close. I got the impression that they will cut the list in half in the meeting today."

"Do we have a better idea where?"

"They didn't name targets, but I'm confident Haider's are Scope and Chrysler Hall, and one of Owais' is Town Point Park. Haider said he prefers an evening attack, so if they go that way, it'll be a nighttime assault during an event at one of those locations."

Charlotte told them what she learned from recent internet activity. "The hit-count on their Google searches confirms that. In the last couple weeks, they've checked out those three areas on Google Maps the most, and they looked at the event schedules for those venues and for Nauticus too. Keep in mind Nauticus borders Town Point Park."

"No military targets?" Grace asked.

"Just as we suspected, the number of looks at military bases dropped significantly in recent weeks. Most likely they abandoned thoughts of attacking hard targets."

"What else did we learn?" Charlotte moved the debrief forward, waiting for Jace to speak.

"One more thing. I detected from Owais that there may be animosity, or at least tension between Owais and Haider, and Bilal. Bilal is keeping them in the dark and they don't appreciate it. Did you sense that, Jace?" Grace nudged.

Charlotte nudged harder. "Tell us what you have. It looks like you have notes there," she said, nodding to his notebook.

"Well, to start," Jace began, "when Haider mentioned he had a preferred plan, he was thinking of Chrysler Hall. I picked up 'concert' from him a few times during that part of the conversation. His target is a nighttime concert at Chrysler. I also sensed November when he talked."

"Excellent — that could nail down when and where right there. What else?"

"Owais had Town Point Park on his mind. I saw a sunny day with lots of people drinking beer. I bet there is a beer fest at the park in October." The park would have thousands of people.

"That'll be easy to find out. That nails a time and place too."

"When he mentioned that timing may be an issue, he thought of Mohammad."

Grace flashed a look to Charlotte. *There's Mohammad's name again.* She asked Jace, "Does Mohammad mean anything to you?"

"No. But when Owais thought of him, I felt despair, and maybe reverence, as though he holds power over Owais."

"That makes sense," Grace directed the statement to Charlotte. "If Mohammad is arriving in mid-October, then it may be too late to direct a strike at Town Point Park."

"What else?"

Jace sensed what they knew of Mohammad, so he didn't bother asking. "Grace is correct about the unease between the two, and Bilal. I sensed resentment, especially from Owais. Bilal is the leader, but he doesn't keep them informed. Haider and Owais share what they know, but Bilal doesn't, and that makes them uneasy."

"Is that all?"

"No. I saw visions from each of them when they were discussing their assignments. AK-47s — they were envisioning using AK-47s. I am confident they are plotting a shooting attack."

"That is the first direct indicator we've had of an attack," Charlotte interrupted. "Until now, based on suspicious circumstances and our gut feelings, we've been assuming they've been planning an attack. Jace's visions of the boys using AKs removes any doubt what they are up to, in my mind."

"There's something else," Jace revealed the reason for his pensive mood. "Grace didn't mention it, but at the end of their discussion, Owais asked Haider if he's looking forward to the end. After a pause, Haider said, it 'depends on the ending.' I felt a great deal of sadness from both. They are afraid and don't want to do this. They don't want to die. Haider and Owais are just college kids who have gotten themselves into something and they think they can't get out."

Chapter 57: The Target

After debriefing the lunch, Jace drove home. He was in a down mood and didn't want to go to work. Besides, it was near the end of the day, and retreating to his study, or maybe relaxing in the hammock to reflect on the day's events was what he had in mind.

Grace remained in Charlotte's office after he left. "As Jace was telling us what he sensed, I glanced at the event schedules for Town Point Park, Scope, and Chrysler Hall, and he's right. There's a craft beer festival at the park on Saturday, October 17th."

"That validates what we were thinking. It's an excellent target, but if Mohammad is arriving around that date, it may be too soon for him to prepare for the attack. He'd want time to understand the target and assess the plan."

"I agree, but we can't disregard it."

"What about Chrysler Hall?"

"There's a symphony orchestra concert Friday, November 13th. That's the only concert that month, but there are two other shows: one in October, and later in November. He was spot-on with that too."

"Friday the 13th, huh?" Charlotte mused at the symbolism.

The afternoon was cool for a summer day in Virginia, so Jace chose the hammock in the shade of the oak tree. The breeze made it comfortably lazy, and he hoped a nap would help lighten his mood. There was still a knot in his stomach, though. The doubt and remorse from both young men at lunch haunted him. They were his children's age. Instead of reveling in their youth and the excitement of college and the promise of unlimited possibilities, they were contemplating their pending deaths. He couldn't shake the sorrow.

As the summer breeze washed around him and the rustling leaves joined the cacophony of singing birds and chirping cicadas, he allowed his anxiety to succumb to sleep. Haider and Owais, though, occupied his subconscious.

He felt Haider's dread of killing innocent people. The warmth that greeted him on campus and in the mosque eroded the hatred for Americans that Mohammad had programmed into his psyche. The longer he lived in the free society in which he was the determinant of his future, not the state and not the state's religion, the less interested he was in Mohammad's jihad. Yet, Jace perceived the torment inside Haider; his sense of honor and obligation to live up to his commitment.

Owais had weakened too. Jace sensed disregard for American lives, not hatred and motivation to kill, but indifference. Owais, though, was afraid to die, and he never believed jihad meant martyring himself for Mohammad's cause. He felt in Owais a desire to run, to disengage from the mission in which he would die far from home.

Jace did not infer from either that they would abandon the cause. Haider's sense of commitment kept him from doing so, and Owais' dread of Mohammad, and the unknown, kept him unwillingly loyal.

Jace's empathic insight of the Saudi boys transitioned to a more vivid, motion picture-like dream. He found himself entering the Scope plaza from across Monticello Avenue. Checking his watch, it was 10 minutes before eight o'clock and nearly dusk. He hurried toward the entrance to Chrysler Hall, scanning the plaza. The sight of his four cohorts approaching the theater from different directions eased his anxiety somewhat. All dressed in business suits and carried courier bags slung around their necks and under their arms.

The plan was to arrive right before the show started. The front doors would be open for late arrivals and most people, thousands, would be in their seats. Jace and his accomplices arrived at the entrance within seconds of each other and presented their tickets to the person at the door. They expected security to at least search their bags, so they decided not to try stealth, but to force their way into the building, shooting the minimal number of security personnel. The five had strapped AK-47s to their shoulders and hung them under their suit coats. Their extra clips of ammunition were in the bags. Bilal was to be the first through the door to eliminate security with a handgun equipped with a suppressor. It would make noise, but not enough to be noticeable over the din made by thousands of concert-goers settling into their seats. Jace sensed Haider knew this to be the case, as he had attended an event there and was confident in his plan.

Haider's scheme played out in Jace's subconscious as though he was taking part in the attack. Once past security, he and the four other gunmen dispersed to their assigned locations in the building's front lobby. One ran to the door of the theater on the left; one to the right, and Bilal ran to the center entrance. Jace moved up the stairwell to the left balcony, and Owais did the same on the right. They had ten seconds to move into position. When they heard Bilal firing his AK-47, the rest would fire and reload until they spent their ammunition. They would then drop their weapons and flee through the exits nearest them and disappear into Norfolk in separate directions. The entire operation was to last only a few minutes. Emptying five magazines from automatic weapons should only take 60 seconds, and infiltration and exfiltration from the building should take less time than that. They could blend into the night before the police receive the first 9-1-1 call.

Jace knew the sorrow in Haider as he pictured firing his weapon at men in suits and uniforms and nicely dressed women screaming in terror, fleeing through the balcony exit that he blocked. The disturbing images and overwhelming emotion of remorse and horror woke him from his sleep. It took a moment for him to orient himself and realize he had fallen asleep in his backyard sanctuary. When he realized it was a dream, his relief allowed the anxiety to leave him, but only for an instant.

"What the hell was that?" he said out loud, more an exclamation than a question, and then hurried into the house to find his journal. *I need to write this in the journal and then call Ike.*

"So, was that a precognitive dream?" Jace asked Ike after he described to him everything that happened earlier in the day.

"It might have been. I'm not sure we can say, but we can be confident you read Haider's thoughts. Maybe you saw the future. Either way, we should consider the attack on Chrysler Hall real."

"I'll tell Charlotte as soon as we're finished. She'll get it to the FBI."

"Have you been practicing your focused meditation?"

"Yes. I've been focusing on Bilal every day, for ten minutes, but I've had no dreams, at least that I can remember."

"Keep at it. What you experienced today may have opened that channel of communication. It will not surprise me when you tell me you had the same type of vision through Bilal's mind's eye."

As he ended the call with Ike, Charlotte walked through the door. The afternoon had flown by, and he didn't realize how late it was.

"Hey. Who were you talking to?" she asked out of curiosity. He was not much for socializing, so if he was on the phone it was with her or the kids — or Dr. Allo.

"I called Ike."

"Why, what's up?"

"When I got home today, I could not stop thinking about Haider and Owais — the despair and sadness. I relaxed in the hammock, and I fell asleep."

"You had a dream." They discussed his sessions with Dr. Allo, and she knew he was working on nurturing precognitive dreams. "Did you record it?"

"I did. You need to see it." He handed her the journal. It was all there. "Read it and then I'll answer any questions you have."

That was fine with her. She had just gotten home and needed time to decompress. She grabbed a chilled drink from the fridge and took the journal into her office.

Jace was hungry. Besides the few bites he had at lunch, he hadn't eaten since breakfast. He was in no mood to cook, so he boiled spaghetti noodles and warmed up their favorite off-the-shelf marinara sauce. It was just the two of them for dinner. The kids had been home for a brief summer break, but were back to school for the fall semester. By the time Charlotte emerged, Jace had dinner ready, including a salad, warm bread, and a glass of chianti. It took her longer than he expected.

"What did you do, fall asleep in there?" he half-heartedly joked.

"After I read your journal, I had to call Grace. She needed to know, and I had to share."

"What questions do you have?"

"Was this a precognitive dream? Is it the future?"

"We don't know. Ike thinks for sure I was watching the attack play out in Haider's mind. So, if they hit Chrysler Hall, that's the plan he developed."

"Tactically, it makes so much sense. In and out in a few minutes — hundreds dead, probably. You did well today."

"I hope so."

"You gave us the place of the attack, the method of assault, the date, and even the time of day. And we learned there will be five terrorists executing the assault. In the journal, you mentioned our guests in Park Place, but no other names. Was Mohammad in your dream?"

"No. I had no perception of who the other two were."

"That seems to tell us we have two unknown, unaccounted for terrorists in our midst," she concluded. "If you're right, we have a month and a half to figure this out."

"What did you think about the first part of the dream?" he wondered. "Neither one of those boys want to do this." Jace hoped for a way to rescue them from, to them, an inescapable reality.

"We know." Charlotte understood his anguish. Despite his introversion, he had always shown compassion for others and would help when someone needed it. He did it without thinking of the imposition it is on him. That's how the two met.

They were both students, and she was behind him in the checkout line at the grocery store. There was a young mother with an infant checking out in front of Jace. When her bill totaled more than she could afford, she removed a package of diapers from her cart and asked the cashier to remove it from the total. The bill was still too much for her, and the woman cried, visibly in despair. Jace saw this, and instead of being annoyed by the delay as most college boys might be, he told the clerk to put the diapers back into her basket, handing over his card. "I've got this. No need to worry, ma'am," Jace reassured the new mom. That overwhelmed her with relief and gratefulness, and Charlotte fought back tears at the display of kindness by the young man ahead of her. Charlotte choked up and said nothing to him, but when he began setting aside groceries from his own cart because he knew he didn't have the money to pay for them, she couldn't hold back. With tears rolling down her cheeks, she ordered the cashier, "Ring that up. I'm paying for it," pointing to the items he had removed from his cart. When he turned toward her to object, he saw her tears, and she saw his eyes were moist too, and he could only squeak out a soft, "Thanks." Taken by her enchanting, turquoise eyes, he couldn't just leave, so he slowly wheeled his groceries to his car, and lingered in the parking lot until she hurried from the store. She was relieved he was there. Their gaze connected instantly, and she made a beeline straight to him. And in her straight-forward, but sweet way asked, "what's your name?"

Chapter 58: The September Call

Grace let Charlotte know that it was time for Minion to call Bossman, but she needed no reminder. They both had been anticipating the September conversation and hoped it would bring more revelations.

Charlotte waited in Grace's office while she pulled the recording from PRISM, and they listened to it together. After the usual exchange of greetings, the candor of the conversation surprised them. Were Mohammad and Bilal getting careless, or too confident in their privacy?

Bilal started. "I am pleased with the progress of our planning. I have chosen one that I believe you will endorse. The plan is complete with only a few minor details to do once you and the Yemenis arrive."

"It meets my desires?"

"Yes, thousands will be seated together with limited exits. The operation takes only minutes, giving them little opportunity to escape. The response will be minimal while we are on-site, guaranteeing success."

"How will our brothers fare?"

"Our plan is too perfect, brother. I do not expect to lose them in the initial action."

"Then you have a plan for afterward?" Mohammad said with a hint of displeasure.

"Yes, we are working on that."

The conversation paused for several seconds. Grace and Charlotte interpreted it as displeasure from Mohammad. Perhaps he tried to find the right words to cloak his statement. "I desire a bold statement against their military," he said, as though he doubted Bilal's plan.

Bilal responded with confidence, "You will be pleased."

After a shorter pause, Mohammad stated his expectations for the next phone call. "When next we speak, I want to hear your preparations for my return home."

The call ended with their usual praise of Allah, and Charlotte and Grace looking at each other with wide eyes.

"That was remarkably less covert than the other calls," Charlotte started.

"Yeah. That was curious. What the heck was that was about?"

With that thought hanging in the air, Charlotte summarized. "Well, we know the two unknown terrorists in Jace's dream are from Yemen, and they are arriving with Mohammad. Their words suggest a terror attack."

"'I desire a bold statement against their military,' Mohammad said. That's close to flat out saying they are planning an attack," Grace agreed. "But how is the Chrysler Hall plan a statement against the military? Everything else sounded like another validation that it is the target."

"What are they up to?"

"Wait a minute. Let me check something." Grace remembered a detail that almost slipped by her. She called up the concert hall's calendar again on her laptop and showed Charlotte. "It's a concert to honor NATO. They'll play military-themed songs, and dignitaries from NATO and our armed forces will be there. It didn't mean much to me until now."

"That is definitely a tie-in. It's not an assault on a military target, but if you're looking to kill military personnel, it's an easy way to do it."

"It's a statement against both the West's and the U.S. presence in the Middle East. It's perfect. I'll run this up the chain to keep everyone informed. Besides our 'illegitimate' secret weapon, this is the first indicator of an attack."

Chapter 59: On Campus

With their focus zeroed in on Haider and Owais, Bilal fell off Grace's radar screen for a while. It was time to turn her attention back to him, hoping he would confirm their belief that Chrysler Hall was the target the evening of November 13th.

She still had the Park Place residence under remote, 24-hour surveillance, and moved the camera vehicle around so the residents would think the car belonged to one of their neighbors. Before the fall semester, Bilal only left for short periods, sometimes with his housemates. The reasons for the trips were obvious from the video. He returned with groceries or other shopping bags, or the group had takeout containers in their hands. When school started, routines set in for the boys at number 218. Grace assumed her window of opportunity for learning something from tailing him had closed, but she felt compelled to try.

After studying his patterns, she found him leaving the house at random times. But a few days of trips to innocuous places like fast-food restaurants and prayer sessions at the mosque had her frustrated. For a change, she dressed in jeans and a casual top, grabbed a notebook and a ball cap, and followed him to campus. Posing as a student was no stretch for Grace. Youthful and attractive, she blended with the diverse population of the school and had been working part time on her Master of Arts degree in International Studies. She knew the university well, and her student ID and parking permit came in handy.

Being on the grounds on a fresh fall day summoned the thrill of the start of a new semester, and she felt the urge to sign up for her next class. But she was in no hurry to finish. The variety of course offerings was too good to just meet the program requirements and graduate. She figured if the FBI continued to pay for her courses, she'd keep taking them.

Grace almost lost sight of Bilal as she soaked in the college atmosphere, but she tailed him to his early class and saw him enter the classroom. She positioned herself in the building's lobby so she could be sure to pick him up again when he left. Afterward, he spent 90 minutes studying in the library, and then went to another class before heading home to Park Place. It was just a normal day for a student who commutes to school.

Grace continued to surveil him in the following days until she was convinced there was nothing to gain from it. The routine varied because the classes were not the same, but there was nothing remarkable to observe. At least she was getting out into the fresh air. She loved fieldwork and the challenge of the tail, and tried to learn something to polish her skills with every surveillance.

The biggest test for Grace was parking. Parking for students living off-campus was scattered, and there was no guarantee she'd get a place in the lot that Bilal used. It irritated her that he stayed away from the large parking garages where most of the commuter parking is located. It would be easy for him to use them, and easy for her to follow. She entertained the idea that he had an aversion to parking structures until one morning he led her to the small garage next to the football stadium. The university limits that structure to on-campus residents and following him in to find a spot to park illegally might bring her close enough for him to notice her. So, she went somewhere else, and that caused her to lose sight of him for 30 minutes. But she knew where his first class was and could pick him up near the entrance to the building. Otherwise, that day, like the others, resulted in nothing to note. She thought it unusual, though, that he was so conscientious about attending classes and studying for someone who knew he would be dead, or at least in hiding in a couple of months.

Grace realized that Millicent and Bilal must be in the same program because Mil had two of the same classes as he did. At one point, she and Mil came face-to-face, each surprising the other. Millicent was with a good-looking young man who Grace recognized as Kent Green, and Mil quickly greeted her with a surprised, "Oh, hi Grace!" Grace responded the same way and hurried away.

Grace relayed her experiences with Bilal to Charlotte. Both were disappointed that the effort was fruitless, other than to discover that he was a diligent student.

Chapter 60: Mil's Friend

The fall semester for Millicent was a new beginning. Six or seven months ago she was enamored with the well-mannered and handsome foreigner, but that relationship left her disappointed and glad it ended. Her bright smile told of her excitement to be back in school with friends and limitless opportunities to have fun and grow. She always expected top grades for herself. Working hard was never in question, but her mentor inspired her more than ever, and the exhilaration she felt was refreshing.

Mil's excitement dampened when she realized Bilal shared two of her classes. She understood it might happen because they were both in engineering programs. Usually, especially for underclassmen, the school offers the same courses at different times during the semester. Mil intended to find out which classes of hers he was in and transfer to the same course with different class times. Until she could do that, she would have to endure being near him. She blocked the possible 'terrorist thing' from her mind and trusted that Charlotte and Grace had it under control. Otherwise, she could not be in the same room with him and be able to function as a student.

She thought he may try to talk to her, so she avoided being in the same place as he was outside a formal lecture. Twice he tried to say hello, but she diverted her eyes and ignored him. She hoped that would be enough for him to get the message, and he would ignore her too. If she had to confront him, she was unsure how she would react. She might say something to draw his suspicion.

Kent Green and Mil had become close, and she hoped he could run interference, steering Bilal away from her. Kent was a sincerely nice guy and knew she wanted nothing to do with Bilal, and he had no love for him either. His loyalty was spiritual while Bilal sponsored him at the mosque.

Something that bolstered Mil's confidence and lessened her fear of running into him was that she frequently saw Grace, the FBI Special Agent, on campus. After she first noticed her, Mil paid close attention and concluded she was there to watch Bilal. One afternoon Mil, walking with Kent, turned a corner and came face-to-face with her. Not knowing what to do, she said, "Hi Grace," in her typical friendly way, and Grace nonchalantly replied the same.

"You know her?" Kent asked with interest.

"Um — yeah, she's a friend." By his inflection, she figured what was coming.

"Can you get me her phone number?"

"Kent! I just can't give you a girl's number."

"Okay. Ask her first. I need her number," he said with an emphasis on 'need.' Mil smiled and laughed to herself. *What kind of mess would that be?*

Chapter 61: Wavering

Saudi Arabia's continued existence depends on economic diversification to reduce its dependence on oil exports, and the military security the United States brings to the Middle East. Trade and investment with the U.S. are key components to its strategy for a diverse economy. Because the Kingdom's future hinges on this relationship, the Saudis maintain strong commercial and military ties with America.

Both Owais al Omani and Haider Khan were raised in middle-class families dependent on the Saudi government, and loyal to its vision. Entrenched in the bureaucracy of the Ministry of Commerce, Owais' father promoted business relationships with U.S. companies. Haider's father held a similar position in the Ministry of Defense, working with American contractors. Their homes favored good relations with the United States and welcomed its culture.

So, with each passing day of summer, the strike against the U.S. grew closer to reality, and both Haider and Owais became more reluctant to die for a cause they did not embrace. Far removed from the teachings of Wahhabism and Mohammad's fanatical desire to kill Americans, their dedication to the mission wavered. As the calendar seemed to race towards October and his arrival, their inner turmoil swelled.

As Jace had sensed, their motivations differed, but their goal was the same — to live. Owais was most comfortable following the lead of others. He worked hard but accepted the ambitions that other people set for him. Wahhabi schooling and the mentoring of Mohammad, and his propensity to follow, led him to the place in which he found himself in Norfolk. For the first time he felt compelled to take control and alter his life's path, but he didn't know how to do that. He had no confidence to step out on his own, but was even more frightened of what Mohammad might do if he tried.

Haider was more independent-minded than Owais and dreamed of forging his own way in business. While he would miss his family, the thought of settling in America appealed to him. In his brief time as a student in the U.S., he relished in the freedom and opportunity presented to him, and daydreamed of endless possibilities, including finding a lovely American bride.

As the strike approached, Haider spent more time at the mosque, enjoying the fellowship of the congregation and seeking guidance in both prayer and from the local religious leaders. The contrast between the peaceful and serving Muslims in Norfolk and the hate-driven holy war of Mohammad's was stark. Haider accepted the idea that he could be pious without a politicized, violent jihad against non-believers, and prayed that Allah shows him a way to reject Mohammad.

Haider and Owais felt the rejuvenation and promise of the new semester, but the specter of October kept those feelings at bay. All in the Park Place house sensed the pall that had seeped into their lives. The sounds of Counter-Strike no longer spilled from the living room. The intelligence gathering was complete, and the bulk of the assault planning was done. They were left to ponder their fate while they waited for Mohammad and the Yemenis to arrive. Bilal had assumed, or hoped, that his brothers were merely preparing themselves to fulfill their duty to the jihad. He, too, found it difficult to concentrate on his studies, and harbored expectations his life would return to that of a student after November. He just needed to convince Mohammad that martyrdom was not the best plan for himself and his compatriots.

One day, later in the afternoon when the sun was crawling to the western horizon, Owais sat on a bench under a tree on the grassy campus mall. Owais had no more classes, but he wasn't ready to go back to the house. It had come to represent doom. The university grounds were peaceful and held promise that lured him to stay. He wasn't aware of Haider until he sat next to him.

"How are you doing?" Haider asked.

Owais' stomach clenched. He loved Haider as a brother and friend, but he was inextricably linked to his ill-designed fate. "I'm okay," were the only words he could to say. Owais was alone. He had no one he could trust to whom he could express his feelings, his faintheartedness. He bottled them inside, and he had no relief.

"This thing we are to do..." Haider's voice trailed.

Owais looked at him for the first time since he sat down, wondering how he would finish the thought. Haider sighed, leaving Owais with more doubt.

"I've been going to mosque lately. These Americans are warm and inclusive. I pray to Allah for guidance."

"And what does he tell you?" Owais was sincere.

"I am loved."

He sounded almost happy and hopeful. *What does that mean? I don't know what he is telling me,* Owais thought, and was still too afraid to ask.

"Come with me."

Chapter 62: The Scheme

"Jace is confident that Haider and Owais do not want to go through with the attack," Charlotte broached the subject with her partner. "Can we use this?"

"How do you mean? Grace asked.

"I'm thinking if we give them a way out, they might take it."

"And that would stop the attack? I'm not confident we can say that. There would still be four terrorists out there, hell-bent on their jihad."

"What if we turned them without Bilal knowing? We could stop the attack and arrest Mohammad and company. Meet with one, or both, and offer immunity for their cooperation."

"I don't know. If we spook them, we blow the entire operation. Bilal aborts and we have nothing."

"We stop a terrorist attack on American soil, in our own backyard. We save lives."

"Yes, but they'll be out there, free to plot another attack. We might stop this one, but what about the next one? Ours will only be a delaying action. We've got nothing on them except what Jace has told us. We don't have enough evidence to even arrest them."

"The last phone call was pretty damning."

"Yeah — that would be enough to get Bilal's visa revoked and kicked out of the country."

"And Mohammad's."

"If we can identify who he is, and if he's entering the U.S. legally."

The two paused their conversation. Neither sure where to take it next. Haider and Owais wavering in the commitment to Mohammad was significant information, but was it useful?

"What if Jace is wrong?" Grace brought up the possibility. She didn't doubt Jace. The other scant pieces of the puzzle they've assembled validated everything he's said. But she needed to say it. "If he's wrong about them, then we've shown our cards to our adversary."

"He's not wrong."

"But we have to consider the ramifications if he is. That's all I'm saying."

"What about the FISA warrant?" Charlotte changed the subject. Grace had requested a warrant to surveil inside the Park Place house under the Foreign Intelligence Surveillance Act. It established the process to allow the FBI to get warrants to spy on suspected terrorists and foreign intelligence operations in the U.S.

"The request is still working its way up the chain of command. It may never get approved. Besides, from the street-side video, there is hardly a time when the house is empty. All three of them have different schedules. It would be tough planting devices in the house."

Charlotte lightened the mood. "Mil called me to check-in. She told me she ran into you at school the other day."

"Right. I was tailing Bilal. I told you that. She was with Kent Green."

"Yep, I remember," Charlotte smirked.

"What?"

"Mil told me he wants your number!"

"Haha — well, he is a handsome young dude."

"Probably not a good idea."

"Nah, probably not."

"But I wonder," Charlotte contemplated, "is that something we can use? He may fill in the gaps we have on Mohammad."

"But Charlotte, we know nothing about Kent. He could be one of them. We would risk alerting Bilal that we're on to him."

"Not if you're clever about it." Charlotte provoked Grace in a good-natured way.

"Oh, brother. What are you thinking?"

"It wouldn't hurt anything if you happen to run into him on campus and stumble into a casual conversation."

"And what, ask him, 'hey, do you know this dude Mohammad?'" Grace threw in some sarcasm.

"No, but you may casually ask what he's doing over fall break."

"Hm," Grace looked at Charlotte with a more serious face, "that is an excellent idea."

For the next hour, Charlotte and Grace plotted how best to approach Kent, and what to say and what not to say. They decided the risk was minimal and to go forward with the scheme.

Charlotte ended the meeting the same way she started it. "I still think we need to exploit the intel we have on Haider and Owais."

Chapter 63: The 'Accidental Meet'

Charlotte kicked their scheme into play by calling Millicent.

"Hi, Mil. Grace is here with me. We need you to do us a favor."

"Sure." Millicent didn't think of not helping.

"I told Grace that Kent wanted her number. We do not want you to give it to him, but we'd like you to set up another accidental meeting."

"An accidental meeting?"

"Yes. The same as before, but Grace will stick around and chat with him for a few minutes."

"Kent's not in trouble, is he? I'm sure he has nothing to do with whatever Bilal is doing."

"No. We want a chance to talk with him without divulging who we are and what we're doing. All we need you to do is get him to a specific place at a certain time. After that, you can leave, and Grace will do the rest."

"Okay. I'll do that." They laid out the plan, and Mil told them the perfect opportunity would be that afternoon, so they ended the call. Showing up on campus dressed as an FBI Special Agent was not part of the strategy, so Grace ran home to change.

Three days a week Kent and Millicent had the same class in the engineering building. Afterward, they made it a habit to walk to the University Center and grab a coffee. The plan was for Grace to be sitting along the path they take through a shady courtyard between the buildings. As arranged, the two women noticed each other and said hello.

"Hi, Grace! I haven't seen you in, oh, a couple of days."

"Hey, Mil. I know — I'm sorry I had to run off the other day. I was late."

"This is Kent Green." She introduced the broadly smiling young man, and Grace invited them to sit with her.

Grace opened the small talk with, "So what are you guys up to?" and after a few minutes of chatting, Mil stole a look at Kent and gave him a quick wink.

"I need to run to the ladies' room. Kent, meet you at Starbucks in 15?" and she left the two alone. Grace took her time and allowed the conversation to arrive naturally to where she intended.

"So, you said you're from Portsmouth," she opened the subtle interrogation, "are you planning to stay here fall break, or do you have plans?"

"I usually just take the few days off to hang around

home and rest, but this year I'm taking a trip."

"Oh yeah? Where?" She sought the information in which she was most interested.

"I'm doing a favor for someone." That answer wasn't what she had hoped, so she kept trying.

"That's nice — giving up your time off for a friend. What will you two be doing?"

"He's not coming with me. He can't do it, so he asked me to pick up his people for him."

"At the airport?"

"Man, I wish! No, I have to drive to get them and bring them back here."

"Oh right, you said you were going on a trip. Not a long one, I hope." Grace worked to get the intelligence she wanted, but he was evasive. She gave him the opportunity to vent, and he took it.

"That's just it. It's a long trip."

"Yikes, that doesn't sound good. What are we talking about here?"

"Two days." She talked to him in a warm and friendly way, as though they had known each other for a while. Kent felt comfortable with this pretty girl with the soothing tone.

"Two days? One way? That's a ton of driving."

"Yes, one way." He appreciated the empathy.

"Oh my gosh. How far is it? Where are you going?" She once more went for the gold.

"I'm going to go to Texas. It's right at two thousand miles." Grace let her jaw drop in feigned disbelief and concern for Kent, then dialed up her sympathy.

"Two thousand miles?" She emphasized the 'thousand,' for compassionate effect, hoping to elicit more info from him. "Kent, Sweetie, that's too far to drive in a few days. You have to travel all that way and then turn around and come back?" She intended to endear herself to him, but her interest became real.

"Yes. I'm not looking forward to it." He had succumbed to her warmth and femininity, and any notion of keeping the trip secret, as Bilal instructed, faded away.

"Do you have to drive it by yourself? Can the people you are picking up help?"

"No. They're coming from another country. I think this will be their first time in the U.S. They won't be driving."

"Holy crap. You are going to have to take lots of breaks. Are you up to this? There's no way I could do that." Grace was sincere. She didn't fake the concern. "You are such an unselfish person for doing this. That's amazing."

"I planned it out. I'll stick to the interstates and stop at the rest areas — at least every other one. And my friend rented me a sweet, new Suburban to use. We'll be comfortable."

"I love the new Suburban," Grace probed more. "The black ones are so cool."

"I agree, but the white ones are sick. We'll cruise in a sharp, ivory ride with dark-tinted windows. I'll be the coolest dude on the road, except no one will see me through the tint!"

"Aww, you can open your window as you roll through town."

"No. I'm not going to be stopped for driving-while-black. Those southern cops will assume I stole a nice, expensive vehicle and run me down."

"Why are you traveling in one, then?"

"My guests need to be comfortable. Bilal wanted to rent an Escalade, but I told him that will draw too much attention to us."

"It's not a big deal, is it? If you get stopped, you won't be doing anything wrong. They can't arrest you for just cruising down the interstate."

"You know that's not how it works!" Kent snapped back. He was a little louder and a tad higher pitched. Grace hoped he would divulge more about his passengers, but thought she may have pushed him too far. She remembered too late that Mil said Kent got easily worked up about social injustice. His agitation lasted just a moment. "Besides, my passengers want to remain incognito. I can't get stopped with them in the car."

"Why is that?"

"I don't know. Bilal wants to keep it down low. I assume it's because they are Muslim and there's a lot of anti-Muslim crap in America right now."

"Well, yeah, that's going around," she said, still trying to build trust.

"Bilal? Is that your friend?"

"Yeah."

"How did you two meet?"

"At mosque. Mohammad referred me to one close

by and asked Bilal to mentor me."

"Oh, are you Muslim?"

"Not yet, but I love the sense of belonging there. Islam is so inclusive."

"So, who is Mohammad?"

"He's a spiritual leader I found online. He sent me to a wonderful community here, and to Bilal."

Grace was not sure how to proceed from that point in the conversation. She felt her next question may push Kent too far, so she asked it indirectly. "So, are you excited to meet him?"

"Who?"

"Mohammad."

"Um."

"I'm sorry. I think I just assumed you were picking him up from Texas."

"No, that's okay. Yes, I am looking forward to meeting him, but I wish he were flying."

"Yes — me too," Grace said, once again showing her interest in Kent's well-being. She felt the conversation had come to its end, and he did too.

"Well, I told Millicent that I'd meet her in 15 minutes. I think it's been longer than that, so I should go."

"Okay. If I don't see you before you leave, have a safe trip."

"I will. See you around campus." Kent started to the University Center, but the Special Agent had one more thing to do to complete Charlotte's scheme.

"I hope so," she called to him in an innocent, but maybe suggestive way.

He stopped and turned to her and then summoned the courage. "Uh, can I have your number?" She hooked her catch. As Charlotte expected, Kent asked for her phone number and they were ready to give him one. She gave him the number to the pre-paid phone Charlotte had grabbed for her as they raced to make the accidental meeting.

As Kent left to meet Mil, Grace used the app on her phone to map routes from Norfolk to Texas cities. The only city she found to be two thousand miles away was El Paso — just about the farthest from Norfolk you can get and still be in Texas.

"So, how did it go?" Charlotte answered Grace's call as they both had grown accustomed — with no social pleasantries.

"I confirmed Kent is picking up Mohammad and driving him here. For sure they are coming from Texas, and I'm 90% confident it's El Paso."

"Wow, so you got what we wanted."

"Yes, and a little more. We know they'll be in a late-model Suburban, white with dark-tinted windows."

"Dang, you must have been extra charming. And the phone number?"

"He has it. And, yes, I was extraordinarily charming."

"Anything else?"

"Yeah. I think Mil is right about Kent not being

involved. He's an innocent bystander being used by his so-called spiritual leader and his mentor. I'll fill you in when I get there."

Chapter 64: Mosque

Both Haider and Owais had neglected salat, one of the five pillars of Islam, that requires prayer five times daily. Not that they abandoned their faith, but the emotional preparations for jihad had distracted them. Besides, they rationalized, war is a legitimate reason to postpone these prayers.

But Haider turned to his religion as his martyrdom drew near to find his purpose and to seek guidance. He joined the men at the nearby mosque for collective worship as much as he could and found solace there. The American practice was far removed from the harshness of Wahhabism and the hate of Mohammad. He realized that the kinship he felt in the congregation was a message from Allah that love is greater than hate. He must reject the jihad, he reasoned, but how can he summon the strength to confront Mohammad?

He sensed the same struggle in Owais and approached him during a solitary moment under the canopy of the trees on the campus mall, away from the house in Park Place. He was unsure what to do, afraid to expose that he no longer believed in Mohammad's holy war. So, he was cautious.

"This thing we are to do..." his thought trailed as he couldn't find the courage to express the words that the attack is wrong. Haider saw confusion and anguish in Owais' eyes as he looked up to see his brother. Haider could only think to say is that he experienced comfort at the mosque and to invite Owais to join him.

So, Owais went with him to the mosque for both sunset and evening prayer. For a few hours, the weight of the destiny chosen for him lifted from his shoulders, and for the first time in an awfully long time, he enjoyed the religious discussion among virtuous men. The camaraderie of the people who gathered to prepare food boxes for those in need was almost overwhelming. Owais understood what Haider meant when he said he felt comfort and realized what he tried to tell him under the trees on the mall.

The next day, when they were alone, Haider and Owais finally had a frank discussion.

"I do not wish to die," Owais started, "I want to see my family again."

"Owais, I feel the same. We should never have taken this path. I have no desire to kill anyone."

"So, what do we do? Mohammad is coming. Should we talk to Bilal?"

"No. I don't trust Bilal. I think he is looking forward to the strike."

"What if we just leave? We could fly home and be done with this."

"That may be what we must do, but I fear what Mohammad would do. Hatred consumes him, and he would punish us, perhaps by harming our families. And we are already guilty of this. We have planned attacks against the U.S. Neither our government nor theirs will allow us to go unpunished."

"Maybe we should go to the FBI and explain to them we followed Mohammad, afraid for our loved ones.

"Would they believe us?" Haider thought out loud. "We could claim we had nothing to do with the planning and just became aware of the attack. Tell them about Bilal and Mohammad and the Yemenis and that it is their conspiracy." But, after considering the possibility, he concluded, "I'm afraid they would not accept that as truth."

"They would send us to Guantanamo Bay. What do we do?"

"We will find a way. At least we know we can count on each other and work it out together."

While both felt trapped and no simple solution presented itself, the two boys from the Saudi middle class found consolation that they were of the same mind.

Chapter 65: The Meeting

Kent figured he would have to travel 16 hours a day to make it to Las Cruces in two days. Driving for that long in such a short time scared him, so he gave himself an extra day to get there. That made it a leisurely trip, and he could scout which rest areas and gas stations would be the best to use when his passengers were with him.

Once he got on the road, his thoughts turned to the woman for which his crush was growing. He found her name in his phone, hesitated a few moments, and then touched the call button. Grace was in Charlotte's office when the 'Kent phone' rang. She had changed the ringtone, so it differed from the other ones on her phone. She wanted to make sure that when he called her, she would know it was him without fumbling for phones.

When the phone rang, they abruptly stopped their conversation, allowing Grace to compose herself and answer the call. In a very warm and inviting way, she answered, "Hi there, Kent! What are you up to?"

Kent warmed as soon as he heard her speak, and

no longer doubted himself for making the call. "Hi, Grace! I'm on the road to Las Cruces and I thought of you. I just want to let you know that I'm off on my little adventure." He had no inhibitions sharing with her. After all, she cared for his safety.

"Wow, so you're on your way. Did you take off early or was it always your plan to leave before the break?"

"Yeah, I left early. I was not looking forward to driving 16 hours a day, so I gave myself a break for the trip there."

"That was smart thinking. I'm glad you did that. Are you doing that on the way back?"

"No, Bilal wants his guests in Norfolk as fast as possible, so that will be a two-day drive. That's fine with me. I'm not keen on making that trip with strangers in the car, anyway."

"So you said Las Cruces? That's in New Mexico." Grace did not miss Kent's reference.

"Oh yeah, it's in the El Paso area, just down the interstate. I'll barely cross into New Mexico."

Grace threw Charlotte a satisfied look, acknowledging the find of another small piece of the puzzle. "Be careful going through Atlanta. The traffic is horrible."

"I decided to go through Tennessee and Arkansas, so I won't be anywhere near Atlanta. I want to stop in Nashville and sightsee a little."

"Nice. Nashville is so much fun."

"You've been there?"

"Yes — once. I was passing through and stopped

for a while. Just walking on Main Street was a blast."

After a minute of small talk, they decided it was best for him to focus on driving, so they said their goodbyes.

Tapping Kent as an unsuspecting source of information was a smart move. Thanks to him, they knew for sure that Mohammad and two others were traveling from Las Cruces, New Mexico; what route they would take; what dates they'd be on the road, and in what vehicle. They would probably track Kent's location with simple and innocuous texts between him and Grace. Charlotte's scheme was working so far.

Anxiety in Charlotte and Grace had been building for a few weeks. Those at the Park Place house had settled into their normal routines as students, prompting no suspicions or actions. There was nothing moving related to the case, and they had been biding their time until Mohammad showed in October. They expected it to move in earnest when Bossman arrived. That moment was almost upon them, and they welcomed it with both relief and unease.

The more Kent thought about his task at hand, the more he questioned it. All the driving when it would be so much easier to fly, the secluded rendezvous in the middle of the desert, and Mohammad and his companions traveling incognito was not normal. He was doing it out of gratefulness to Mohammad and Bilal for guiding him to Islam, but Grace was right. Maybe he is too accommodating, too nice of a guy, and lets people take advantage of him. *I'll be glad when this is over*, he said to himself as he cruised south on Interstate 81.

It was after dark when a vehicle pulled up outside the Las Cruces house. Kent peeked out the window to see an older Toyota Highlander park behind his Suburban. Three men got out of the SUV and unloaded their backpacks. They walked to the rear of the home to use the back door, so he stepped away from the window and toward the kitchen to greet them. He heard a muffled thwack that came from outside toward the vehicles. He wondered what in the hell that could have been and then reasoned that someone must have opened and then slammed the tailgate of the truck.

Kent waited in the kitchen by the door, expecting to see three men, but only one man entered. He recognized Mohammad from photos on his websites. He half expected him to be wearing a thawb, the long, white, robe-like shirt worn by Saudi males, but he wore darker pants and a loose shirt more suitable for being in America. Mohammad greeted him graciously, holding him by the shoulders and thanking him for guiding him through this last leg of his journey. As Kent greeted him, he heard the doors to the Highlander slam shut and the vehicle drive away. A curious look on his face caused Mohammad to explain. "Our friend who drove us here is leaving. My companions are seeing him off." Kent nodded his head and then began preparing dinner for his guests.

Bilal had given him specific instructions about what food and drink to buy and sent a large cooler packed with foods he knew his leader would enjoy. As he set the dining room table, the other two men came through the kitchen. They were rougher looking and acknowledged Kent with nods. Mohammad spoke to them in Arabic, and they disappeared down the hallway that led to the bedrooms.

Mohammad explained, "Friend, we will pray and then indulge in the food you have prepared for us." Kent was embarrassed that he hadn't thought they would have to pray when they arrived. He knew that missing a prayer was acceptable, but they must make it up as soon as possible. If they were traveling during the normal prayer time, they would pray at the first opportunity. Mohammad followed the others to the bedrooms for the ritual washing and change into clean clothes After a lengthy wait, the travelers emerged from the back and sat at the table. Kent noticed they had cleaned-up and changed their clothes and must have said their prayers before they came to eat. While he visited the mosque in Norfolk and engaged in spiritual discussions, he had not yet committed to Islam by stating the Shahada, the Testimony of Faith. Converting to Islam is a simple thing. A person only needs to say the Shahada, but his mentors at the mosque advised Kent to cite the Testimony only after he had studied and understood the conviction required of Muslims. So, it did not surprise him that Mohammad chose to do evening prayers with his companions, and without Kent in the room.

The meal was ready, and they ate as though they were famished. The rough-looking men only spoke in short bursts of Arabic, so Kent assumed they did not speak English. He could tell that Mohammad was well-educated, and he spoke English fluently. After satiating their appetites, Mohammad engaged him in a spiritual conversation over their meal.

"Bilal tells me you are studying with him and others at mosque to prepare for stating the Shahada."

"Yes sir. I want to understand and prepare to make the commitment to Islam."

"It is the only legitimate religion in the sight of Allah. The word Islam itself means submission. One achieves harmony of mind and steadfastness of heart only through submission to the one true God."

Kent expected nothing less from the man who professed to be his spiritual leader. The dinner conversation consisted mostly of Mohammad stating examples of proof that Islam is the religion recognized by God and encouraging him to say the Shahada. He fidgeted in his chair as he grew uncomfortable, thinking Mohammad wanted him to state his commitment right there in the New Mexico desert, but Mohammad relented.

"To be a faithful Muslim, you must comprehend what it means to submit to Allah. You only do that when you are willing."

Kent was grateful for the concession and allowed himself to relax. He had read and had been told all that which Mohammad had imparted, but he had trouble accepting the concept that God held Islam as the only true religion. That would mean 2.2 billion Christians, including his mom and dad, who had always been active in their Baptist church, were wrong. The interwoven connections between Christianity, Islam, and Judaism fascinated him and he could not wrap his mind around the idea that Islam was the only true word.

"Friend, when do we leave this place?" The discussion pivoted.

"It will be a really long ride. We should get up early and go before sunrise."

"Of course; we will leave right after Fajr."

Fajr is the morning prayer said before dawn. Kent knew the travelers would need to know, so he had looked up the required time of Fajr for that day. "Sunrise will be 7:09 tomorrow morning, and Fajr starts at 6:02. We'll need to get going as soon as we can, if that's okay."

"Yes, we'll eat a morning meal, say our prayer, and be off by 6:15 am."

Chapter 66: The Ride

The passengers woke early the next day, ate their breakfast, said their morning prayer, and were ready to go by 6:15 as promised. When he loaded his gear into the Suburban, he noticed several more duffel bags than he saw the men carry into the house the previous evening. He crinkled his brow with curiosity and almost moved his hands to unzip one of the bags when he sensed someone standing behind him. He turned to find one of the rough ones staring at him, so he jostled his own bag as though he were making sure it was secure and closed the tailgate of the truck.

Relieved to be on the road, Kent drove southeast on Interstate 10 toward San Antonio, and would soon turn onto Interstate 20 and start the trek east. His goal was to make it to Memphis before they stopped for the night. Soon after they had left, he heard the rough one speak Arabic to Mohammad, and it made him uneasy.

"The American saw the bags. He looked curious," Fadel said.

"Do not distress, brother. We only need him to

bring us to Virginia. We must monitor him so that his curiosity does not cause trouble."

That raised the hair on the back of Kent's neck. He didn't speak the language, but he recognized the word for American. The guys at Park Place used it many times. *They're talking about me.*

That prompted him to address Mohammad. He was unsure of his expectations, and it was as good a time as any to ask.

"Sir, we're going to be driving until around 10 or 11 tonight. You won't have the opportunity to pray until the evening prayer. Is that okay?"

"Yes, that's fine. Since we are on a journey, we can pray when time permits."

"We should be on the same schedule tomorrow. We'll stay in Memphis, Tennessee tonight and be in Norfolk by 11 p.m. tomorrow."

"That's fine. Bilal warned me of the long drive."

"We have enough food for the entire trip, so we don't have to eat at restaurants."

"Excellent."

"Bilal never mentioned to me the purpose of your visit. Do you have anything planned?"

"Ah yes. There are exciting things on our itinerary."

"Will you be sightseeing?"

"I expect we'll see things of interest."

"How long do you intend to stay?"

"It may be a few weeks. I am not quite sure yet."

"What is your destination after Norfolk? Will you be flying?" Kent's interest was more than curiosity.

He hoped he wouldn't have to make a return trip to El Paso, or anywhere else.

"Oh no, I won't be flying. We made other arrangements." Mohammad read his purpose of the question. "You are serving me well now, and I will not require more from you."

Require? I'm doing this because Bilal asked me to help. I'm not serving anybody. Mohammad's choice of words offended him. He spoke only of himself and did not include his two companions. *What about the two goons?* Kent thought. He immediately felt guilty for judging and labeling them, much like he had been many times in his life. He reasoned away the answer to his question, *it's just that he's their leader.* Since he had him engaged in conversation, he almost asked about the extra bags in the back, but the prospect of it caused him chills, so he decided against it. *I don't think I want to know.*

The rest of the day transpired mostly in silence. Kent chose a large rest area for lunch with picnic tables a suitable distance from the visitors' center. It allowed them to get out of the truck and move around unnoticed for more than a few minutes and gave him privacy so he could text Grace.

The evening brought an uncomfortable moment. As instructed, he reserved three rooms next to each other at a Hampton Inn outside Memphis. He checked in while the others waited in the vehicle. Once they were settled and the food brought to Mohammad's room, he announced his intention to drive to a Wendy's they had passed on the way to the hotel. The strange look and objection from Moham- mad startled him. Mohammad insisted that he keep the Suburban parked outside their windows so he could see it and held out his hand for the keys. This sudden and irrational lack of trust insulted Kent, and he objected.

"But I just want to get a burger, and I thought I'd give you privacy to wash up and get your prayer done before you eat. What's the harm in getting a burger?" The rough ones noticed Mohammad's out- stretched hand and heard the tension, and closed in on Kent in a way that frightened him.

"There is no harm, but we need to keep the ve- hicle safe to ensure we complete our journey. I mean no offense." Mohammad's hand remained palm up, expecting the keys to the SUV, and Kent obliged. The goons won the dispute. Mohammad waved off Abu and Fadel, and Kent retreated from the room. He hurried out of the inn and down the road and couldn't help looking over his shoulder every minute or two. He found himself at Wendy's and realized how hungry he was. After a leisurely din- ner at the restaurant and a calming text conversa- tion with Grace, he walked to the hotel, slower than when he left.

Kent heard nothing more from the travelers that night. As a passive-aggressive protest of how his guests had treated him, he intentionally arrived at the Suburban at 6:20 am — five minutes late. He could see the relief from the three when they saw him approach. *Message sent; message received,* he thought with satisfaction, and loaded his bag into the SUV with a rough one peering over his shoulder. The expressions on both goons' faces changed from relief to anger, and that gave Kent more satisfaction. He got into the driver's seat without saying a word and waited for Mohammad to hand him the keys.

He was in no mood to talk, so the day was quiet except for short bursts of Arabic, and another exceedingly unsettling incident for Kent that caused him to doubt his entire relationship with Mohammad and Bilal. It occurred as they crossed the Virginia border on Interstate 81. A trooper driving a Ford Taurus with the iconic blue-on-gray paint of the state police pulled in front of their vehicle. The foreigners took notice, and their spooked, rapid chatter caused the unease inside the truck to crescendo. Mohammad said something terse that caused them to be quiet, and he asked Kent what the police officer was doing. As reassuringly as he could, Kent told him he was patrolling the highway as usual. He was doing what troopers do. But chills ran down his spine when he spotted the goons in the rear-view mirror reach under their loose shirts and clutch their belts. Beads of sweat formed on his forehead as he checked his speed. He knew he wasn't speeding. He had set his cruise control to the speed limit to avoid giving police any reason to stop him, but the tension compelled him to keep looking at the speedometer. When the officer turned on his light bar, and flashing blue lights filled his field of vision, his mouth went dry and his sweat turned cold as the blood drained from his face. He felt lightheaded before his adrenal glands pumped adrenaline into his bloodstream, intensifying his awareness and helping him maintain his wits. Just as quickly, the trooper sped away, leaving the illicit travelers in the Suburban far behind. Kent's hands were shaking, and he needed to pull over, but there was no rest area on that stretch of Interstate 81. He dared not to look at the others, so he stared straight ahead.

When the sweat rolled from his forehead into his eyes, he swung his head toward Mohammad to wipe it on his sleeve, and he glimpsed Mohammad staring at him. At that moment, a rush of regret coursed through his body. He regretted searching for Islam on the internet and reading Mohammad's websites. He regretted everything. Kent knew thugs when saw them. He grew up with them, and he knew what they were clutching under their shirts. Thugs are thugs — they are all the same, and he was driving them across the country, into his hometown. He thought of his mom and dad. They believed in law and order and respected the police. The gang-bangers in their neighborhood angered them. What would they think of him now? *Pop is rolling in his grave.*

As they emerged from the Hampton Roads Bridge-Tunnel into Norfolk, Kent called Bilal and told him they were minutes from Park Place. A little past 11:00 p.m., they arrived at 218 W. 30th Street, and the Saudis, who were waiting outside, warmly greeted Mohammad. As nonchalantly and as quickly as he could, Kent retrieved his bag and hurried to his car parked on the street. In the formality of greetings between the Saudi men, he left unnoticed by them. Not so by the thugs. Abu and Fadel watched him hurry off but were unsure what to do in the strange neighborhood in an unfamiliar land.

Charlotte and Grace watched the arrival on her laptop in real-time — thanks to the surveillance camera across the street from the house.

Chapter 67: October 15th, Thursday

"**L**ook at that. Kent took off like a bat out of hell," Charlotte said as they viewed the live feed of Bossman's arrival. "He was out of there in less than 15 seconds."

"Yeah, he was spooked."

"Check out those duffel bags."

"They're heavy, but it doesn't look like there's much in them," Grace said.

"How many are there?"

"Six."

"There will be a full house tonight at 218 West 30th Street. Those two must be the Yemenis."

"We have a house full of terrorists in Park Place. Six of them." Grace's said, pondering what was to come.

"And six duffels." Charlotte made the connection out loud, adding to the trepidation. "I guess we know what's in them."

Grace picked up her 'Kent phone' and called him. He answered after two rings.

"Hi there," she sang into the phone in that way that charms men. "I figured you should be home by now and thought I'd check on you. Are you back?"

"Finally. Got in a few minutes ago."

"Good. Are you home and resting?"

"Almost."

"So, how did it go?"

"It was creepy. I am so glad that's done. I hope I never see those people again." Since the task was complete, he had no inhibitions talking about it.

"Why? What happened?" Grace wanted him to talk.

"You were right. I'm too nice a guy and I allowed Bilal to take advantage of me. That was a horrible trip."

"Tell me."

"The three of them were nothing but bullies. The two thugs with Mohammad didn't speak English, and they were carrying."

"Carrying? Guns?"

"Yes. I grew up around thugs and I know when someone has something tucked in his belt. They scared the crap out of me."

"How? What'd they do?"

"Earlier today, right when we crossed into Virginia, a trooper pulled in front of us and turned on his lights. Those dumb asses were jumpy as hell and reached for their belts like they were going to shoot it out with the cops."

"Oh my God, what happened?"

"The cop must have gotten a call, and he sped

away. They were afraid, and that had me shaking. Why would normal people be so jittery about a state trooper?" he asked without expecting an answer. "And that's not all," he continued to vent. "These mysterious duffel bags just showed up in the Suburban, and they kept a close eye on me when I was around them. Last night I tried to drive the truck to Wendy's, and they wouldn't let me. They forced me to park it outside their windows so they could guard it, and Mohammad made me give him the keys. They are sketchy and I don't trust them." After he got that off his chest, he went quiet.

"Well, you're safe now, right?"

"Yeah."

"Where do you live, Kent — on campus, or what?" She worried he may be in danger. It sounded to her as though his passengers showed too much of themselves and will try to fix that.

"No, I live with my mom in Portsmouth. Why?"

"Oh, I just want you safe and sound after that long drive," hoping she covered her true concern. "I'll let you go. You need to rest."

"Alright. Can I call you tomorrow?"

"Please do, and if you realize you're in trouble with these dudes, call me. They sound scary dangerous. Keep me posted on that."

"Okay, I'll do that."

After she ended the conversation, Charlotte looked at her in a 'what the heck was that' expression. Grace answered without her having to ask.

"He left so fast after they arrived at Park Place. I

was curious what was happening with him."

"You're worried about him."

"I think he's in danger." Grace explained what he shared, and they agreed they should take precautions to protect him, but they weren't sure what.

"Should I tell him I'm a Special Agent?"

"Not yet. Let's think through this." Charlotte approached this problem the same way she does most problems — with a little time and a lot of critical thinking.

Chapter 68: October 16th, Friday

Now that Mohammad was in Norfolk, Bilal was restive. It was one thing to embrace the holy war against Americans and plan violent strikes in secrecy, but the realization of executing an attack in which his friends will die was frightening. Bilal had looked forward to replacing his father as the head of his construction company and living a life of comfort and relative wealth. Mohammad assured him that was still in his future; that after the strike, he could return to Saudi Arabia to resume his schooling. But that was not the plan for the Yemenis, Haider, and Owais, for they were to martyr themselves in the name of Allah and the jihad.

Bilal had convinced him he would have to leave Norfolk the way he arrived, by vehicle, and he needed Bilal to navigate their way out of the country. He felt sorry for his friends. He knew they did not want to die, and it would be easy enough to survive a lightning-fast strike and escape into the city before the police could be on the scene. Dying in the attack would be more difficult, as they'd have to wait for first responders to arrive and allow law enforcement to shoot them.

The Park Place cell had been waiting for months for their spiritual leader to arrive, and it was time to show him the results of their effort. After their morning meal, they tried to brief him together, but he wanted to hear only from his lieutenant. Haider and Owais were told to go to their classes as though it were a normal weekday, robbing them of their best chance to convince Mohammad that they need not be martyrs on this mission. Abu and Fadel were told to stay inside and out of sight, so they sunk into the couch in the living room, fascinated by American television playing before them on the 50-inch screen.

Before they discussed the assault, Mohammad had to address the pressing business at hand.

"Kent Green is a loose end and we must eliminate him," he started. It had been on his mind since Kent disappeared so quickly after their arrival. Mohammad didn't like leaving clues to his whereabouts and intentions. Max Lopez was already a victim of his cautiousness.

"How do you mean?" Bilal was taken-aback, never expecting to have to 'eliminate' individuals he knew.

"He knows too much and suspects we are not who we claim to be."

"I don't understand. We trusted him with your

safe travel, and he lived up to his commitment. Should we not reward him?"

"He has seen too much and does not trust us. That is why he left us in such haste last night. If we do not silence him today, he could expose everything."

"The police will investigate the killing as a murder and it may announce our presence here."

"American society is filthy with crime and murder. It will be another murder, like every other murder. I'll have Fadel do it, but you must take him to Kent Green. Do it today — this morning."

"Yes, brother, it will be done." Although surprised at the personal tasking, he was resigned that he had to do something he never imagined doing — killing someone he knew face-to-face. "But Fadel will be too conspicuous and must stay here."

"Leave now then."

Grace's workday started around 7:00 a.m. so she could get to the office before the crazy traffic, and ready herself for the morning meetings. She briefed the latest information on her case, the persons of interest at Park Place, and the arrival of the visitors, but had no firm evidence for her chain of command that these men were terrorists. The September phone call prompted interest and was the reason she worked the case unencumbered by other assignments, but not enough to garner more attention from the Special Agent in Charge.

After her meetings, she checked her disposable phone, hoping to see that Kent had called, but he hadn't. She felt compelled to call him, but resisted the urge. She and Charlotte had not had time to talk to decide what they should do to protect him, and she didn't want to say something that may be counter to what Charlotte thought.

Bilal was well-versed in using a nine-millimeter semiautomatic handgun. While in Yemen, he trained with both an AK-47 and a Glock 9mm, one of the most reliable handguns available. He grew to enjoy shooting the full-sized Glock 17 with a suppressor. The silencer not only muffles the noise made when firing the gun, but it reduces the kickback, allowing the shooter to be more accurate. From the duffel bag that he claimed for himself, he retrieved the Glock and the suppressor that came with it. The weapon easily concealed on his belt under a light jacket, and he put the silencer in his pocket. His mind was racing, unsure when and where to kill Kent. He preferred to plan things in advance, and this spur of the moment killing left him extremely uneasy. When he got in his car, he stopped to think. *Where would he be right now?*

After considering options, Charlotte thought it

best to tell Kent that Grace was an FBI Special Agent. There was no need to tell him about their investigation, but letting him know she has experience in personal protection and dealing with thugs may give her concern for him added weight. Charlotte called Grace to discuss it, but she didn't answer. *She must be in her morning meetings.*

Kent slept late that Friday. The trip to Las Cruces and back was grueling, and his body and his mind needed to refresh. His first class was after lunch — the same as Millicent's. He didn't want to go, but he took his studies seriously and felt an obligation to himself not to miss class if he could help it. So, his plan was to sleep late before starting his day.

Bilal reasoned that it was early, and Kent needed rest from driving such a long distance in a short time. He would most likely be in bed, recovering from the trip. Fortunately for Bilal, he had his address. When they first met, Kent provided his contact information so that Bilal could send him material that they used to recruit followers. He mapped the way to Kent's house on his smartphone and then started his car.

Grace grew impatient waiting for Charlotte and started to call her when realized she had missed her call. She should have checked when her meetings ended, but checking the burner phone distracted her. There was no message, so she touched the screen to return the call. When Charlotte answered, Grace replied with a rushed, "Whattaya got?"

"Tell Kent you are an FBI agent. Don't tell him anything regarding the case and what we are doing. You are just a cop going to grad school. That should legitimize to him your caution about Mohammad."

"Okay. I'm calling him now."

Grace immediately dialed Kent and let it ring ten times before hanging-up and trying again. He didn't answer.

She called Charlotte, "He's not answering."

"I bet he's sleeping. He had a rough week."

"Do you know where he lives?"

"No. I'll call Mil."

"Good. I'll see what I can find on this end."

Millicent's phone rang. She was in bed and was going to ignore it, but couldn't resist looking to see who was calling. To her surprise, it was Charlotte, so she answered.

"Hi Mil. Where does Kent live?"

"Uh, he lives in Portsmouth," she answered, sleepy and confused. "Why?"

"Where in Portsmouth? I need his address."

"I don't know it, but I know it's in a neighborhood near the shipyard, and he went to I.C. Norcom."

"Okay. Do you know where he'd be right now?"

"Well, I guess he's home. He doesn't have class until this afternoon."

"Thanks, Mil." Charlotte hung up with no explanation, and Millicent tried to go back to sleep, but her mind was racing. *Oh my God, Kent.*

"He lives near Norfolk Naval Shipyard in Portsmouth, but I don't have an address," Charlotte relayed to Grace.

"Okay, I'm leaving now and going that way. Someone here will find it and send it to me."

"Grace."

"Yeah?"

"Good luck." The concern Grace had for Kent caused the same anxiety in Charlotte, and it had evolved into angst for both.

Grace hurried to her car and sped towards the Chesapeake Expressway. Once she got on the highway, she figured she could make it to Kent's neighborhood in 15 minutes.

The drive from Park Place to Portsmouth was a shorter distance but used mostly city streets. Depending on traffic, the drive time was close to that of Grace's. Bilal used the drive to plot how to carry out his task without getting caught or bringing suspicion on himself, and thus the entire operation. Once he reached the Prentiss Park neighborhood, he drove around the block to scout his best approach. Relieved to see that the street was quiet, he saw not one person outside. He assumed most had left for work, leaving the neighborhood to himself. Bilal found an ideal place to park. It was on the street across from an empty church parking lot, and next to a residence with boarded windows. There was no one to see or question a stranger's car parked under a shade tree, one house from Kent's. He got out and gently closed the door so as not to disturb the quiet, and while he walked toward his target, he reached in his pocket to palm the silencer.

As Grace raced down Interstate 464 toward the Jordan Bridge, a colleague sent her directions. She only needed to get there to deter any potential action against Kent. After that, she had to figure out what to do next, and work out what to say to him after she barges into his home to find him alive and well. She's an FBI Special Agent and worried about what he said regarding the thugs. She called to check on him, but she got no answer, so she thought it smart to be better safe than sorry and check on him. That thought reminded her to try again, so she dialed his number. There was no answer, and her anxiety level continued to climb.

As Bilal approached the house, he walked straight to the rear. It was more hidden from view than the street-facing front door, and trees and bushes hid him from the neighbors. Before he tried to enter, he screwed the silencer onto the Glock and returned the weapon to his belt. The door was locked, so he broke a pane of glass in the old-style, nine-pane window, reached in, and turned the lever to unlatch it. Bilal's knees weakened as he slipped into the kitchen. It was quiet except for the tick-tock sound of a clock coming from the hall that led to the front door. He froze for a moment to calm his nerves and listen for signs of life.

Grace was a minute away, but she tried Kent's phone one more time. It would be easier to explain to him she was coming over than to show up unannounced. She drove as fast as she dared down Deep Creek Boulevard through Prentiss Park and was only a few blocks away when doubt crept into her head. After all, she was acting on a gut feeling. *I'm probably making a fool of myself.*

Bilal had drawn his weapon and snuck up the stairs to the bedrooms on the second floor. The door to the room at the top of the staircase was wide open, and he saw Kent sleeping. He slipped to the side of the bed to get a last look at his face to make sure he was ending the life of the right man. As he raised the gun to Kent's chest, the phone on the bed table vibrated, causing a seemingly deafening buzz to break the silence in the room. Bilal could not help but divert his eyes to the source that had caused him to jump and noticed 'Grace' on the caller-ID. Kent interrupted the cursing of Grace in his head was when he heard him say, "Bilal?"

Kent finally woke to the soft vibration on his bed table. After talking with Grace the night before, he said hello to his mom and then settled into his bed for a good night's sleep. On her way to work that morning, his mother tiptoed past his room and down the stairs, being careful not to wake him. She wanted to hear about his trip, but he needed his rest, so she could wait until that evening.

Grace raced through the intersection of Deep Creek Boulevard and a cross street and found Kent's home on her left. Paying no attention to oncoming traffic, she crossed the opposing lane, screeched to a stop, and exited her car. She opened the gate of the chain-link fence, bounded up the porch steps, and pushed the doorbell three times, hearing the 'ding-dong' coming from the front hall. After a few moments of no response, she attempted to open the door, but it was locked so she hurried around to the rear of the house.

Kent looked up from his sleepy daze to see Bilal standing over him. He managed a confused, "Bilal?" before he realized what he was holding. When he saw the gun pointed at his chest, his eyes grew wide and he began to protest. In a rush of panic, he shouted, "what the f..." but he could not finish the word.

The sudden buzzing, and then Kent waking startled Bilal. With his heart racing and his hands shaking and slippery with sweat, he squeezed the trigger of the handgun three times, cutting Kent off mid-word. He looked at him, stunned at the violence and suddenness of what he had just done. Unable to think or move, Bilal watched as Kent lie bleeding from chest wounds of his making. It was the sound of the doorbell ringing that shocked him back into reality. He ran down the stairs, through the kitchen, and out the door in a matter of seconds. He leaped over the three-foot-high fence into the neighbor's yard and around the corner to emerge right where he had parked. Without looking back, he hurried to his car and drove away in the very direction from which Grace had come just moments earlier.

Chapter 69: Friday
— Park Place

As he rushed from Kent's home, Bilal was too unnerved to think clearly. The Glock was still in his hand as he approached his car, so he just threw it in the passenger seat and sped away. When he stopped at the main road, he realized he had been speeding and if he had passed police, he would have drawn their attention. Pausing at the stop sign to collect himself, he finally decided that turning right would take him to the tunnel and back to Norfolk. He drove the entire way through city streets and traffic lights with the handgun and silencer in plain view and didn't realize it until he parked in front of 218 W. 30th Street. He engaged the safety, removed the suppressor, and concealed both before walking into the house. Mohammad was in the study, waiting for his return.

"Is it done?"

"Yes, brother. It is done." Bilal felt a surge of pride that he had carried out Mohammad's orders, and he did it under duress. Now that he had killed someone face-to-face, he was certain he would not falter in the assault. "I shot him three times in the chest. No one saw me." He thought of the doorbell ringing and hoped he had escaped unnoticed. He did not share that detail.

"Did you make sure he was dead?" Mohammad pressed.

"He is dead." Bilal avoided answering the question directly, otherwise he might have to divulge that someone was at the door when he shot Kent.

"Good, it was for the cause. Clean your weapon. Then we will prepare for the noon prayer and can discuss our action against America after we eat."

At that moment, a wave of panic rolled through Bilal's mind. *Kent saw me. What if he's alive?* He turned the television to a local station so he could see the breaking news, and he waited.

The target and detail of planning for the strike on Chrysler Hall pleased Mohammad. At first, he objected. He had envisioned a direct assault on the U.S. military, but Bilal convinced him of the futility of doing so with just five men. All of them would likely die with few American casualties. It would be an operational and symbolic victory for the infidels, and the attack would disappear from the news headlines in a day. Mohammad's goal was to make a lasting impression on the American public, and another failed attempt, like the one in Corpus Christi, would not do that.

"Yes, I understand. The symbolism of martyrdom is important," Bilal tried to ease his mind, "but it is lost on Americans. They do not share our faith and belief in the honor of dying in the name of Allah. Besides, the anger and desire for revenge, and the dread of another attack will linger for weeks if we disappear."

The logic of Bilal's words was sound, and Mohammad relished the idea of lingering panic in his wake. Perhaps the plan was perfect after all.

"Bilal, you thought this through well. I like what you say. But if our soldiers walk away after the strike, what happens then? Where do they go? What do they do?"

"We have a month to work on those details, but I have ideas. It would be a simple thing for Haider and Owais to leave the country. We must make special plans for Abu and Fadel."

Bilal indiscernibly drew a deep breath and exhaled, relieved and grateful that he changed Mohammad's mind, and his friends would not die. He was excited to tell them when they returned from campus. Mohammad approved the entire plan as they had hoped, and they would live to return home to their families. He had been hoarding cash, expecting clandestine travel to the U.S. border — and freedom. Now he could complete those preparations openly without fear of being discovered.

Chapter 70: Friday — Prentiss Park

Something just below her consciousness nagged Grace as she made her way to the back of the residence. It didn't register, but it made her slow down and proceed with caution. She noticed the back door was ajar and the broken windowpane next to the lock. Then it hit her. Just before she rang the doorbell, she heard a faint thwack-thwack-thwack. When she realized someone had broken-in, that sound forced itself into her awareness. Those were suppressed shots. She unholstered her service weapon, a 9mm Glock 19M — favored by the FBI, smaller than a full-sized handgun and easier to grip and to conceal. Special Agents are the most highly trained law enforcement officers in the world, and her training took control. She entered the house calmly and carefully, climbed the staircase, and found Kent. Grace grabbed bedsheets and used them to apply pressure to the wounds. He was unconscious, and she saw he was struggling to breathe. She assessed that at least two of the wounds were lung shots. If he had any chance to live, he had to receive urgent medical attention.

She dialed 9-1-1 and handled the emergency as though it was a training exercise. She made it clear that she needed EMTs urgently and advised the Portsmouth police that an armed federal agent was on the scene. That was important information — there was no desire for tense locals to rush in with guns drawn.

Fortunately for Kent, a Portsmouth Fire and Rescue station was less than a mile away, and they arrived two minutes after she called. Maryview Medical Center was a quick run on Frederick Boulevard, allowing him to be in the hands of doctors in a brief period of time.

Tears welled in Grace's eyes after the EMTs left with Kent, but she immediately gained control of her emotions. She could not allow the local police to see her act in any way other than professionally. She waited seven minutes for them to arrive — her training prompted her to check her watch as events unfolded. Apparently, their thinly stretched force had no one in the area at the time of the call. She wanted to talk with her partner but was unsure that she could without getting emotional, so she waited.

Jace was at his desk in Town Center, 12 miles from Prentiss Park. He tried to review a report, but he was experiencing a sudden, familiar chill, and an ominous wave of trepidation. He at once related it to Bilal. It was the same feeling he's had twice before, both in his presence. Jace had been practicing the focused meditation as Ike told him to do, focusing on Bilal. But the point was to trigger precognitive dreams, and as far as he could remember, he had none.

A rush of grief plowed into him, forcing a sharp, but brief vision in his mind's eye. He saw Grace standing in a bedroom, alone and with tears in her eyes. An empty bed was covered in blood, as were her hands and blouse. And then the vision was gone.

Jace grabbed his phone and dialed Charlotte.

Grace's phone beeped. It was Charlotte, and she knew she had to answer it.

"Are you okay?! What happened?" Charlotte's urgency startled her, as though she knew something had happened.

"Someone shot Kent. I found him in his bed with three bullet wounds to the chest." Her voice faltered, but she held her composure.

As sorrow swelled inside her, Charlotte's initial thought was to ask, "Is he alive?"

"Yes, he was alive when he left here for Maryview, but..." Grace didn't finish the sentence, and Charlotte didn't want to hear it.

"So, he's alive."

"Yes." Grace's professionalism overcame her emotion, and she described what had happened. "The local cops aren't here yet, so I have to stay with the crime scene until they arrive. Once they're set, I want to check on him, but it could be an hour before I'm finished with Portsmouth PD. How should we handle this?"

"We need to talk through this. I'll be over there in a few minutes. What's the address?" Charlotte felt things were happening far too fast, and they had to get on top of it. She saved telling her about Jace's vision for later.

When Charlotte arrived, the patrol officers had the site secured. The local detectives showed up just as she got out of her car, and she showed them her credentials when they tried to shoo her away. She followed the investigators inside and up the stairs to the bedroom where they found Grace waiting for them. Charlotte listened as she walked them through what she did and saw that morning, including hearing three suppressed gunshots. Of course, the cops wanted to know what she was doing there. That's when she hesitated and looked at Charlotte, so the detectives turned to her.

"Ma'am, why are an FBI Special Agent and an Assistant U.S. Attorney at my crime scene?" The senior detective asked. Charlotte and Grace had no time to discuss how best to handle the situation, so she stuck to the facts.

"Special Agent Madson and I are collaborating on a federal investigation and the victim of this shooting is a person of interest."

"So, is this murder case ours or yours?" The detective's use of the M-word cut them both.

"Murder?" Grace asked. "Did he die?"

"No, excuse me, ma'am, not that I am aware." The cop detected a note of concern. "We're from Homicide Division, but we investigate all gun violence. It's just a habit. Almost everything we work turns into a murder case at some point."

"I know some guys in Homicide," Grace said. The cop spurred an idea, and she flashed a look to Charlotte to be tagged-in to the conversation and then continued. "PPD Homicide has a rep on our Joint Terrorism Task Force. Do you guys know Charlie Fields?"

"Sure."

"Charlie's been briefed through the JTTF on the case Ms. West and I are working. Can we call him in on this one? I'd prefer PPD investigate this as a local shooting and have him coordinate with us. We'll keep it in the JTTF and maintain case integrity, but it will appear to be a local matter. That is extremely important. We don't want the public to think this case is being investigated by the feds."

"Is this guy a terrorist?" The junior detective could not contain his curiosity.

"No, not at all. He's a good guy that rubbed bad people the wrong way. That's it." Grace set the record straight.

Charlotte wanted to get moving, so she settled Grace's suggestion with the cops. "Officer, we're going to Maryview. You have this for now, but the expectation is Charlie will take over and link-up with us." It was a directive statement, but she said it in a way that made it more palatable than an order might sound.

"Yes, we'll do that."

"Thanks, guys," Grace took Charlotte's cue and walked towards the door. "Charlie and I talk frequently, so I'll call him and fill him in on details," making sure the locals knew that she expected them to bring Charlie Fields in as the lead investigator immediately.

"Oh, one more thing," she added as she walked out of the room, "the victim lives in this house with his mom. She must be at work right now. Please find her and help her through this."

"Yes ma'am, will do."

The police presence at the Green residence had drawn a crowd. By the time they stepped out the front door, curious neighbors young and old, retired and unemployed, and kids who should have been in school had gathered around the police tape with their cell phones held high, recording their next videos to post on social media. Charlotte and Grace needed time alone to discuss their next steps, but they would find no privacy there.

"Let's get out of here," Grace said with urgency, and not realizing the amount of blood still on her hands and clothing.

"I'll call you as soon as we're on the road."

Chapter 71: October 17th, Saturday

"**I**'m sorry, Grace. I didn't understand how real the threat to him was." Charlotte felt responsible for Kent's shooting. If she considered the events of the day Thursday evening, they could have asked him to spend the night elsewhere. That would have been easy to do and given them more time to think of solutions. But she wanted to sleep on it. And now he was near death.

"There's no reason for you to apologize. Neither one of us thought it was urgent that night." Grace rebuffed her apology, feeling responsible herself for what happened.

"How is he today?" Charlotte asked.

"The hospital told me he's stable, but he is still unconscious. They don't know when he'll wake up."

"Do you know how his mom is doing?"

"Charlie says she's doing well. Kent has a close-knit family, and his brothers and sisters are there with her."

"It's good to hear that." Charlotte found some

consolation in that — but not much. "What security is in place?"

"One uniformed PPD officer at his door, 24/7. It has aroused suspicions. I wish there were a better way."

"We don't have the manpower for something more subtle. So, let's see who left the house yesterday morning, shall we?" The conversation turned to the reason they were working the weekend.

Charlotte met Grace early Saturday to get ahead of the terror cell. From the moment Mohammad arrived just two days ago, there had been a new dynamic and they worried they had lost their advantage.

The video footage from the Park Place surveillance camera showed Bilal leaving shortly after 9:00 a.m. They watched him pause inside his car and then drive away. He was the only one who left around that time.

"Grace, do you remember seeing Bilal's car parked near the Green's place?"

"Crap. No, I don't. I focused on getting to Kent. I drove up to the house so quickly I almost went by it. There was a car in the driveway, but it was Kent's. There may have been a vehicle in front of the neighbor's, but I was distracted. That's something I should have noticed." Grace was hard on herself. She finished near the top of her class at Quantico and was proud to be a Special Agent. But she didn't do a complete 'awareness of her surroundings' observation when she got to the Green residence.

"That's okay. Maybe it wasn't in sight. He probably parked around the corner." Charlotte tried to reassure her partner and friend. "Even if we had hard evidence, we wouldn't move on him. Stopping the attack and arresting all the terrorists is the highest priority. We'll get him then." At that point, she realized she had not told Grace about Jace's vision. Not that she thought it helped, but Charlotte needed to mention it to her.

"I forgot to tell you. When I called you while you were in the bedroom," she paused, "Jace called me seconds before that. He saw you standing in that room, alone, and blood all over the bed."

"That's why you sounded alarmed and with such urgency. That makes sense now. So, he had a vision?"

"Yes, but the most important part is his empathic event just prior to it. He experienced that dark feeling he gets with Bilal right before he saw you."

"So that ices it then. We thought Bilal shot Kent, but Jace confirmed it — at least to me."

"He's been working with his parapsychologist to develop precognition — to see what will happen in the near future. If he can do that, he may prevent things like this from happening."

Grace detected remorse, so she responded to Charlotte with appreciation. "It amazes me he can do what he does. He's been a tremendous help to us already. We would not be on to Bilal if not for Jace."

Charlotte and Grace both believed if Bilal suspected Kent was alive and able to name him as the shooter, then panic would ensue in the Park Place house, creating a dangerous situation. Fear destroys well-laid plans and predictable behavior. Their leverage of knowing the cell's intentions and anticipating what they do would evaporate. That was a frightening consequence for them.

In another time, perhaps not too long ago, the hospital and the PPD could have released to the press that the shooting victim had died without gaining consciousness, and not too many folks would be the wiser. Bilal might feel he's safe and the terrorists would stick to their plans. That is impossible today. Controlling the news around Kent would be an enormous challenge. Family, friends, and acquaintances from the neighborhood, his mom's church, his school, and mosque were commenting on his condition on their social media accounts. Announcing to the world that he was dead would require them to maintain that lie with all those people who care about him, for a month.

As they pondered that dilemma, Charlotte remembered Millicent. "Oh my gosh, we need to call Mil and explain what happened."

"I hope she hasn't already heard it. Word spreads like wildfire on social media. It's hard to know what's true and what's not." That caused Charlotte to look up and turn her head towards Grace.

"Hm," is all she said as she called Mil. She put it on speaker to let Grace join the conversation.

"Charlotte!" Mil answered with a quiver. "What the hell? Is Kent dead?"

Surprised, but not so much, Charlotte was gentle but firm with her. "No, Mil. Kent is not dead. He's hurt, but he is not dead." They shared what they could with her. She was in the middle of this through no fault of her own, and she needed to be aware so she could protect herself from Bilal.

Charlotte had to ask, "So, why did you think he was dead? Did you see it on the news or what?"

"It's all over Instagram and Facebook. People are saying he was shot in the head, and it was a gang-style shooting."

"He was not shot in the head. Is anyone setting the record straight on social media?"

"I had to get off. There is so much crap on there. No one knows what they're talking about." Millicent spit out the words. "I even saw video of you two leaving Kent's house."

"Us?"

"Yeah, two people posted videos of you hurrying to your cars and driving away. They said you were feds and you are investigating drug gangs."

"Well, that was my day job..." Charlotte lost herself in thought for a second. "One more thing. Until we talk again, please stay as far away from Bilal as you can. If you must, that includes skipping class. Consider staying with your parents for a few weeks. I'll call you later."

After they ended the call, Grace asked, "you think he'll come after Mil?"

"I don't know. There should be no reason to unless he thinks she will connect him to Kent. Based on how swiftly he acted on Kent, I don't trust them.

Mohammad must be driving the bus now. I want to check out the social media activity on this. I wonder if we can use it to our advantage?"

"We have a social media guy in our section," Grace offered. "His job is to find persons of interest using their social media posts and to track trends. I'll call him today and ask him to give us a report. He can get it to us tomorrow."

Chapter 72: October 18th, Sunday

Bilal felt the blood drain from his face when he heard the local news report a man shot in the chest at his residence in Portsmouth was still alive. The fact he remained unconscious gave Bilal some relief, but Kent now posed a danger to the jihad they had planned for so long, so far from home.

Bilal reasoned Mohammad would be extraordinarily upset when he told him of this personal failure, and the resulting serious threat to their cause. He hoped beyond hope the internet would bring him news the man had died, and the need to inform Mohammad of the complication will have passed with no consequence. So, he said nothing of the unfolding drama when he saw the reports Friday afternoon; nor did he tell him Saturday as internet communities exploded with speculation of Kent's connection to a drug gang. If he remained comatose, there would be no breach of operational security, so Bilal waited and watched the social media pages of Kent's family and friends.

◆ ◆ ◆

FBI agents gather and analyze signal intelligence, but Grace's 'internet guy' was an analyst who considered being called a geek a high compliment. Steve loved anything he could do on his computer and developed a talent for not only mining the wealth of information people post online about themselves, but using social media as a tool to influence people's behaviors. He liked working weekends — that just meant he would get paid for doing things he'd be doing at home, anyway. He particularly did not mind working for Grace, who had always been nice to him and shared credit with him when it was due.

The task was to summarize the social network conversations surrounding Kent Green and his shooting, and any connections made to Grace and her colleague, Charlotte West. That was a simple assignment. He completed it in a few hours and sent it to her that day.

Grace received the report on Saturday but was too tired to study it. She'd had a rough couple of days, and she hoped for a night off to clear her mind. She did a cursory review and noticed nothing that needed attention and forwarded it to Charlotte.

The internet chatter surrounding Kent was typical, especially for those around his age. There was outrage directed at authorities, as though they were responsible for the attack. There was the rumor and insinuation that he must have been mixed up with the wrong individuals. He was a young, black man in Portsmouth and that was all you needed to know. And there was the outpouring of support and love from well-wishers who knew better than to assume the worst about him. Two things were of note to Charlotte. One was the family was tight-knit and private, and bothered little with the social media storm. The other was the small group of conspiracy theorists, a subgroup who occupied both the outraged crowd and the innuendo bunch. These people floated theories centered on the attractive, professional-looking women, one smeared with blood, seen leaving the Green home after the shooting. Most suggested they were federal agents who shot Kent because of his involvement in drug gangs, social justice protests, or anti-government anarchists.

Charlotte presumed Kent saw the person who fired shots into his chest. And if it was Bilal, they could use the misinformation on social media to confuse him and potentially freeze him with indecision. If he kept hearing from 'reliable sources' Kent was dead or comatose, he may relax and stick to his plan. Likewise, if the narrative was that he had unsavory relationships with gangs or other groups, then people would not notice his link to Bilal.

The trump card, though, that overrode everything else were the videos of Charlotte and an FBI agent leaving the residence. Bilal knew her. He had dinner with her in which she peppered him with conversation for two hours. And he was not pleased. He would surely remember her as the prosecutor who investigated his brothers in jihad, whom she called terrorists. If he saw the videos and made the connection, then she was sure it would spark an unpredictable and dangerous reaction.

Sunday morning, she left Jace in the den with a cup of hot coffee and the newspaper, and excused herself to her office. She could not shake the sense of urgency she had that they need to make the next move in this game of chess with Bilal and the new player, Mohammad. She wanted to talk it through with Grace and dialed her number.

"Good morning," Grace answered with a greeting with which the two of them rarely bothered. Charlotte assumed she had gotten rest and was feeling better.

"Has there been any movement at the house?"

"None since Bilal's trip on Friday. Looks like they're holed-up."

"Cars are all still there?"

"Yes. What are you thinking?"

"If there's no activity, then they have yet to be spooked into doing something unplanned."

"Yeah, agreed." Grace knew there was more on her mind. She wouldn't call just to ask that. She knew she would be informed of any change at the house. "So, what?"

"The social media report says there are videos of us, and conspiracy theories about why we were there. One, I want to use that, and two, if Bilal sees me at his crime scene, he's going to run, or do something stupid. And since Mohammad is giving the orders now, I'm betting it's something stupid."

"Yeah, I had that thought too. You think he'd recognize you?"

"No question about it. I'm sure I left an impression on him."

"Any ideas?"

"The best we can do is to cause them to hesitate and watch when they move." Charlotte laid out her thoughts for her partner to consider. "We need to place doubt in Bilal's mind about why I was there with a federal agent. If he thinks my job is to investigate terrorists, then he may realize we're onto him and he goes stupid. If he believes I'm there for another reason, then maybe it helps us."

"The conspiracy theory that Kent is a gang-banger." Grace realized where she was going.

"Yes. Officially, I'm still assigned to the Criminal Division investigating organized crime."

"We could have our internet guy strengthen that thread — just bump it a little."

"That sounds like what we need. How would he do it?" Grace had Charlotte's attention. They were on the same page.

"It's easy. Steve has fake social media profiles he uses to establish phony accounts. He'll create an account that looks as though he belongs in the discussion and then make comments to those conspiracy threads that push the idea we are investigating gang activity. He can even make multiple accounts on different platforms, depending on how much of a bump we want."

"When could he do it?"

"He'd have it done before noon today if we asked him. We'd have to tell him what to say."

"That would be cool. We'd want to confirm you and I are investigating a gang-related hit, but not be too obvious about it."

"We can conference Steve in and explain what we want this morning."

"Good, but if Kent regains consciousness, all bets are off. He can probably identify who shot him. If he names Bilal as the shooter, then Mohammad will be forced to act. Can Steve help with that?"

"Yeah, sure. He could spread the word Kent is still unconscious, and the longer he stays that way, the more likely it is he won't wake up. No matter what happens in reality, we can plant doubt."

"We also need to talk to the family and the hospital. They have to stay silent on Kent's condition and they have to know that." Charlotte added the last piece of the solution. Even though it would be easy to influence the narrative, it was still a sketchy proposition. All they could do was try to introduce doubt into the terrorists' decision making and hope they gain an advantage from it.

"Did you see? Kent Green is alive," Haider whispered when he found a private moment with Bilal.

"Yes, but he is unconscious. He won't be talking to anyone."

"Have you told Mohammad?"

"No. There is no need. We are not compromised."

"But he will find out. He sees the news on television." Haider swallowed hard with apprehension, afraid of Mohammad's reaction when he finds out Bilal failed to cover his tracks.

"If that happens, let me handle it. The shooting is being investigated as a gang hit. Federal agents say it is related to organized crime — a Mexican cartel." Steve's handiwork was convincing.

"Did he see you? Can he identify you if he wakes up?" Bilal's assurances did little to soothe Haider's jitters.

"No." Bilal lied. "I shot him while he slept in bed. If he awakens, he'll have no idea what happened to him. I have this under control," he said more firmly. With that, Haider's distress eased somewhat.

"What should I do?"

"Nothing. I'm closely monitoring his condition. It will be fine."

Steve spoke as an ex-con who commented in the 'federal agent' conspiracy threads that those two women sent him to prison for drug distribution. He recognized the FBI agent and federal prosecutor who put him away. He got caught up in their transnational organized crime investigation because the cocaine he was selling came from a Mexican cartel. Using another account in a thread that discussed Kent's condition, Steve claimed to be a Maryview

Hospital employee, and assured the readers Kent had died. He stated with authority they were keeping it a secret because the FBI wanted the gang-bangers to try to finish the job and fall into the trap they had set. Those posts were enough to convince a near-panicking Bilal to rest easy and believe everything was going to be okay. Besides, he thought, Kent's family is not disputing any of it, so it must be true.

Charlotte and Grace had no idea the elegance of their charade hit the mark. Steve's posts, combined with the silence of those who should know the truth, gave Bilal a desperately wanted sense of security, and at least for the time being, postponed any rash decisions by the leaders of the terrorist cell. All they could do was wait and watch for the terrorists' next move.

Chapter 73: October 19th, Monday

B ilal recognized the woman in the videos. How could he forget that unpleasant dinner in which she continued an unwanted conversation with him? She was that forward, American woman who said she was a prosecutor. At first, it surprised him to see her at Kent's house, and it alarmed him. What did that mean? Was it just a coincidence? But the social media thread explaining she was investigating organized crime made sense. If the local authorities thought the shooting was gang-related, then they would have called U.S. federal agents to the scene. It made enough sense in Bilal's mind to explain away her presence at the scene and justify not telling Mohammad about the developments. There was no need for him to know because Bilal had everything under control. That is what lieutenants do.

It was Fadel and Abu who alerted Mohammad to Kent's condition. They were not used to living a soft life, relaxing in a house with nothing to do, so they remained transfixed to the television. Haider and Owais taught them how to play video games, so much of their time was occupied with feeding that obsession. But they also enjoyed looking at the attractive and leggy women on the TV news shows. It was their habit to watch the local morning news, and on one of these shows they saw a photo of Kent on the television screen. Most of what the news reporter said they didn't understand, but they excitedly called for Mohammad when the photo appeared on the screen. Mohammad and Bilal were across the hall and hurried into the living room to hear most of the news report.

Mohammad looked at Bilal with icy, unblinking eyes. Bilal felt his stare bore into his spirit and braced for the onslaught of anger. Mohammad did not wait to have a private discussion with his second in command. He confronted his cell leader in front of the Yemenis and Haider and Owais who had entered the room, drawn by the commotion.

"You told me you had killed him."

"I thought I had — three bullets to the chest. He shouldn't be alive."

"I told you to be sure."

"I was sure when I left him. I don't understand how he is alive."

"If he wakes from his coma, he could end us all."

"He didn't see me," Bilal lied again. "He does not understand what happened."

"But he witnessed too much during our journey here. He suspected that we were not who we said we were."

"It doesn't matter. He is in a coma, or already dead, and cannot tell anyone anything."

"The entire mission is in jeopardy. We must kill Kent Green before he can alert authorities. Fadel will go to the hospital to finish what must be done."

Bilal's fear of Mohammad turned to indignation. He was in control of the situation, but Mohammad was not listening. Bilal's judgment and leadership of the cell was being dismissed in favor of a Yemeni who does not even speak English.

"No, that will be very bad," Bilal said in a defiant and steady tone. Before Mohammad could respond, he made his argument. "Kent Green is incapable of talking to anyone. The police believe his shooting to be a drug-gang killing. There are reports that he is dead, but they are keeping it a secret to capture gang members who return to kill him. If you send Fadel, you will send him into a trap and expose us, and then our mission will fail." Feeling emboldened by his newfound will to stand up to Mohammad, he added, "We must wait!"

Mohammad, shocked by his deputy's insolence in the presence of his charges, fell silent. He stared with his cold eyes, unsure how to respond, and used the quiet to decide his recourse. Still staring at Bilal, intending to portray wisdom and strength, Mohammad chose a tactful exit from the confrontation.

"Trusted lieutenant, you have presented to me information of which I was not aware. I accept your counsel. Please tell me all you know. Let us discuss it privately."

With those words, the conflict ended. Bilal won the day, and Mohammad saved face and maintained ultimate control of his jihadis. The two Saudis retreated to the study for what would be a tense, private conversation.

Chapter 74: October 20th, Tuesday

L ate October in the Tidewater area of Virginia can be pleasantly warm in the daytime and bone-chilling at night, especially when a wind is blowing from the northeast. It would not be unusual that the three residents in Park Place shopped for overcoats Tuesday morning. But the Special Agent tailing them reported they bought six coats of different sizes, all medium-length. It was a notable bit of information for Grace and Charlotte to use to piece together the terrorists' next move. The obvious connection — six duffels, six people, and now six jackets — was not lost.

After shopping, the three went back to their house and carried the packages inside, but Bilal soon returned to his car and left. The Special Agent followed him to the campus but returned to West 30th Street when Bilal once again parked in the narrow garage next to the football stadium. Despite being closed to commuter parking, it had become his favorite place to park. It was part of his routine, and instead of risking exposure to his target in the garage, the agent dropped the tail.

The only other observation was the lack of activity. Haider and Owais typically spent Tuesday afternoons on campus, but on this day, they stayed home. It was curious that those two skipped classes while Bilal did not.

"Reserve round-trip flights out of Charlotte to anywhere that has a connecting flight home. I suggest London if you can. Book the earliest flights available on Saturday — the sooner the better. Pack your bags and bring them with you when we leave. Drive your own cars." Bilal gave instructions to his friends. "Immediately after the strike, go to the Charlotte airport and catch your planes. It is only five hours away, so you have plenty of time. Do not speed. You would look very suspicious speeding on the interstate highway out of Norfolk. Once you are out of the country, take a flight to Riyadh and you will be free. Do you understand?"

The sudden change in plans surprised Haider and Owais, and the distress showed on their faces. It had not yet sunk in and they both were still trying to process what they were being told.

"Make your reservations today, brothers. Do you understand?" Bilal repeated.

"Why do we make round-trip reservations?" Owais asked in a daze.

"Because one-way tickets are a flag for security officers. If you are traveling one way, they single you out for questioning. The same goes for paying in cash. Don't use cash. Use your credit card. And be sure you bring at least one bag to check. If you pay in cash or have no bags with you, those are security flags too. You must appear to be normal passengers. Travel as if you are going on a holiday. Are you okay, brothers?"

Reality hit them like a punch in the stomach. Both Haider and Owais nodded.

"What of you, Bilal?" Haider asked.

"I must drive Mohammad to safety, but I do not know where. We haven't worked that out yet. Moving the attack has given us no time to plan our escapes. But you two are legal students here. You can leave with no problems. Just be normal travelers."

"What of the Yemenis?"

"They will martyr themselves. If they don't, they will ride with me and Mohammad. We still have the white Suburban and plan to leave directly after the assault. This evening we are briefing the strike, and we will all know what to do and how to escape."

"Bilal," Owais asked, "why are we doing this?"

"Because Mohammad thinks we must strike right away since Kent Green could wake up and report us to the U.S. Government. We can't wait to execute our plan at Chrysler Hall weeks from now." Bilal paused, and with genuine sincerity apologized to his friends for causing their perturbation.

Chapter 75: October 21st, Wednesday

Having been briefed on the new assault, the jihadi cell spent the next day preparing, working out minor details Bilal didn't have time to resolve. The plan was a contingency Bilal had prepared on his own. He intended to present it to the others to consider with their proposals, but the Chrysler Hall attack was too good not to select, so he never divulged his plans. He did his due diligence in his plotting, as his brothers had done, including taking videos of the target and surrounding areas. When Mohammad insisted they execute a strike with urgency, Bilal's alternative was the only choice. The timing of the other targeted events developed earlier in the summer did not allow for immediate action.

"I don't like it," Charlotte had an uneasy feeling. "No activity at the house at all?"

"None. No one left the house; they didn't go to class; didn't get food; nothing," Grace reiterated.

"If you were a terrorist and your attack was imminent, what would you be doing right now?"

"I'd be lying-low, walking through the attack with my fellow terrorists, and getting ready."

"Yeah, that's what I'd be doing," Charlotte knew Grace would validate her thinking. "Double check with your guys. Make sure we have live eyes on that house 24/7."

Haider and Owais found an opportunity to steal away a private moment later that evening and prayed to Allah to show them the way forward.

"Owais, I do not want to kill anybody. These are good people. They have nothing to do with their government's policies." Haider had convinced himself he could not go through with the attack.

"Yes, I know, brother. Just get through this and get on the plane home. Mohammad will kill us if we don't do this."

"I will shoot no one. I'll empty my clips, but I won't shoot these people."

"Do what you must to go home to Riyadh. We will meet there in a few days, and this will be behind us." Owais had accepted that the only way out was to carry out the assault and then run for the airport.

Chapter 76: October 22nd, Thursday

It was later in the afternoon. Jace was in a meeting reviewing a proposal West Clean Energy was to submit to build a solar field in western Virginia, but a restlessness kept him from focusing. He was thankful when it ended. Those briefings lasted for hours and by the time it was over he thought of nothing else but leaving for the day. He told his team he was tired and left work for the 25-minute drive home. He called his wife when he stopped for one of the traffic lights near Town Center.

"Hi, Char."

"What's up?"

"I'm on my way home. I just don't feel right."

"What do you mean?"

"I feel — discombobulated," he couldn't find a suitable word, but 'discombobulated' was as good as any.

"Haha, what?" she chuckled.

"I don't know. I can't think straight."

"That's weird. Do you need to go to the doctor?"

"No, I want to relax in the study, put on some music, and meditate. I thought I'd let you know what I'm doing."

The call with Jace had just ended when Charlotte's phone beeped. It was Grace calling, and she had no time to contemplate what was happening with her husband.

"Still nothing," her partner updated her on the status of the surveillance in Park Place.

"No activity the whole day?"

"No one's left the house."

"Something is about to happen. I can sense it." Charlotte was new to the fieldwork side of law enforcement, but her instincts were always right. "No phone calls?"

"None. They may be using fresh burner phones, but we have no way to know that."

"I checked. There is one event at Chrysler Hall in the next week." Charlotte searched for any clue that might hint at what Bilal and Mohammad were thinking. "It's a comedy show tomorrow evening. That's not exactly NATO night with the symphony."

"They may be desperate, grasping at whatever is available," Grace offered.

"What about the other venues? Did you find anything?"

"No. There's nothing at Town Point Park and nothing at Scope. Nauticus is always an option with Wisconsin, but the crowds there in October are sparse."

"Damn. What are they up to?"

All Charlotte and Grace could do was wait.

The only thing left to do for the young Saudi men in Park Place was to ponder their fates. The final preparations were done and the mental walk-throughs of what they had to do and how they would do it had been replayed in their minds dozens of times.

Haider prayed that the bullets fired from his AK-47 find no human flesh, and that his father, mother, and sisters are blessed with peace and well-being. Owais, fatigued from the preparations, lost himself in one last game of Counter-Strike. And Bilal, emboldened by his courage to shoot Kent and influence Mohammad, looked forward with anticipation to a successful mission in the jihad against the Americans.

Jace was extraordinarily unsettled and wondered if he was experiencing an anxiety attack. The doctors had warned him it was common for people who have been through what he has, and that medication helps. But he never needed it. Meditation worked well, easing his stress and settling his mind, so he turned on the smooth jazz mix the kids had made for him and reclined into his favorite chair. The music washed away external stimuli and a breathing technique helped him bring to mind the calming image of leafy trees swaying in the wind. This method had worked many times and usually resulted in a restful nap. Habit, though, formed by his daily meditation exercises focused on one individual, caused him to think of Bilal.

It was dusk when Charlotte got home from work and the house was dark. Jace typically would have lights on, reading the newspaper or cooking dinner, but when she opened the door, it was eerily quiet. She dropped her things on the kitchen table and stepped silently into the hallway. She noticed a dim light in the study and peered through the French doors to see him furiously writing in his journal by the glow of a single desk lamp. She thought it best not to disturb him, figuring he would come out when he was finished.

She changed into her comfortable clothes and went to the kitchen to start dinner. Jace was waiting for her there. His hairline was wet with perspiration and he stared at her with a serious look. She felt her stomach knot — something was wrong. That was not like him. He was a calm and easy-going man, quick with a smile. She knew when he was troubled.

"What is it?" she managed to whisper.

"The attack is imminent. I saw the attack," he blurted.

"Tell me — what did you see?"

"Of course. I can't believe we didn't think of that," was Grace's reaction when Charlotte told her of Jace's dream. "I've got to talk to the Special Agent in Charge."

"Yeah. Call me back."

Grace was not sure what she would say to her boss. Does she tell him the husband of an Assistant U.S. Attorney had a vision and knows what the terrorists plan to do? Does she explain that the entire investigation has been driven by what Jace has seen and heard in his mind's eye? If she divulges that to the man in charge will he lose confidence in her and pull her from the case? She could not risk that. She had to get resources to the target.

Grace presented the logic of their observations and hoped that it was enough for him to agree to devote more agents to help prevent a potential terror attack. She started with the September phone call between Mohammad and Bilal in which they discussed hitting a military target and losing their brothers. She reviewed Kent Green's trip to Las Cruces, and his more than coincidental shooting the morning after they returned. Grace theorized the sudden lack of activity at the Park Place house soon after Mohammad's arrival pointed to an imminent attack, and they deduced what the most likely target would be. They needed resources to surveil the suspects and apprehend them before they wreak havoc.

The SAC agreed with her assessment, but thought it was weak. The identification of the target and timing of the assault were merely informed guesses. He couldn't initiate a full-scale response without something more substantial, but he assigned two more agents to Grace for Friday, and he agreed to contact the Norfolk police to request help with physical security. She was satisfied. Considering the circumstances, it was what she had hoped.

Grace called Charlotte as soon as she finished with her boss.

"He gave me two agents for tomorrow, and I'll have uniforms from Norfolk to help."

"Well, that's something." Charlotte understood the predicament and had no complaints. They were on their own. "How are we going to approach this?"

"I don't know, but we have all day to figure it out."

"You realize that Jace and I have to be there."

"Charlotte, we can't do that."

"Yes, we can. You need us. You'll need all the eyes you can get, and we know who to look for. Besides, Jace may be the secret weapon that decides who wins — them or us."

"You're right. Meet me at 6:00 a.m. and we'll work this thing out."

Chapter 77: October 23rd, The Day Of The Attack

C harlotte and Jace loved college football, so even though they were not alumni, they had been Old Dominion season ticket holders since ODU started their program. The game began at 6:00 p.m., but they met Grace and her team for a pre-operation briefing four hours before kickoff. They arrived at the stadium an hour before the gates opened to ready themselves and take their positions. They were all fitted with radios and earpieces for instant and clear communications.

The plan had Grace, Charlotte, and Jace strolling the concourses, waiting and watching for Bilal and his cell. Besides the few off-duty cops that worked security at the games, they had four uniformed Norfolk police officers available to them. Grace stationed two to patrol the east concourse and two on the west. She didn't add extra protection to the south-end loge seats and luxury boxes. Fans who use those accommodations pass through another layer of security, and she figured terrorists wouldn't bother with it. They would hit the denser crowds in the other parts of the stands that are easier to access.

The blue-shirted event staff, who scan the tickets of the people entering the stadium, do cursory searches for contraband. But Grace asked the campus police to post at least one officer near each entrance with the warning that the FBI had credible information that a few students may try to enter the game with weapons.

The two Special Agents were to stake out the Park Place house and follow whoever leaves. They drove separate vehicles in case the suspects use more than one of their own. If it worked as planned, the agents would tail the subjects to the stadium and the team would coordinate a takedown with the help of the uniforms. Things could get dicey, Grace told them, if the terrorists split into groups. Each agent had predetermined responsibilities if that happened. She would stay on Bilal, and the others each had a Yemeni to take when the time came. Plans tend to fall apart within the first few minutes of any op, so she implored them to be alert and listen for instructions as the action developed.

Grace's direction to Charlotte and Jace was to deploy to their concourses and scan the crowd. In case the subjects slip their tails or get lost in the throng, their job would be to respond to the last known location, spot the terrorists, and call it out on the radio.

This football game was the annual salute to the U.S. military. The halftime presentation included the marching band playing the hymns of each branch of service, while veterans stand as their service's hymn is performed. At the start of the show, in Jace's dream, gunmen opened fire into the crowd from the west concourse. That is where Grace and Charlotte roamed with uniformed escorts, guarding against the jihadis leaking past security and into the stadium. Jace positioned himself near the student section in the east stands. He believed part of his vision takes place from that perspective. A young woman wearing a red hat and red mittens in a sea of ODU blue will die a gruesome death when a bullet fired from across the field strikes her head. If the opportunity presented itself, he wanted to be there to prevent that.

The time had come. Their bags were packed, and they waited. The six men at 218 West 30th Street said their prayers as a collective and ate their meals together — Mohammad insisted. He was in his glory, already rejoicing in his strike on American soil. His soldiers in jihad were less joyous, perhaps contemplating their end of days, or maybe their escape. As the day grew old, they gathered once more for their sunset prayer. For most, it would be their last.

The sun was low in the sky, just barely visible over the upper level of the west stands. LED lights lit the field as though it were daytime, and the air filled with the buzz of twenty-two thousand excited football fans. The brand-new stadium was small compared to those of big-time college programs, but it was intimate, with the sell-out crowd sitting close to the field of play. The fans cheered the kickoff with a deafening roar, and the game was underway. Three people in attendance, though, knew of the sinister contest playing out in secret and were on high alert; their nerves already frayed.

The two Special Agents on stakeout in Park Place watched as all six subjects emerged from the house and loaded their vehicles with suitcases and duffel bags. The lead agent radioed Grace.

"Stadium 1, this is Tail 1. We have movement." Grace, Charlotte and Jace each felt a jolt of awareness; sounds seemed clearer, odors more poignant, and vision more acute. Jace thought of Charlotte and she of him, willing 'good luck' to the other from across the field of play. Both said it aloud, but neither could hear.

"Tail 1, Stadium 1. Copy that." Grace responded in their earpieces. Her call sign was Stadium 1, Charlotte's was Stadium 2, and his was Stadium 3.

"Stadium. Tail 1. They are loading into three vehicles."

Damn it. Grace almost said it over the radio. "Copy that. Who's got what?"

"Tail 1. I have the Suburban with Bossman and Minion."

"Tail 2. I have the Nissan with one student and a friend." They avoided using names to keep operational security. Everyone on the net knew that Haider Khan drove the Nissan, and his friend was a Yemeni.

"Stadium 1. Copy."

"Tail 2. The third vehicle is a Toyota Camry with one student and a friend. Both the Nissan and the Toyota are now in motion west on West 30th."

"Tail 1. Suburban is headed east on West 30th."

"Copy," Grace acknowledged over the radio net, and then released the key to the mic. "What are they doing?" she said to no one. *So much for best-laid plans.* Her NPD escort knew the question was not directed to her and remained apprehensively silent.

"Tail 2. Both Nissan and Toyota are north on Colonial Ave."

"Copy that Tail 2." *They're coming this way.*

"Tail 1. Suburban is south on Granby." That call had Grace's mind racing. Mohammad and Bilal were driving straight to Chrysler Hall. Jace's heart was in his throat. Did he make a mistake? Did he divert everyone to the stadium when the target is Chrysler Hall after all? *Damn it!*

"Tail 1, this is Stadium 1." Grace was calm and un-emotional. "If they get out of the vehicle at Chrysler Hall, pursue on foot with urgency and take them down. Consider them armed and dangerous." Tail 1 knew that, and the scenario played in his mind. He let his thoughts turn to his wife and baby, but quickly returned to the urgency at hand. Grace had briefed them to wear their vests, and he was glad he did.

"Tail 2. Nissan and Toyota are headed west on 35th Street." Jace's pulse slowed, and he pulled himself away from second-guessing. Haider and Owais were coming to the stadium. *Calm down. Be ready.*

"Copy." Grace then stated what may have been obvious, but times of high stress need clear direction. "All on net, we potentially have two simultaneous attacks. Tail 1, be advised Norfolk PD is responding Code 1 to Chrysler Hall." A moment before, she had asked the police to help stop a potential attack but respond to the scene without lights and sirens. She did not want Mohammad and Bilal to get spooked and flee.

"Tail 1. Copy," his answer succinct and professional as he mentally prepared for what lay ahead.

"Tail 2. Target vehicles are north on Killam, at the campus now."

"Copy. Tail 1, what is your status?" The clock had run out on the first quarter of the football game and the second quarter was about to begin. That meant halftime, and the attack, was roughly 20 minutes away. Grace needed to know where the Suburban was.

"Tail 1. Approaching Scope. ETA one minute." *One minute. Good luck Tail 1.* Grace didn't say it on the radio, but action was imminent. She thought of her friend, the Special Agent who was now Tail 1 and who had volunteered to help her with surveillance.

"Tail 2, status?"

"Tail 2. Both vehicles are turning left on 41st Street toward Hampton Boulevard. They are coming your way."

"Copy." Grace paused for several seconds as she forced herself to breathe. She turned to the police officer whom she had asked to stay close, "tell your guys suspects are approaching the stadium. Be alert."

Grace's boss, the Special Agent in Charge, decided not to mobilize for this exercise — he thought it was based mostly on conjecture. That didn't mean he wasn't concerned, and he tuned to the radio communications of her team from his desk in Chesapeake. He and his second in command listened to the op as it unfolded, and he turned to his deputy with a steeled look in his eye. "Spin up all free agents and send them Grace's way. At least two to Chrysler Hall and the rest to the stadium." He hoped he was over-reacting.

Jace's stomach was in knots. It seemed like the second quarter was going much too fast. A familiar voice interrupted his thought as he watched the game clock speed towards halftime.

"Jace! Hi boss." It was Millicent with her effervescent smile and cheery personality. "What are you doing, chillin' with the students?" The sight of Mil horrified him, and at once filled him with relief. She wore a red knit cap and matching mittens against the chilly October evening.

"Mil," he didn't know what to say. The only thing he could muster was, "you're wearing red."

"Yeah, these mittens are so warm. They're my favorites." Jace was still stuck for words. What could he tell her? 'Don't go sit down. You're going to get shot?'

"Um, can you hang here with me for a while?" he asked as his gaze shifted to the scoreboard.

Millicent caught his diverted eyes and saw his rapid breath in the crisp air. She sensed something was wrong, so she told him she would. Then she noticed an earpiece in his left ear, and he appeared to react to whatever it was he was hearing.

"Just stay with me please," he was more insistent.

The team held their collective breath as they waited for Tail 1 to report. Finally, the radio came alive.

"Tail 1. Suspects are turning from Granby toward Chrysler Hall on East Charlotte Street." This was it. In seconds, Mohammad and Bilal would be at their target. Tail 1 placed his right hand on his service weapon as the Suburban's brake lights lit in front of him. When they got close to the Scope complex, he had maneuvered directly behind the vehicle so that he could react quickly when they stopped to get out. The radio was silent as the team kept the airwaves clear for him.

"Tail 1. Suspects just turned right on Bank Street." *They're turning away from the target. What are they up to?* Grace wondered. Tail 1 surmised that they must be parking, and his anticipation peaked. *This has to be it.* But the driver didn't stop. He turned right again, and the Suburban went back in the direction from which it came.

"Tail 1. They just turned west on Freemason Street."

Bilal made the mistake of mentioning simultaneous assaults to create chaos in the city, causing confusion, and slowing the response of the authorities. During the hectic, previous few days of re-targeting and re-planning, Mohammad incorporated it into their new plan. A quick, superficial strike on Chrysler Hall would distract the local police and increase the probability of success at the primary target. He declared that he would personally execute the diversionary action while his jihadi brothers moved on the stadium. The caveat, though, was that he must escape before law enforcement arrives so he could continue the jihad with future strikes.

Grace's instinct saved lives at Chrysler Hall. By asking NPD to respond Code 1 to the target, she prevented the attack. As they approached the venue, Bilal and Mohammad noticed a heavy presence of police throughout the entire Scope complex. They assumed there must have been an event or incident earlier in the evening to warrant the attention. The hall is across the street from a housing project, explained Bilal, that attracts crime to the area.

So, he turned around and made for the stadium to help execute the assault as he originally planned. He called Haider as they drove to Hampton Boulevard to let him know he was on his way.

"Tail 1. Suburban is north on Granby. Hold on," he paused. If the terrorists were going to attack, they would do it in the next few seconds. They would turn right, back to the theater. He waited for his target to pass East Charlotte Street, then Bute, another cross street, before he called his status.

"Tail 1. Still north on Granby." A moment later he made the radio call that gave those on the net immediate, although temporary, respite.

"Stadium. Tail 1. Target vehicle has turned west on Brambleton. It looks like we are coming to you."

Grace heard the relief in his voice. There would be no shootout at Chrysler Hall this night, but the stadium was about to be under siege.

She wasted no time. Tail 2 had been radio-silent as the drama unfolded around his partner. "Tail 2, what is your status?"

"Tail 2. Subjects parked their cars in the 43rd Street parking garage. Four individuals are walking your way on Hampton Boulevard. I am pursuing on foot."

"Stadium 1, Copy. ETA?"

"Tail 2. We should be there in five minutes. Be advised, the subjects are wearing dark-colored, bulky, medium-length coats and beanie caps."

"Copy that. Consider targets armed and dangerous," Grace reminded her teammates just to make sure everyone was prepared. She passed the information to her NPD escort, who relayed it to the other uniformed cops.

Grace, Charlotte, and Jace each instinctively looked to the video board to check the game time. There were six minutes before halftime, and the clock had stopped for a timeout on the field. The drama was playing out just as Jace described. The only thing to do was to react to the terrorists' next moves and hope no one gets hurt.

"Tail 2. Subjects are on campus a block south of the stadium. They've stopped and one is talking on a phone."

"Copy that. They may be coordinating with the Suburban. Tail 1, status please?"

"Stadium, Tail 1. Suburban is on Hampton Boulevard two minutes from your location."

"Stadium, Tail 2. Four subjects are now on foot headed west behind academic buildings."

"Copy that," Grace warned her crew. "They are going around the south end to the west. They can approach the west entrance from there."

Charlotte and Jace both began drifting to the south end of the stadium; he on the east concourse and she on the west.

"Jace, are you okay?" Mil asked as he walked south, paying more attention to his earpiece than to her.

"Yes. Stay with me. It's almost halftime."

"Tail 1, status?" Grace spoke into her radio with measured, reassuring calm.

"Tail 1. Suburban is passing the stadium right now." That made sense to her. *They'll circle to the west side from the north.*

"Stadium 1. Be advised they will likely turn left on Bluestone Ave just north of the stadium. They're going to circle to the west."

"Tail 1. Target vehicle just turned left on Bluestone."

"Tail 2. The four walkers are approaching the west entrance on Bluestone. ETA one minute." As the tension grew and action became imminent, the training and professionalism of the Special Agents maintained control.

"This is Stadium 2. I see the Suburban. It slowed on Bluestone, northwest corner of the stadium."

Charlotte called out the terrorists' position as instructed in Grace's pre-op brief. She was on the west concourse, one tier above ground level, looking down on the vehicle. She had reversed her way and walked back north when the agent on the radio said Minion and Bossman were approaching from that direction. Hearing Charlotte reminded Jace that his love was in danger. Despite the cold weather, he loosened his jacket seeking relief from a sudden wave of perspiration. Knowing there was nothing he could do to protect her, he stopped in his tracks and cursed out loud, surprising Mil. She could feel the blood drain from her face, and her hands quivered. Something bad was happening, and she didn't know what.

"This is Stadium 1. I have eyes on the four walkers. Tail 2 close-in." Grace was on the first level concourse too, looking down on the unfolding attack. She reached for her Glock 19 and unholstered it. The NPD officer heard Grace's side of the radio calls and saw her reach for her service weapon, so she did the same and called to her fellow officers on their net to alert them of impending action.

"Tail 1. Minion is out of the vehicle walking to the west entrance." He rushed out the words, knowing he had only seconds to react. He sped around the Suburban that had stopped near the northwest end, jumped from his car, and closed in on his target on foot.

Grace ran from her perch on the concourse to the stairs leading to the gates. Her officer was close behind, summoning the other uniforms on her radio. Charlotte's NPD escort reacted to the call and raced to the north stairway closest to them. Not thinking, and unsure what to do, Charlotte followed. The two cops on the east concourse bolted for the southeast stairs, following their training to run to the danger and to aid their fellow officers. Jace, thinking of Charlotte, took off after them. Mil realized that people she cared for were in harm's way. She walked to the stairs, choking back tears, not wanting to follow, but unable to not.

The stadium plan had flaws, unlike that for Chrysler Hall, and is why Bilal shelved it. He was confident that his brothers would disappear after the theater assault and be free to return home to Saudi Arabia. They would have walked past the token security, been in the concert hall in a matter of seconds, and blasted into the crowd with their AKs. It would not be that fast and simple at the football game. While the event staff manning the gates would be easy to dispatch, getting to the mass of fans in the stands would take too much time. The jihadis would have to storm through the gate, run up a long flight of stairs to the main level, disperse the length of the concourse, empty their clips and then retreat the way they came. That would consume significantly more time than at Chrysler Hall, and there would be tens of thousands of people to avoid once the shooting stopped. Bilal also worried there could be an immediate armed response. He had been to earlier games and noted several campus and Norfolk police officers with sidearms. The stadium assault needed good luck to go perfectly and allow his soldiers to escape. Of course, that was no burden of Mohammad's. He preferred his soldiers die in the strike, willing to martyr themselves, instilling terror in the souls of the Americans.

Bilal's plan was to approach the west entrance with suppressed sidearms in hand and AK-47s slung over their shoulders under their coats. Shoot the event staff at the gates and any law enforcement officers nearby, with their handguns. With luck, few, if any people would notice the gunshots through the roar of the fans watching the game. They would disperse throughout the west concourse and as soon as the salute to the military show started, they would fire their AKs into the crowd, killing hundreds. They would then discard their rifles and run for the exits, defending themselves with the handguns. Mohammad would wait for them in the Suburban on the west side of the stadium and drive them to safety. Haider and Owais were to be dropped off near their cars, and the rest would flee north on Granby Street to Interstate 64 and out of the city in a matter of 10 minutes.

The radios were now silent as the Special Agents transitioned from surveillance to immediate response. The west entrance had three pedestrian gates accessible at halftime. Bilal hurried to the one closest to him, while his four comrades ran to the other two. The gates were wide open and offered no resistance to the terrorists. Bilal was the first to draw his weapon and shoot the event staffer at his gate. There were only two other ticket checkers, each manning their posts, and he noticed them go down in his peripheral vision as he watched his victim fall. He wasn't sure who shot them, but thought it was a good start to their strike against the infidels.

Grace and her officer were the first to arrive at the west entrance. As she rushed down the stairs, she saw the terrorists storm the gates and shoot the unlucky souls assigned to scan tickets at that moment and place. She raised her Glock 19 while descending the last few steps, pointed it at Bilal, and fired.

Bilal turned from watching his first victim fall to see police officers rushing towards him and his brothers. He lifted his gun to engage, but felt and heard several thuds hit his chest, and he crumbled to the concrete floor. Grace's shots were true, avenging the shooting of Kent Green.

She pivoted to her left to train her weapon on the four remaining jihadis, but she was exposed. In the open, with just air and space between her and the assailants, she fell in a firestorm of lead and brass. The seconds it took her to recognize the threat from Bilal, aim her 9mm and squeeze the trigger was enough for Owais and the Yemenis to swing their AK-47s from their shoulders and spray bullets towards her and the Norfolk police officer behind her. Both women fell as multiple 7.62x39mm rounds ripped through their bodies.

Tail 1 ran to the gate with his weapon drawn in

time to see Bilal drop and then watched as Grace and her NPD escort violently jerked to the ground. The horror took his breath away, but his training compelled him to engage the gunmen to his right, who had just shot Grace and the officer.

Tail 2 also arrived a second too late. From his vantage point behind the terrorists, he heard the gunfire before he saw the weapons and began firing at his targets, striking one in the back of the head.

Haider had no thought his life was ending. He was dead before his body succumbed to gravity. His prayer was answered, though, for he did not pull the trigger, and no bullets from his AK-47 tore into the flesh of another.

Fadel had just eliminated the ticket checker at the middle gate. As he admired his skill, proud that he used only one shot to the head, his accomplices opened fire with their rifles. He looked up to see two adversaries fall and then heard gunshots from behind him. He ran to his left to escape the field of fire while Abu and Owais engaged in a gun battle with the Special Agents.

They exchanged their spent magazines for fresh clips, causing both agents to seek the cover of nearby stadium walls. Abu finally perished in the deadly crossfire of Tail 1 to the left and Tail 2 to the right.

Owais retreated south through the ground-level plaza. In the fight's chaos, he threw his AK-47 to the concrete and ran toward the south exit, joining fleeing fans who had been at the nearby concessions stand when the shooting started. The escape plan was to run north where Mohammad would be waiting in their vehicle, but it did not matter. Their leader had driven away as soon as he saw the Special Agents draw their handguns and fire into the entrance.

Fadel was the last of the cell. He moved to his left and kept running north through the stadium plaza. His intention was to climb the stairs at the north end to the main concourse and complete his mission. He surmised it was up to him now, since his brothers were otherwise engaged, and he would soon be a martyr in the eyes of Allah.

As Charlotte's uniform descended the north staircase, he heard the gunfire coming from south of his position and drew his weapon. Above the din of the battle and the roar of the still oblivious crowd, his sister in blue stationed with the FBI agent declared in his ear the radio call that no cop wants to hear. "Officer down," she said weakly. He steeled himself and charged in her direction, toward the raging gunfight. Charlotte, running on instinct and nothing else, was close behind him. Within a second or two, the officer faced the barrel of Fadel's AK-47.

Fadel was intent on reaching his assigned position for the attack. He had shouldered his automatic rifle as he ran so he could kill anyone who got in his way. As he neared the bottom of the north stairs, a policeman emerged from a small group of people with his handgun ready. Fadel fired but missed his target from 15 feet away. His adrenaline driven rush, and his labored breathing from the exertion conspired to off his aim. The split second it took to settle and squeeze the trigger again gave his opponent an opportunity to fire two rounds. One bullet penetrated Fadel's chest, causing him to jerk, firing a quick burst into the officer's torso. The force of the rounds threw the officer to the ground and jarred his service weapon from his hand.

Charlotte had just descended the stairs and turned to follow when the shots were fired. She saw two football fans fall from the first belch of the AK, and then her escort dropped in front of her, his handgun landing at her feet. She looked up to see the burley terrorist she recognized as one of the Yemenis, wounded in the chest and on the floor, sitting up to level his rifle at her and the fans still stunned from the shooting in front of them. As composed as if she were prosecuting the thug in court, she picked up the officer's 9mm, stepped two paces forward, aimed the handgun, and emptied the clip into the terrorist. Being a federal prosecutor of organized crime, it was almost obligatory for her to own a weapon for personal protection and know how to use it. She did.

Chapter 78: The Aftermath

Mohammad knew the strike had been compromised when he saw men draw their weapons and close-in behind his jihadis. There was no cause for him to wait for his soldiers to return. He turned the vehicle around and went back to Hampton Boulevard. Driving in the U.S. was no different than in Saudi Arabia. The rules of the road were the same, so he was at ease at the wheel.

Bilal had mapped out two escape routes for exfiltration. The primary route dropped Haider and Owais off near the parking garage so they could get in their cars and drive south. The secondary was the quickest way to the highway and out of the city. So, as the gun battle raged at the west entrance, he turned north on Hampton Boulevard and in only a few minutes was on Interstate 64 going northwest. Before NPD was able to issue a BOLO — to be on the lookout — for the white Suburban, Mohammad was through the Hampton Roads Bridge-Tunnel and speeding towards Williamsburg at 70 miles per hour.

❖ ❖ ❖

In the confusion of the gun battle and the immediate response to aid the fallen, Owais ran out the south gate with a crowd of fleeing fans. He ducked into the adjacent parking garage where, under the cover of cars and walls, he shed his coat and beanie, put on an ODU ball cap to match his ODU hoodie, and walked away. It was all he could muster to not run to the 43rd Street garage where he left his Toyota. He quickened his pace as the commotion behind him crescendoed. The surrounding streets erupted with flashing lights and screaming sirens, and he heard the public address announcer at the football game calling for a calm and orderly evacuation. He looked over his shoulder to see people streaming towards him from the site of the attack.

Owais, now slightly ahead of an evacuating throng, crossed Hampton Boulevard at the direction of traffic cops who were desperately trying to direct cars and people away from the stadium. Once in the garage, he ran to his car and drove faster than he should have to the exit on 41st Street. Ahead of the crowd, he turned left, opposite from the now frenzied Hampton Boulevard, and very quickly maneuvered through the backstreets of Norfolk to Interstate 264 and through the Downtown Tunnel. In no more than an hour and a half, he would be driving south on Interstate 95 to catch his flight in

North Carolina.

Millicent, tears streaming down her cheeks, tried to follow Jace, but event staff and campus police blocked her path. Forced to join the stream of evacuees, she mingled outside the stadium with the crowd drawn to the cause of the commotion. She hoped to glimpse her friends, the Wests, but could not get close.

Jace rushed to the point of the assault with the Norfolk police officers stationed with him on the east concourse. Before they hit the ground-level pavement, fans looking to beat the halftime rush to bathrooms and concessions crowded the plaza, impeding their way to the west entrance. By the time they arrived, the attack had been thwarted, but weapons were still drawn. Jace spent an agonizing three minutes before law enforcement declared the immediate scene secure, and he could look for his wife.

First responders pushed him and others back so they would not walk through the blood and bodies. FBI and Norfolk police continued to flood the area to secure the stadium. Medical personnel, who were already on-site to respond to football game injuries, were directed to the wounded. Jace watched a group of officers and agents frantically helping the EMTs attend to wounded lying at the bottom of the stairs.

In the cacophony of sirens and shouts and someone behind him screaming and crying, Jace heard her call his name. He looked across the ground-level plaza to see his beautiful wife, her long blond hair in her favorite ponytail, standing with others attending to another group of victims. She feebly raised her hand to tell him she was alright and tried to force a reassuring smile but was unable to muster it. With the crowd still evacuating the west side, and the area of attack cordoned off, there was no way for him to reach her, so he signaled to her with a raised palm. The relief of seeing her left him lightheaded. His knees weakened, and he felt out of breath, so he sat on the concrete to rest from the sudden fatigue. From that vantage, he could peer through the legs and bodies, and realized Grace, their friend, was down, and he watched a well-rehearsed ballet of first responders working to save two of their own.

Charlotte shot Fadel dead. She kept the empty 9mm trained on him until an officer carefully removed it from her hands. The shooting had stopped, people were sobbing, and the crowd began to leave their seats and witness the carnage. Before she realized, officers had swarmed to control the scene and administer aid to her NPD escort and the women who had been unlucky enough to be in the line of Fadel's errant burst. More paramedics arrived from the Norfolk fire station just one-half mile from the stadium. FBI Agents helped Charlotte step aside, and sent someone to get her water, and then peppered her with necessary questions. With the help of Tail 1, Tail 2, and the SAC who had monitored much of the operation through the radio calls, the FBI rapidly pieced together what had happened. It was not fast enough, though, to realize the white Suburban was missing and Mohammad and Owais were not among the dead or wounded.

All told, there were eight dead, four wounded, and two terrorists at-large. Three gate attendants perished, having been mercilessly executed at point-blank range. Grace's NPD escort, the officer who instantly relayed critical information to her brothers in blue, causing them to converge on and engage the terrorists before they could scatter, surely saved lives. She died from her wounds. Her vest stopped five bullets, but AK rounds ripped below her armor and through her body. Grace killed Bilal before he could kill more innocents. Special agents Bill Ross and Amad Frazier, Tail 1 and Tail 2, with the help of NPD and campus police, killed Haider Kahn and Abu al Salami, stopping them from reaching the 22 thousand fans in the stands. Charlotte killed Fadel Abdu, who was seconds from accomplishing his part of the terrorists' mission.

The two fans struck by Fadel's first burst suffered flesh wounds and recovered. Charlotte's NPD escort, who likely saved her life and those of countless others by slowing Fadel with a round to the chest, also recovered, thanks to his body armor. His vest stopped all three bullets from penetrating his torso.

Her body armor, and the quick action of her fellow first responders, saved Grace, who heroically blunted the assault head-on, allowing others to finish the job. Her vest stopped four AK-47 rounds, knocking her off her feet and unconscious, while more rounds tore through her legs. One bullet severed her femoral artery and if not for the immediate action from her colleagues and the emergency medical technicians on the scene, she would have bled out, ending her young life.

Chapter 79: Epilogue

Grace had an odd satisfaction in killing Bilal. She thought it wrong to be content in taking another's life, but the knowledge that she avenged the death of Kent Green made it feel right. Kent died from his injuries at the hand of Bilal about the same moment Grace's Glock 19 loosed four hollow points into Bilal's chest.

Her recovery from her physical injuries took much less time than being emotionally ready to return to duty. The events of the past months weighed heavily and drew a mix of powerful emotions that caused her pause. She allowed herself to become too attached to Kent, and his death saddened her to tears. Yet, she felt no remorse in killing Bilal — he deserved it. While her training took control when her stress levels elevated, she sensed fear trying to influence her decisions. When it was apparent that her friend, Bill Ross, may be alone in engaging two terrorists in a gunfight, she thought of his young family. She feared for his life while guilt slapped her in the face. But she had no fear when she rushed to confront the five terrorists crashing the gate at the stadium. Her only thought was to stop them from doing harm. And the exhilaration of practicing her craft, piecing together the puzzle, working with her partner to track and stop evil men was unmatched. Innocent people — good people — died, but it would have been much worse if not for her and Charlotte. Her parents were proud of her. And she was proud of herself, and knew that her brother would have been proudest of all as she carried on the fight that he could no longer.

When she returned to work, the FBI Director called her to Washington, and the President of the United States presented her with the FBI Medal of Valor. He recognized her for meritorious service in identifying a terrorist cell in the U.S. and stopping its attack, saving hundreds of lives. That alone would have earned her the Medal for Meritorious Achievement, but her exceptional act of heroism of engaging the terrorists before they launched their strike, putting herself at great personal risk, won her the highest honor conferred to Special Agents.

During her debrief of the full investigation, she detailed the invaluable contributions of Mr. Jace West and his wife, Assistant U.S. Attorney Charlotte West. She made sure her command structure knew that without Jace's telepathic readings and precognitive visions, she and Charlotte could not have identified the terrorists and uncovered their intentions. She recommended that Jace be a trusted resource in investigations going forward.

The FBI awarded Jace its Medal for Meritorious Achievement for his contributions to preventing the assault, and in doing so, recognized his unconventional investigative skills.

Returning to work after the lightning strike was difficult for Jace. At first, it took effort to repress his clairvoyance to focus on running his company. During the terror investigation, he came to understand the power of what he could do — something most people could not. His ability was extraordinary, and he could no longer imagine himself working every day without using it in meaningful ways. It compelled him to want to help people. He knew it would be a challenge. There was still much he didn't understand, but Ike would be there for him, mentoring him along the way.

Charlotte agreed that he should let his trusted management team run West Clean Energy, so he could use his gift for something bigger than himself. She told him it was now his obligation. Besides, the company was doing very well, and he could visit his team whenever he wanted. On January 2nd, Jace was a semi-retired man, no longer burdened with day-to-day responsibilities. But at 43 years old, he opened a new chapter in his life. Both Charlotte and Grace had plans for him. The fear he felt for Charlotte's life that day at the stadium strengthened him, and their bond. If she was going to continue in this line of work, he had to be there to help.

As an extrovert, Charlotte loved performing in

the courtroom. Her mission in life to put human trash in prison was fulfilling. Almost as important to her was making the lawyers who defend these immoral criminals look foolish in court. It was not enough for her to take the gangsters off the streets. She had to punish those who tried to prevent her from doing that. She did not want to join the Joint Terrorism Task Force as it would mean less of that, but her sense of duty compelled her to go where she was needed. She found her new task just as thrilling, but much more stressful. The race against time to prevent the horror, rather than punish those responsible for it, added urgency that did not exist in the aftermath. But she was still removing bad people from society. Killing the burly thug from Yemen was no different. She took him out, and that's what mattered. It was her mission, and she had no regrets.

For her courage in the face of grave danger, preventing a terrorist from wreaking untold death and injury, the FBI Director bestowed Charlotte with the FBI Shield of Bravery.

Kent's death struck at Millicent's heart. The investigation into his shooting proved that Bilal was the perpetrator, and it sickened her. Jace, Charlotte, and Grace sat in her parents' living room and explained everything to her with mom and dad at her side. Her effervescence had left her. Gone was her natural joy. How could she have been so close to a terrorist; someone who took Kent from her, from the world? She apologized to Jace, and her parents — she couldn't find the will to go back to work, or to school. She needed to be away from those things. She needed time.

With a great deal of luck, Owais made it to Charlotte Douglas International Airport without being discovered by law enforcement. The FBI issued a BOLO for the Toyota to nearby state agencies, but he drove at night on a highway with other sedans that resembled his. No one noticed. He parked in long-term parking and slept in his car, leaving it behind forever when it was time to leave for the terminal. Upon landing at Heathrow, he found the Saudia Airlines counter and booked a flight to Riyadh. He was home in time to sleep that night in his own bed in his family home. He tried not to think of his friend Haider.

Mohammad benefited from Bilal's foresight in planning their exfiltration. Weeks before Mohammad and the Yemenis arrived, Bilal purchased a five-year-old Lincoln Navigator. It was in pristine condition with low miles and perfect for a drive to the southern border, or wherever their escape led them. Bilal paid a fellow Saudi national studying at William and Mary to allow him to park the Lincoln in the student's driveway. As an unexpected bonus, it came with a vehicle cover that the previous owner used to protect it from the weather. So, Bilal covered the Navigator and parked it in a driveway in a neighborhood in Williamsburg. An hour after the gun battle at the stadium, Mohammad arrived at the address that Bilal had entered into its navigation system and exchanged the white Suburban for the sleek, silver Navigator. The cover hid the Suburban in plain sight for months afterward, and Mohammad disappeared into the night. Mohammad and Bilal had discussed heading to Jersey City, New Jersey. With a large population of Muslims, and in the metropolitan area around New York City, it was a perfect place to melt into the fabric of urban America. They reasoned they could wait out the ensuing manhunt there and then make it to the border and out of the country when the time was right. Once he found safe harbor there, Mohammad recognized it was a rich environment from which to recruit disillusioned Americans and politicized Muslims, and was in no hurry to leave.

ACKNOWLEDGEMENT

This book was made better by my beta readers, Heather and Kelsey, and my proofreader, Zach. Thank you to all.

ABOUT THE AUTHOR

D. S. Wall

DAVE WALL is an engineer and MBA with 38 years' experience writing technical and professional documents of every sort. With his debut novel, On American Soil: Jihad, he fulfilled a decades-long desire to write creative fiction in his favorite genre. He lives in Vir-ginia with his wife of 38 years. They are proud parents of a son and a daughter.

You can contact the author at dave@davewallwrites.com, and visit his website at davewallwrites.com

TO MY READERS

I hope you enjoyed reading this story. Your feedback is important to me. Please consider leaving a review for On American Soil: Jihad on Amazon.com.

You can also email me at dave@davewallwrites.com.

Made in the USA
Middletown, DE
20 December 2020